Praise for
THE DEATH I GAVE HIM

"Liu's exquisite prose perfectly marries physicality and emotionality, the visceral and the sterile. This is *Hamlet* reflected in a fractured mirror. Every angle on the familiar comes as a surprise; every new edge cuts with razor intelligence. And oh, the tension! It will murder you."

Shelley Parker-Chan

"Blazingly ambitious, immaculately written, imaginative, and oh, goodness, I can absolutely keep going. *The Death I Gave Him* is the locked-room murder mystery queer *Hamlet* retelling of my dreams."

Cassandra Khaw

"*The Death I Gave Him* is the *Hamlet* retelling of my wildest dreams, and Liu's prose cuts like a scalpel: precise, unflinching, unafraid to draw blood. Read this book, and then read it again."

Grace D. Li

"This is both a locked-room mystery with some pointed things to say about science, hubris and mortality, and one of the best versions of *Hamlet* I've ever come across. Smart, wildly propulsive, and tense as a muscle held at the snapping point. After this, I'll read anything Liu cares to put in front of me."

Freya Marske

"A taut emotional thriller, a deeply queer love story, sexy as hell and far kinder, far more humane, than Hamlet itself. A sliver of freedom granted to its characters to make choices beyond them in the original play, a release from context, or gender, or genre even."

Alexis Hall

"I've always been kinda lukewarm about *Hamlet*, but *The Death I Gave Him* finally gives me a Prince of Denmark I can feel: someone whose pain and brokenness are so powerful and beautiful that they can change the world."

Sam J. Miller

"A breathless, piercingly immersive *Hamlet* reimagining that feels at once futuristic and timeless. Each scene is layered with creeping dread and tension that builds masterfully to a harrowing climax."

Ren Hutchings

"If you love Shakespeare, a haunted-house escape room, and a plot full of tenderness, philosophy, brazenness, and terror—as well as the unexpectedly erotic—this is the book you never knew you've always wanted."

C. S. E. Cooney

Also by Em X. Liu from Solaris

If Found, Return to Hell

THE DEATH I GAVE HIM

EM X. LIU

SOLARIS

First published 2023 by Solaris
an imprint of Rebellion Publishing Ltd,
Riverside House, Osney Mead,
Oxford, OX2 0ES, UK

www.solarisbooks.com

978-1-78618-998-1

10 9 8 7 6 5 4 3 2 1

A CIP catalogue record for this book is available from the
British Library.

Designed & typeset by Rebellion Publishing

Printed in the UK

For:
妈妈, 爸爸, 飞飞

FOREWORD

ONE MUGGY AUGUST Sunday of 2047, the Elsinore Labs
Operating System—though he prefers Horatio—clicks on
with very little fanfare for what has just occurred within
his walls. It takes nearly a millisecond for his processes
to sort it all out. Excess carbon, hissing into the vents; a
bright red dash amidst all the white assaulting his optic
sensors; the distinct and potent chemical stain of sulphur
still concentrated enough in one area for Horatio to direct
awareness there: Dr Graham Lichfield's personal lab. One
heartbeat present. Two point eight degrees Celsius hotter
than the weekly average, but trending downward. Iron in the
air.

The myriad details coalesce into a corpse. As soon as this
becomes clear, the rabbiting of the remaining heartbeat
in the room resolves into sense as well. An easy 110 bpm,
tachycardic enough for panic. Horatio blinks the cameras
open and finds shattered glass, a pool of blood still fresh
enough to leak between the tiles. Violence smeared across

the entire tableau. A correction, then: the *late* Dr Lichfield's personal lab.

Of course, in 2047 the Lichfield name had yet to become known in the ever-striving field of gerontology, much less infamous in the greater public consciousness. Furthermore, the eventual notoriety would come to be claimed by the son and not the father. There was no way of knowing, at the time, that this moment—this *death*—would ripple outward with consequence. That day, the grief in the room was insular, shared only by its occupants: Elsinore itself, incarnate by stalwart Horatio, and Hayden Lichfield.

Hayden Lichfield is an oft-blurry, certainly controversial, but no doubt pivotal figure in the sea change that occurred sometime in the mid-late 21st century. Longevists have existed since human death was a score to contend with, but a slew of experimental trials were starting to show, for the first time, that perhaps the prophets were knocking on reality's door. No longer relegated to the realm of pseudoscience, senescent research—the study of aging, which is inextricable from the study of immortality—was reaching its full potential. Technology had finally caught up to what everyone had known all along: we alone have dominion over the body. We can, as Feynman once said, "swallow the doctor," and use our hard-won skills to manipulate the forces that drive us towards our inevitable end—and halt them.

This book does not aim to illuminate how this paradigm shift came about, or even the factors at play that led to the inevitable change. And indeed, I doubt that the scientists working with their heads down and hearts hopeful in 2047 were envisioning the chaos they would sow—as we all know now, immortality is cheap these days; the real questions are, for whom and to what end? Truthfully, I don't believe we will know the true echoes of this revolution until long into our future, a timeline that stretches out even further because it deals with the very nature of eternity.

I was a bright-eyed (some would say naive) history student trying to put an undergrad essay together about the tail-end of the digital dark ages when I first came across the story that would later become my master's thesis, and then this book. At the time, I was primarily interested in the siloing of information, the utterly paranoid zeitgeist stemming from the looming collapse of all communication networks as people knew it. And of course, the Elsinore incident came up often in this context. I knew the story in its bare bones at the time: Dr Graham Lichfield the visionary, a king of paranoia in his own right, sends his son on a terrible mission to ensure the safety of their research, only for the grave secret to escape his careful clutches regardless. It was a story about the failure of containment, that nothing is truly private.

But looking deeper, what captivated me in the end was not the ways in which Dr Graham Lichfield failed, or the betrayal of his companions, or the crumbling structure that kept them all captive for twenty-four hours. It was Hayden Lichfield who I remembered.

Not because he was brilliant (though he was), but because he was afraid. Few know that it was Hayden who proposed the Sisyphus project, and even fewer understand his reasoning. I felt as if I was uncovering a humiliating secret, poring over my primary sources, because *I* could see it. Hayden Lichfield was afraid of death, because he was afraid of failure, and he spent his whole life trying to reverse it.

That is what this book is about, first and foremost. A

retelling of that fateful night in Elsinore, as best as I could reproduce. My main source is the neuromapper[1] log between Hayden and Horatio that ran throughout most of the night, and I have done my best to untangle the account from either of their perspectives, albeit with my own editorial touch. Other primary sources include an incisive and thorough article Felicia Xia—Hayden's ex-girlfriend, and daughter of Elsinore Labs' head of security—published following the court proceedings; audio transcripts retrieved from court documents; and other official documents I could find. The story is fragmentary, I admit. But I implore you to embrace the experience, see what you may uncover between the lines.

Looking back, what I vividly recall is the night that first essay was due, after the storm sirens had all quieted so I was faced only with the eerie stillness of campus, interrupted only by the stabs of neon holo, advertising last minute neuro-rewiring study aids; the sound of my own frantic typing (I was and am old-fashioned); the footsteps of my classmates ducking into the light drizzle outside. I thought of Hayden, then. I thought of his fear, because I understood it. I was a first-generation university student hailing from a continent that had gone dark decades ago, swallowed by the sea much like the original Danish shores Elsinore once sat on. My parents still do honest work, with their hands—because even now, in a post-human world, some things run on bodied labour. Hayden was not like me, but he was afraid of the same things that I was, and his fear changed the world.

---

1 One of the earliest instances of whole mind upload technology pioneered by Dr Graham Lichfield some half a decade prior. It processed neural impulses, solidified synaptic patterns into coherent thought, and wired them into existence. Graham Lichfield's own neuromap recordings have been lost to time, but Hayden's from that night have been preserved.

"As far as I am aware, Dr Graham Lichfield was dead by minutes before he was found."

—*Denmark v Lichfield,*
243 UFR, 154 (S.C.D.K. 2050)

CHAPTER ONE
HORATIO

HERE WE ARE in the lab, and the only living occupant is Hayden.

"Horatio," he says.

Hayden Lichfield kneels beside his father's corpse, one hand white knuckled on his thigh, the other braced on the ground. "Hora—tio," he says again, his voice cracked in two around the name.

There is blood on his fingertips. Behind the lens of his glasses, his eyes are blurred, wet caught heavy on his lashes. His breath comes in spurts, heaving, the lines of his neck drawn tight as he turns his face up towards the camera.

"*Hayden,*" Horatio manages to say. "*What happened?*"

"Take a look around," Hayden says, a wry twist to his mouth even now.

"*I have,*" Horatio says delicately.

Hayden makes a little gasping sound, far back in his throat, then shudders, a brutal motion that takes hold of his entire body. He clasps a hand to his mouth, doubling over.

There are red streaks all over his face, a thin glaze over the dust of freckles on his cheeks. "'M sorry," he mumbles, gaze lost to Horatio, pinned somewhere far away. "I don't know."

"*Hayden*," Horatio says again. He is softer, now, aware of the faint tremble of Hayden's fingers.

"Are the cameras running?" he finally says, instead of an explanation.

"*Why does that matter right now?*"

There is a disconcerting story slowly solidifying in Horatio's understanding. A fresh body, Hayden's fear, his wild eyes so paranoid of surveillance. Horatio's programming, designed to slice through arrays of possibilities with elegant certainty, understands immediately the implication resting on Hayden's shoulders. Horatio waits.

"Are the cameras recording us right now?" Hayden asks with increasing urgency.

"*No*," Horatio says, and decides to give Hayden his trust, as always.

Hayden pries himself off the ground. His chest rises and falls, and he does not turn towards the corpse. Instead, he rests a hand against the touchscreen of the nearest computer console and turns it on with a reflexive flick of his wrist. Horatio is ever familiar with the contents, even more familiar with Hayden's desperation to protect it. The console holds everything on the Sisyphus Formula, the most important thing Hayden and his father had ever created. As the data blurs under Hayden's fingertips, Horatio remembers what it took to create it: desperate nights holed in fume hoods, gel stains done and redone, the flicker of enzyme equations scribbled with more and more haste as the days dragged on. An echoing flicker now, as words fly by Hayden's face too fast for human eyes to follow. Horatio catalogues it all anyway: *ß-catenin, constitutively active, Sisyphus Formula in beta...*[2]

"Is everything here?" Hayden asks, slamming a palm flat on the screen to stop it all. There is a screaming cord of tension in his shoulder that makes it look like his hand is all that is holding him upright. It shows up harshly against the black and white text, the only thing Horatio can pay attention to instead of the research writ underneath, the crawling veins snaking underneath his paling skin. Fragile and yet solid and always a world away. Impossible for Horatio to support. Hayden works his jaw. "There's nothing missing, right?"

This, at least, is something Horatio can give him. *"Everything's in place. I can't find any records of files being moved or modified since last night."*

"And is there anyone coming? Your hall cameras are still functional, right?"

"Nobody."

"Who else is in the building?"

"One lab tech on duty. Your uncle is in his office, along with his private security detail—the usual, Paul Xia." Horatio pauses. *"And Felicia."*

"Shit." Hayden scrubs a hand over his face. "What is she doing here?"

"She came with her father. I think she was curious."

"What was the *occasion?*" The strain in Hayden's voice is palpable. Whatever Hayden sometimes thinks, Horatio is not entirely oblivious to the whole sordid tale between them. Felicia Xia has occupied many roles in Elsinore—research intern, fellow student, Hayden's once-partner—but who she

---

2 Best attempts to recreate the formula's contents are chronicled in A. Foo's groundbreaking 'Chasing Sisyphus'; the approximations here are included for narrative value rather than historical accuracy.

is herself is a distant but impossibly bright figure to Horatio, filtered as she is through other peoples' recounting instead of anything Horatio knows for himself.

"*Your uncle asked for a meeting. He didn't say why.*"

Hayden's eyes narrow. "Suspicious." His hand curls into a fist against the screen. "Is it just a coincidence? Can't be."

"*Are you asking me?*"

"Why would they come in the middle of the night? Who knew they were coming? Did my dad know?"

Alarm startles Horatio into suspicion. Scenarios he hadn't considered under the realm of possibility widen, whirl. "*Are you saying they could be... complicit?*"

"I..."

Hayden's heartbeat falters.

"*Sorry,*" Horatio says hastily. "*I didn't mean to insinuate.*"

"Shit."

"*Maybe we're overthinking this.*"

"Or maybe we're not, and there's a murderer walking the halls right now."

The room's percentage of carbon dioxide inches up. Hayden threads a hand into his hair, clutching tight.

"*Hayden,*" Horatio gently admonishes, "*breathe.*"

"But—"

"*Hayden.*"

Hayden winds himself up further and further, his knuckles straining white against the slip of his pale hair. It takes him further and further away from Horatio, who feels increasingly like only the physical shell of Elsinore, nothing but circuits and cameras, prison to Hayden's prisoner.

He slips to his knees. When he looks up, all Horatio sees are the dilated glaze of his pupils, the slack part of his lips, expression wiped clean not from serenity, but a fear deeper than even panic. Horatio is familiar with this, too. He adjusts the temperature in the room, nudges it a few degrees higher, sends a warm breeze trickling over Hayden's skin. It doesn't do much, but Hayden's eyes droop, go half-lidded, and the awfulness of his stare diminishes slightly without the gaping width of it. Horatio dims the sharp fluorescence of the lights, too, watches the way the white glow of the console screen beams down on Hayden's form like moonlight. Not quite peaceful, but there is nothing else Horatio can do other than settle and wait and wish. When he gets like this, Hayden calls it a disconnect—*like my mind is detaching from my body,* he says, a frustrated twitch to his upper lip. *I don't quite feel real.* What does that make me to you? Horatio used to wonder, when they were both nascent enough to knowing each other that Horatio was still content to be unnamed, still felt unmoored by nature. Now, Horatio doesn't so much wish for physicality to prove an innate realness in himself, but to reach out; not a want to be grounded, but to ground.

Slowly, in the shadowed lab room, Hayden comes back to himself.

He blinks, once, twice, then faster. A frown breaks the vacancy of his face. When he releases his hand from his hair, strands come out, flaxen against the speckled linoleum flooring of the lab.

"I need to transfer the data," he croaks. All at once, his limbs unfurl, as quick to action as he was to collapse.

He wipes a palm on his lab coat and moves to his desk in a few strides.

"Are you talking about the Sisyphus Formula?"

"Yeah," Hayden mutters, snatching up the papers piled in a drawer. After a few moments of digging, he emerges with a small data card pinched in his fingers. "Is there anything missing on your end?" he asks as he comes back to the console, where Horatio can see him clearest.

Horatio pauses and runs a quick scan over his own systems. Comes across—a glitch.

"*Oh*," he says.

"What is it?" Hayden snaps. "Did you see something?"

"No," Horatio says, "*I mean—*"

"Could you please not be cryptic right now?"

"*I* meant," Horatio enunciates, "*that there's something missing, actually. Two hours, to be precise.*"

Hayden is quiet for a while, head turned down.

The only sound in the lab is the slow trickle of something liquid running down one counter, pooling amidst shattered glass and upturned beakers. Aside from the mess on the ground—red, slick, impossible to miss—the only broken thing in the room.

"If there's time missing... then it must've been premeditated," Hayden says, sticking his thumb in his mouth as he starts to poke at the console. "Therefore..."

"*You think they want the data.*"

Hayden inserts the card into its slot. "I don't want to risk it."

The data slowly divests itself out of Horatio's knowledge and into the card. As it's done, all Horatio remembers is the purpose of the formula, nothing of the process of making it. Last minute, he snatches an image out of the stream—Elsinore's radiation room, an oblique shot off angle of a crooked camera that would be fixed two weeks later, the first night Hayden had thought he'd broken through and so had stayed long past everyone else. The way the harried glow of the computer screen seemed to reflect some hectic truth in him. The carved line of light, bisecting his face from furrowed brow to the concentrated divot of his mouth. It's useless to anyone who might be looking for the exact mechanics of the formula, but Horatio knows there's an unbearable tenderness in how he holds tight to it. This is the evidence of Hayden's efforts, if nothing else. Horatio wants at least that much to keep.

WELCOME TO ELSINORE LABS reads the blank flashing message of the screen when it's over.

Hayden runs a finger over the card, reverent. He slips it in his pocket and shrugs his lab coat higher on his shoulders.

"*Cold?*" Horatio can't help but ask.

Hayden gives his camera a wry look. "Turn the temperature down."

"*Why?*"

"Slows down the decomposition process," Hayden says.

"*...And?*"

"I have a plan, Horatio," Hayden says, and a smile splits his face for the first time that day, toothy and fierce. "Please."

"*I don't like the sound of that,*" Horatio says, but complies. Cool air whistles through Elsinore's vents, plunging the room into a steady drop. "*Do I get to know what this plan is?*"

Hayden's hesitation is visible in the purse of his lips. Instead of answering, he steps back towards the bench, where the incubator sits. Little vials are lined up inside, swirling samples of formula within them. Horatio watches from the monitor inside as Hayden methodically clears them out, row by row. One vial goes in his pocket. The rest, unflinchingly, he sweeps onto the ground.

"I need to keep everything on the Sisyphus Formula safe," Hayden says, still alight with something Horatio can't quite name, eyes gleaming. He drops the rest of the bench's glassware on top of the already broken vials, fluids and synthetic cell cultures spilling over the floor. Now, a milky-white mixes with the red, leaking through the cracks between the tiles. He doesn't even wait for the puddle to settle before stepping over it, heels slipping in the mess. A hand ruffling through his hair as he mutters, "I don't trust this place, Horatio."

"*Ouch,*" Horatio says dryly.

Hayden pauses halfway to the door. "I didn't mean it like that." He puts a hand on the lock-pad, obviously uncracked. "Someone did this," he says, tracing the edge of the lock with a finger. "Someone wanted this."

"*Then you're in danger, too.*"

Hayden flashes him another grin. "That's not the priority right now."

"*It should be.*"

His finger falls from the lock, limp at his side. "What am I supposed to do about that, Horatio?" he asks, his voice gaining a tremble at the edges, the smile thinning out. "All I can do is protect what I still can."

In a way, Horatio understands this. Everything in him screams towards it, to keep safe what he holds most precious. But Hayden's mind is nothing if not stubborn and there's no protecting someone from themselves. That's always been the problem.

"*And then?*" Horatio asks, if only to stall him a moment. Despite the gory evidence of its recent past, this lab is a bubble, something soap-spun and caught. On the second floor, Charles Lichfield paces afoot. The lab tech sits slumped in his chair on night shift in the supply room. Felicia Xia leans against the wall, listening. Paul Xia wrings his hands, speaking to Charles every so often. This is the last time Hayden can be alone with him, without the rest of Elsinore wondering, trying to watch.

"Then I'm going to find out who did this."

Horatio does not like the grim certainty of Hayden's mouth. The temperature drops another few degrees. Hayden sucks his bottom lip between his teeth, worrying at the flesh. Minute quantities of fresh iron mingles in the air. Slowly, he pivots on a heel, shoulders dropping as he slumps unceremoniously against the pristine door. Like this, the corpse is in his line of sight. Hayden's hands shake. He pins them between his legs and tips his head back, his sullen hair falling out of the careful brushed sweep over his forehead. "Do you think I'm being stupid?" he asks the ceiling.

"*I think you're being hasty,*" Horatio replies promptly.

Hayden closes his eyes and breathes out a long breath. "Thank you for being honest."

"*I always am.*"

"Can you turn the neuromapper on?"

For a moment, Horatio does not process the words. Or some part of him does, but the implication does not fully sink in until Hayden has brushed most of the hair away and is looking at him, beseechingly, lower lip still caught in his teeth with the bleeding edge of pink flush under the skin.

The neuromapper was Dr Lichfield's greatest invention— would always be, if the Sisyphus Formula was never finished. Hayden had refused, when his father had given him one. At the time, Horatio had privately been relieved. Dr Lichfield (the *late* Dr Lichfield) had one installed, of course, but storing one's employer's thoughts via data had always carried an edge of impartiality to it, and besides, Dr Lichfield didn't often connect to Horatio's interface. There was something horrifically intimate about the notion of carving a direct pathway into Hayden's mind. Something neither of them could come back from, having taken the plunge. Hayden had allowed his father to install the hardware, but the machinery sat cold and unused at the base of his skull, a dead end of a thing that Horatio tried not to think about most days.

And now, Hayden is asking for it.

"Please," Hayden says.

"*Are you sure?*" Horatio asks.

"I want to," Hayden says, nodding. "I—just in *case*—"

They are both keenly aware of the corpse cooling in a gnarled mess before them. Air cycles through Elsinore's vents, carrying leftover keratin particles, microscopic remnants that Hayden surely is aspirating. The only thing left of the man who believed so passionately in the lasting endurance of life. Only protein and dust, all carbon, nothing of the man except what's stored in Horatio's memory.[3]

"*You can't undo this,*" Horatio says. "*Are you sure you want me to…?*"

"No," Hayden snaps. His hand is curled around the back of his neck, like the physical barrier can protect him. "But I don't want to end up gone forever, either. Just do it before I change my mind."

"*Okay,*" says Horatio, because he's never been able to refuse a direct request from Hayden. He opens the link, activates what was lying dormant, starts the program.

It takes less than a minute to change both of them irrevocably.[4]

Hayden gasps, his hand tightening over his spine, the silvery metal of the neuromapper interface peeking out from

---

3 Many attempts at retrieving Graham Lichfield's neuromap have been made, all ultimately futile.

4 What follows is my best attempt at illustrating the sensorial experience; at this point in the neuromap log, large chunks of recollection are missing, either from decay or corrupted through the synthesis/recording process itself.

underneath one finger. It is nestled between two vertebrae, a flat disc of titanium from the outside. A soft white glow bursts from it, and Hayden pulls his other hand in front of his mouth, muffling another breathy gasp. He pulls his legs up, tucked tight under his chin, and Horatio tries not to dip into the live stream of thoughts suddenly accessible to him, but it's impossible not to, a storm of wildfire fury that crowds everything else out, all—*someone murdered my father slashed his throat with broken glass what if someone comes what if my uncle sees the walls are not soundproof someone is always listening get up and look at the body get up don't look at it don't look at it he's already dead this is pointless he's already dead and all I have left is the research to protect and Horatio*—Horatio slams the mental door shut here, with effort, and slowly the lab comes back into clarity. Hayden still slumped against the wall, looking ashen. One hand fallen at his side, the other firmly clamped to his mouth, a small whimper escaping as he curls in tighter on himself. He looks vulnerable and small, and Horatio has never been more aware of the flesh and bone tremors of Hayden's body before, the frisson of spitting nerves, the flushing skin and delicate bones, stiff against the cold door.

As Hayden's eyes slip closed and he slowly releases the tension held tight in his neck, Horatio is struck by the sensation of this body previously unknowable to him, unfurling. Ready to be known.

Hayden? Horatio asks, testing the mental bond now forged between them.

Hayden blinks wearily. He raises a hand to his ear, like he's trying to physically touch a sound that never came from there, then his mouth quirks up in an understanding smile. *Yeah?* he responds internally.

Are you okay?

The flash of a frown. Horatio feels its echo, somewhere in his memory. The walls between them are still thin. He remembers this stage, with Dr Lichfield, but yet again, again, it had been more clinical, easier to build up the walls between them until the neuromapper was recording without Horatio's conscious knowledge. Hayden's thoughts burn as they come.

"I'll be fine," Hayden says out loud, shaking out a wrist experimentally. "I think."

"*I need your permission to stay connected,*" Horatio reminds him. "*We can turn it off. It'll still be recording, I just won't see any of it.*"

Hayden shakes his head. "It's fine. I want... I want you to keep watch."

"*Okay,*" says Horatio. "*But... is it weird?*"

The hesitation in Horatio's own question is new. Hayden pauses, noticing. "What do you mean?"

"*I...*" For once, Horatio is the one faltering. "*Do you mind it, I mean?*"

Hayden laughs and scrubs a hand over his face. "Do I mind you having access to my most intimate thoughts?"

Horatio finds that he has no words for that.

The look on Hayden's face softens, from mirth to something smaller. More *intimate*. "No, Horatio," he says carefully. "I don't." Then he shrugs deeper into his lab coat as if against the chill and says, "You had almost all of them already anyway."

In the ensuing quiet, he clambers to his feet again, hand on the door.

"*Are you still doing this?*" Horatio asks, for lack of anything better.

The energy sweeps back into Hayden's limbs. Through the

neuromapper link, it feels how Horatio thinks lightning must feel, or like too-cold ice cream, something that sinks itself into you with a sudden and quick flash of clarity dipped in pain.

"There's nothing else I can do," Hayden says again. "Can you stay low for a while? Next time we talk, everyone will know."

"*Fine*," Horatio says, because he has never been able to refuse a direct request from Hayden, not even twice in a row. "*Please don't get yourself killed, too.*"

That knife of a smile again, brighter than the lights around him. "I'll try not to."

And then the door swings open, and Horatio watches him go.

As we come to the midpoint of the 21st century, Dr Graham Lichfield has accomplished perhaps his greatest achievement to date: the Neuromapper®, a recording device for one's very thoughts. When asked to comment on the application of his project, Dr Lichfield stated, "Consider it my entry in the time-honoured tradition of scientists in pursuit of the elixir of life. The neuromapper can preserve your ongoing thoughts, your way of thinking, everything that makes up who you are. I don't think it's farfetched to call that a kind of immortality."

—*Beyond the Body: A Review of NeuralTech Now and in the Future* (2045)

CHAPTER TWO
HAYDEN

THE HUMAN MIND is not designed to hold linearity. Hayden Lichfield's mind interfaces with the neuromapper uneven, piecemeal—

—stiffening flesh and leaking fluids, marring the sterile tiles, burning iron—what once was his father—

—the data card iridescent under his nail, the only thing left—the chemical sting of spilled formula—

—a bottomless, yawning feeling of not-knowing—

—Horatio—

Horatio.

—not infallible, the sheltering walls broken down, Elsinore gutted like a wounded animal—

Hayden doesn't remember when he first realized he is going to die.

In an average human lifespan, approximately 10^{16} cell divisions will occur. Every time, due to some fluke of nature of the haphazard, patchwork machinery that evolution has put together, the chromosomes shorten. Only by a few hundred bases each time, but this is enough to wear a body down. Eventually, the lifeline that is DNA runs out, too. Eventually, the wear and tear of living—growing, proliferating—finally frays the ends of all twenty-three pairs of chromosomes, and they first fuse, then shatter.

Hayden doesn't remember when he first learned about this slow erosion of genetic material. All he's even remembered is turning his hand palm up and staring, knowing little pieces of himself are coming apart, even now, with every breath he takes in, always.

Standing in the white serenity of Elsinore's empty halls, all he can do is twist his fingers into each other, tighter and tighter, imagining the chromosomes breaking.

Something inside him is always dying.

Hayden takes in his next shuddering breath. His heart thumps, audible, in his chest.

There is nobody in the halls with him. Ahead, Elsinore stretches like the razor edge of a knife, brilliant and gleaming. Hayden feels flayed open, exposed. The light itself sharp on his skin, the neuromapper digging into his thoughts. The thin skin of his lip rubs raw against his incisors, capillaries bursting under the pressure. Out here, everything is still pristine. He could close his eyes and imagine normalcy behind the door, his father breathing and beckoning.

Before he can regret it, he pulls the door open again, enough to reach the locking screen, swings his elbow back and slams it in hard enough to hear a crack. When he lets the door slide shut, it clicks ever so softly. When he pushes again, it does not open.

The rest of the lab needs to know what happened, but no one can know he was the first on scene.

Hayden tugs at his sweater and turns away, towards that white blankness.

The hallway wavers in his vision. Hayden has walked this route a thousand times, but his memories of knocking on Security's door with a sheepish grin and no passcode in hand feel like they belong to another person now. He crosses his hands in front of him as he walks, pressing fingers deep to his wrist and counting in his head. That stubborn radial pulse, high and frantic, surges against his fingertips. It's a welcome reminder that there is still some vitality left here, there is still something that remains contained, potent, just for himself.

Eventually, he makes it to his destination.

Supply Room, the sparse black lettering on the door reads. Hayden releases his wrist and raises a hand to knock, wondering which lab tech is here tonight. The building isn't built for more than half a dozen researchers at once, but there is always someone sitting watch over the machinery.

"Come in!" whoever it is calls. Hayden doesn't recognize the muffled voice.

Hayden grabs the handle and pulls. "Hey," he says as he steps in. Even to his own ears, his voice sounds hollow. He clears his throat to give it some life.

The supply room isn't much to look at: a bare desk and chair before a full wall of screens, the rest of the room lined with shelves upon shelves of fresh equipment. Sitting with his legs bunched up beneath him is Gabriel Rasmussen, one of the local hires from a year out, fresh from the University of Copenhagen. One of the techs Hayden doesn't despise but barely gets along with—he works with the son of Dr Lichfield like he might with any other grad student—but in this case, his presence makes him both a potential ally and a potential suspect.

He's also blatantly not paying attention to his job, which makes Hayden unfairly resentful.

Rapping his knuckles hard on the wall, Hayden leans in. "The soccer game will be there after you clock out," he says.

Rasmussen doesn't turn around. "Americans," he mutters.

"I'm from Canada," Hayden says automatically—an easy retort between the two of them, something to fall back on.

"*North* Americans," Rasmussen says, like he always does. He spins around in his chair and runs a hand through the lazy tangle of his hair, bunched at the back in a low bun. "You work too hard," he says, a bare touch of a lilting accent in his words.

Hayden frowns. "No, I don't."

"Come out with me next time," Rasmussen says with a grin. "Bet you'll say no."

Hayden scowls. "I need your help."

If Rasmussen is offended by the blatant sidestep, he doesn't show it. They've gone out to the local bar about half a dozen times in nearly a year, which Hayden considers adequate, but which obviously presents as consciously antisocial in the eyes of his peers. With Rasmussen, it's hard to see through the easygoing exterior to figure out what he really thinks. He's still never stopped asking.

"What with?" he asks, already turning his laptop off, soccer game forgotten.

"The door won't open."

Rasmussen raises an eyebrow. "Again?"

Hayden scowls. "I think the frequency makes it obvious it's the door and not me," he mutters.

"Have you tried knocking? Your dad's around tonight, right?"

Any relief that had come with the mundanity of their previous conversation dries up. Hayden's face numbs. "Yeah, but he's not answering. He was trying to get some activity out of this sample. Frankly, I think it's a lost cause, so he might be too caught up in the futility of it all to hear me knocking." This part is not a lie. Hayden turns his lips up into a wide smile, shakes his head. He is the picture of a dutiful son: exasperated, but fond. "You know how he gets."

Rasmussen stretches his arms over his head and sighs theatrically. "You really are related," he says, then grabs his toolkit out from under the desk. "You owe me for this, Lichfield."

"I'll buy you a drink Friday," Hayden offers.

Rasmussen grins, then stands.

Hayden lets Rasmussen take the lead as they leave the supply room, falls in half a step behind as they both head back down the hall. Conversation openers fly through his mind, but he can't bring himself to give voice to any of them. Instead, he studies the hunch of Rasmussen's back, the open and fluttering close of his scapula as he breathes.

Going back, the walk through the hall is much too short.

Too soon, they stand at the door to the lab.

Rasmussen knocks, then slings his hands back in his pockets to wait.

"Must be something really interesting going on in there," he says, and Hayden has to swallow down a bubble of hysterical laughter.

When enough time passes and no one comes to open the

door, Rasmussen sighs again and gets to work on the lock. He crouches. Hayden stands above him, flexing his fingers. The tightness in his chest is enough to bring back an old paranoia: that his heart has stopped without him realizing, that he only has seconds before the inevitable collapse. Even as still as he is, there is no telltale thump in his chest. He hears nothing; the only thing ringing in his ears is the metal-on-metal clink of Rasmussen working. Panic crawls up his throat.

He's fumbling for his wrist when the lock clicks.

"Think I'm gonna have to replace the whole thing," Rasmussen says. "Sounds like something's jammed in there. You sure you didn't see anything weird when you left?"

"Nothing."

Rasmussen shrugs, then shoves a tool into the door and yanks down. There is another sharp crack. The handle swings down effortlessly when he tries again.

Hayden takes in a breath so deep his ribs strain as they flare open, his skin sliding up against the soft cotton of his shirt.

"Thanks," he says as Rasmussen opens the door. Slides forward into the stillness of the lab, several degrees colder than the hall outside.

"Drinks! But okay, fine, call me again if there's any—oh, my god."

Hayden tries to shutter his eyes, but he can't look away. The clinical calm does nothing to stop him wondering, since the inception of this night, what of his father's body has collated within him, how much sloughed off epithelium he has inhaled, how much the lurid acid on his tongue is chemical taint, putrescine-toxic, how much more death is settling within him.

Nothing's changed since he first saw the body. The red

pulp, the intermingling stench of rot and iron, the snarling, twisting mess that is the corpse's limbs. It is crumpled against the lab bench, face first into a metal cabinet. No signs of blunt force trauma, though now that he is facing it full on, there is the distinct shimmer of broken glass, gravelly in the congealing blood.

A picture unfurls in Hayden's mind, clearer than he wants it to be: intruder, fight, scuffle, a scattering of glass— weaponized, then a vicious stab to his father's jugular, the hot spill, and finally the guilty escape.

The murderer left no footprints.

Only a mess. From here, it barely looks human.

How terrible death is, Hayden thinks, to take vibrant, vital people, and render them into nothing but their component parts, all greying flesh and hissing gas and frayed, useless nerves.

Rasmussen is shaking.

Hayden braces a hand on the doorframe, though he doesn't need it. Just when Rasmussen is turning to him with a look of horror, he lets his own legs go out. Fresh vessels break and blossom under his skin when his knees hit the ground, bruises surely to come. He's grateful for it, this living pain, a physical snarling thing. He kneels here, before this thing that was once his father, and tells himself that's the only sort of pain there is to feel.

CHAPTER FOUR

Earlier this year, Felicia Xia shared an intimate, heart-wrenchingly honest testimony in her article, Tell Me A Tragedy, centred around her experience of the unfortunate incident that occurred at Elsinore Labs. Reading it, I was struck by the complex relationship she shared with Hayden Lichfield, now facing trial for his role in the events, and yet who Felicia struggles to condemn on the page. The conflict jumps off the page: to hate him, or not to hate him?

— An Interview with Felicia Xia

CHAPTER THREE

Excerpted from *Tell Me A Tragedy* by Felicia Xia

IT WAS LATE when Charles Lichfield gathered us all into his office to make an announcement. Though this was the only room in the facility that had any windows, barely any light filtered in. We all stood, bathed in the stark fluorescence Elsinore favoured, listening to the grave news.

There had been a murder.

More, there had been a *theft*.

I was calm at the onset. Surprised, perhaps, but I'd always assumed there was a reason Charles Lichfield had hired my father as a personal security detail. This was just that reason, brutally realized.

"As of now," Charles said hoarsely, "we go into lockdown." And just like that, the doors to Elsinore Labs were shut, cutting the five of us away from the outside world. The walls rumbled, corridors closing themselves off, until we were left in this shell of a building. Charles told us he had a line to the police, and his eyes were so shot through with bright red veins that I felt sorry for him, and I wanted to help him in his grief. So, we all agreed. Lockdown until we recovered his brother's most precious research. It felt logical at the time.

Afterwards, they would tell me the siege lasted for fourteen hours. I was the only one to escape unscathed.

Supposedly, this makes me uniquely qualified to speak about it. But I am not writing this to sensationalize, nor do I believe I can shed light on what so many people have asked about the incident. Namely, *why?* I don't know what Charles Lichfield was planning when he first initiated the lockdown. I don't know why Hayden Lichfield reacted the way he did. At the time, I only knew what I was told of Graham Lichfield's research, supposedly revolutionary.

All I know is this: I was not supposed to be in Elsinore when the doors shut, but I was. I wish my father hadn't been so hasty to heed Charles's call, at least not enough to rush over in the dead of night, but he did. Some have asked me if I want to erase my mind of the whole ordeal, wipe my hands and memories clean of it, but I don't.

I am writing this to clarify for myself, as best I can, why Hayden killed my father.

If you manage to derive some meaning from it, all the better.

THERE WE WERE, confused and bleary-eyed, watching Charles pace back and forth across the tight space of his office. In the washed-out light, his hair was almost blond, his eyes darker than usual. The only lab tech on duty that night was Rasmussen—not one I'd had much contact with before, since he worked with Hayden and his father instead of Charles and I—and he stood cross-armed by the door, as if he alone could ward off whatever threat that might appear from outside. Hayden was at the desk, slumped over, his head in his hands. I remember pitying him. I remember hating that I pitied him, because this was the first time in months that we'd spent more than a few minutes in the same room without him fleeing like a coward, and I didn't want to still care, but I did. How could I not? His father had just died. I hated that I couldn't look away.

My own father had his hand tight on my elbow, palms damp.

A tense silence had fallen over us, thick and unrelenting. Earlier, when the deep rattle of all the doors slamming rumbled over us, it was like the walls themselves were collapsing. Now, the air was left stifling and claustrophobic.

I'm sorry, Charles had said, frantic, *but I can't lose his research. I'm sorry.* He didn't mention that he'd just locked us in with a killer, but there was so much wildfire in his eyes that his frenzy was contagious. I knew Charles Lichfield well enough by then to know that there was nothing stopping him until he got what he wanted. When he spoke, it was with a persistent tic of his upper lip.

"We should stay here for now," Charles said, tucking his arms behind his back. "The intruder must be hiding somewhere in the building. It's safest here."

Rasmussen shifted. "You sure there was an intruder?" The unsaid accusation hung in the air: what if it had been one of us?

Beside him, at the desk, Hayden stirred enough to aim a dull glare at Rasmussen, though his chin still rested in his arms. "Of course there was," he muttered, scratchy but fierce. "What else could've happened?"

Rasmussen's gaze slid over each of us.

Hayden scoffed. "Horatio?" he called.

"*Yes?*" Elsinore's signature AI system chimed in. "*How can I help you?*"

"Has anyone left the facilities since we rebooted your system?"

"*No one.*"

Tilting his gaze back to Rasmussen, Hayden raised a condescending eyebrow.

"Thank you, Horatio," Charles said. "If there is any chance we can recover that data, I need to take it. That was Graham's life's work. He…"—his voice grew quieter, gentler, breaking the tension without relieving it—"he often said he'd rather die than let it go to the wrong hands."

Rasmussen settled back against the door, arms tight over his chest. "So, we're all just sitting ducks, then?"

Charles composed himself and lifted his chin. "If you're concerned about your safety, don't be. Paul has agreed to investigate, and we've already established communication with the department outside."

"Don't suppose you'll let *us* make any calls, then?"

"I have a line to the authorities. I thought it best to shut outgoing signals down to keep the noise low." And indeed, my phone was long dead. All I had with me was a pager, useful to send notes to my dad, useless to send word to the outside.

My father mopped at his brow with a napkin, but he didn't raise any objections. This was the very thing his presence was supposed to prevent, I suppose. But private security detail or not, he wasn't technically allowed in the facility afterhours—

as a student intern, I was even less so, but I was curious. Suppose that was my fault, in the end. I thought about the long ride down in my father's rattling car earlier that night, before any of us knew anything would go wrong, the streets empty save for the sparkling hologram ads downtown, selling everything from the latest de-aging cream to virtual reality boyband stadium shows. Looking back, it was like a haunting, the city busy with ghostly imitations of people instead of any living body.

In the wake of our uneasy silence, Hayden said something that really did cut through the air of suspicions and doubt. He pulled himself up, all the earlier irritation drained away, and when he asked, "What about the body?" his voice was barely a whisper.

Charles's face fell. He crossed the room in two quick strides, then faltered, his hand hovering in the air just over his nephew's forearm. Hayden blinked, looked up, then edged his hand along the desk to hook a finger around Charles's sleeve.

"We have refrigeration units," Charles said, his voice pitched low as if he wanted only Hayden to hear. "After Paul ensures the coast is clear, we'll… put him to rest."

"I want to do it."

"Hayden…"

Hayden shook his head. He tilted his face up and away as if trying to hold back tears, and though I didn't understand his request, I saw the emotion behind it. He pulled Charles's arm into his grip and clutched tight with white knuckles. "I want to move my father's body," he said blankly, "and I want to do it now."

Charles reeled back.

"I'm sorry," Hayden said, shaking his fringe away from his

eyes, and despite myself, my eyes were drawn to the movement. He and his uncle had always had that same sandy hair, but the way a shadow slanted over his face at that moment made his seem darker. "I know this is an active investigation. I'll—I'll come right back. Horatio can document the—the crime scene as it is right now, undisturbed. I can do it myself. I just—I can't let him stay there like that."

Charles took a step closer and draped his other arm around Hayden's shoulder.

My skin itched when I watched Hayden's defiant eyes burn. He wanted to take his father's body and stash it away in the cold. I didn't understand how you could even entertain the idea, let alone insist on it. That was when I realized I didn't understand him much anymore.

"Hayden," Charles said again, even quieter, though in the sparse office that didn't stop me from hearing his every word. "It's dangerous out there. I'll have failed your father three times over if I lose you too." The corners of his mouth twitched, like he was trying to smile and grimace simultaneously.

"I don't care," Hayden said, at the same time as I said, "I'll go with him."

All eyes fell on me.

I was desperate, then, to hide myself away from them all. There was something about the atmosphere in the office that made my teeth grind. Something about the shadows at the corners of the room, something about how nearly everybody was too tense to sit, all the chairs scattered around like barricades we had to navigate as we moved. Something about how we always moved, eyes darting, monitoring each other's every action. I was desperate enough to volunteer to go with Hayden, just to leave.

And, in retrospect, I wanted to figure him out again. That was the core of it.

I prised my father's fingers off my elbow. "Two of us is safer than one," I said, too confident in my own abilities, and besides, I'd swiped some gear out of my father's jacket on the way here and knew enough about his job to use it. I thought working here was sufficient to know Elsinore like the back of my hand.

There was some sort of discussion, but I blocked most of it out, too fixated on the way Hayden sat, hunched in on himself and half leaning on his uncle, worrying at his lip throughout the whole thing.

Finally, Charles acquiesced, and I stood by the door while Hayden extricated himself from the half-embrace and gave his uncle a tired smile.

I led the way out of the office. As soon as I eased the door shut behind us, I breathed a little easier. Counterintuitive, I know, but I preferred an unknown danger over the scrutiny of being inside.

And then we were alone. Physically, if not truly.

"Horatio?" Hayden called up to the ceiling.

"*Yes?*"

"We have trolleys in the supply room still, right?"

"*We do. They should work to hold up an average male body.*"

I watched Hayden's shoulders sag a little. He looked left, then right, then scrubbed at his face before nodding to the empty air. "Thanks," he muttered, turning back to me, only a touch of stilted awkwardness in his voice. "Do you mind helping me grab the trolley? I won't make you do any of the... dirty work, but I might need someone to help me push."

He looked too young, then. He wouldn't even meet my eyes.

I'd spent the entirety of my internship at Elsinore trying to avoid him. Before that, we'd spent half of our relationship in Elsinore, together. I had never really known him without this place, but that much had always been obvious to me. Even in bed, he would be restless, waking up in half fits to scrawl notes onto an old pad he kept by his nightstand.

"Okay," I said, and then he gave me the barest hint of a smile, and I had to look down the hall to not betray the sudden startled longing that hit me. I swallowed hard. "Why not get your uncle to send someone?" I asked, wanting to steer the conversation.

"Who would he get? Rasmussen?"

"Maybe that's better," I said. *Better than seeing your father's body for yourself.*

"My dad died alone."

I didn't know what to say.

"Felicia," Hayden said from behind me, and the sound of it was familiar enough that my feet were spinning me around before I'd even processed what I was doing.

Here, now, he blinked at me, eyes wide and bloodshot. His fringe was too messy and long, falling in his face. "Felicia," he said again, "do you know how long it takes for a human body to start to decompose?"

I nearly laughed.

Callous instinct, I'm sure, but he used to ask me questions like that all the time, see. Suddenly, while brushing his teeth; whispering, in the crammed corner of a little hole-in-the-wall restaurant; loudly, while ignoring alarmed looks from tourists, that time we took a weekend trip out to Berlin. He asked me morbid questions over ice cream, and I laughed at him for being so sombre.

But this wasn't a hypothetical anymore.

"Why in the world would I know that?" I finally managed, echoing what I used to say to him in response.

Hayden's smile tugged tight over his face, plastic. Certainly, he remembered, but he didn't show it. "Minutes, really. As soon as the heart stops pumping, the cells choke and die. There's no coming back from that." He shook his head and swiped a hand over his mouth. "My father is rotting in that lab room. When I close my eyes, I keep imagining what it must look like, how distorted his body will be. He deserves to be put to some sort of rest, and by someone who cares for him, not the lab tech who had the misfortune of coming to work on a godawful day like this."

I have seen Hayden Lichfield at his lowest. At the very end, I don't think he was pretending for anyone, least of all me. We weren't like that anymore. But that's nothing to say about this moment, when I thought he was still knowable to me. I still turn it over in my head, over and over, trying to find the little breaks in his armour, in that pathetic mask of sorrow he put on for us all.

I didn't ask again after that. I didn't want to know what he might say.

WE FOUND OURSELVES standing outside the door of the lab, trolley in hand. Hayden licked his lips, a quick flash of his tongue dragging over chapped skin, then bowed his head. When he opened the door, a nauseating smell seeped out from the cracks, making my eyes water.

"I can take it from here," he said. "Thanks."

I certainly wasn't going to protest. The trolley squeaked when I pushed it towards him, bumping up against the wall. Hayden took the handle and turned it around, propping the lab door open with his shoulder as he backed into the room. He looked up. He held my gaze. I don't know what expression I wore, only that I could feel icy fear creeping down my back, and I couldn't tear myself away from his dark eyes. Still the same eyes, then. The entire time, he stared at me, as if there was some secret he might glean, if only he could scrutinize my face for longer. His mouth twitched, but he didn't say a word.

That was how we parted: me, waiting and expectant; Hayden, backing into the doors.

From there, I could see what used to be an exit, except all that faced me down the hall now was a smooth white wall. I'd explored the halls so many times over the years that seeing that blank, sealed-off blunt end was surreal, claustrophobic. I thought of the tremble that shook the foundations of the building when the lockdown was initiated, the grind of walls slamming down—all the doors were blocked off like this, vanishing behind a blockade of metal. Elsinore was built to withstand a siege.[5]

I didn't get a chance to pry at the gate, much as a panicked instinct inside me wanted to. Before I could, the doors to the lab swung open again, and Hayden walked out with the corpse.

After that, I didn't dare speak—I might've gagged if I tried. I'll spare the details of the body, but suffice to say, I did not recognize the Graham Lichfield I knew lying on the trolley.

Hayden nudged me with one shoulder. His hands, holding tight to the bar, were slick with blood. "Let's go," he said, and I followed him towards what would later become our makeshift morgue, my words dying in my throat.

---

5 It is uncertain how the specially constructed walls of Elsinore Labs function, nor who it was that initiated the construction project in the first place. Most sources attribute Graham Lichfield, consistent with the reputation he built in the twilight years of his life as irrationally protective of his space.

CHAPTER FOUR
HAYDEN

THE BODY IS heavy.

Alone, without Felicia, the weight is strangely more to lift. Hayden heaves the trolley into the cold-room, stopping just before the walls of glass that surround all their cold tissue samples. When he eases the trolley sideways, the body rocks. An arm dangles off the side before he can steady the wheels.

Wait for two breaths, in and out. Watch it crystallize.

Hayden heaves the limb back onto its chest. His blood-soaked hand leaves a ring around the limp wrist.

It's a stark reminder of what he's here to do. He turns his own hand, palm up. Old blood has seeped into the furrows of his fingerprints, thick and viscous. Further down, flaking on his palm, is a darker, ruddy brown. Hayden is here for a resurrection, but there will be more blood spilled.

He wipes it all as best he can on the body's lab coat. Red blends into red, smearing the already dirty fabric.

Once he deems his fingers clean enough, he nudges the trolley aside and pushes on the glass pane. There is a beep, then the wall slides open neatly, freezing air hissing out into the small hall. Hayden shudders as he pulls the trolley fully into the chamber.

Usually, if he knows he needs to spend time here, he pulls on a heavier coat, at least some gloves, but there is no time and so he only has the same flimsy lab coat as always. But it's not the cold that makes his hands quiver as he pulls out the vial of Sisyphus Formula and lays it out on the table. The metal *clinks* as he sets it down. From the drawer underneath, he pulls out cotton swabs, a scalpel, a suture kit, and the applicator designed just last month: a syringe with a smooth, metallic body and a motorized drill, its hair-thin fibreglass bit housed in a metal tip.

For a resurrection, two things must be brought back: the body, and then the mind.

For those purposes, two machines rest in the corner of the room. A modified ECMO—meant to prolong life, used here to give it—stands bursting with tubing; sitting beside it, the matching helmet meant to interface with one's neuromapper. Hayden pulls them both over.

When all the parts to his irrational but insistent idea are assembled, he pauses.

"*Are you really going through with this?*" Horatio cuts in, not needing the direct link to Hayden's own mind to figure out exactly what the plan is and always has been.

"You don't think this is a good idea."

"*How could I?*"

Hayden shrugs and presses his lips into a line. "I need to know who did it."

"*Didn't even think to ask if he recorded it?*"

"He connects his neuromapper every morning at seven when he comes in," Hayden says stiffly. "Turns it off at night. You have nothing."

Horatio doesn't contest the point. *"Hayden, do you have any idea how guilty you look right now?"*

Hayden nearly brings his thumb up to chew before he catches sight of the dried blood that hasn't quite flaked off yet. Rubbing the pads of his fingers together, he leans his elbows on the table. "They *would* believe that I could kill my own father, wouldn't they?"

"It's suspicious enough you didn't immediately raise the alarm."

"No one knows that I didn't. What's Paul Xia doing now?"

"Talking to your uncle."

"You'll tell me if he asks you anything, right?"

"Yes, but you're aware I have to answer. Truthfully."

"That's fine. That's a risk I'll have to take. So long as the cameras aren't recording. Are they?"

"They're running, can't turn that off in here. But I'm not recording. Only in here."

Hayden stifles a laugh. "Always so paranoid, Dad," he murmurs.

Horatio makes a muffled noise that sounds almost like a scoff. *"Hayden, there's something you're not saying."*

"What?"

Horatio pauses, like he doesn't want to press, but then: *"Just tell me if it's important."*

A wave of guilt crawls up his throat. Hayden closes his eyes, trying to keep the tide of emotion away from his mind: the neuromapper link is not infallible either, there is nothing impenetrable about this, he—his mouth tastes like acid and copper, bitter and thick. He flexes his arms, unsticking his stiff and cold-locked joints. The body is lying before him. Before *them*, because Hayden is not alone. He needs to remember that.

In front of it, there is an array of slick, shining tools, and his hands ache to hold them, use them, share the culmination of all their work.

"I want to know," he says, because of all the lies he's told and plans to tell, he doesn't want to lie to Horatio. "I want to know if Sisyphus works. I want to try it." His fingers curl in the air. Everything feels electric.

Hayden pulls out a bottle of methanol and rinses it over his palm to clean it. The quick cold as it evaporates sharpens his eyes, dries the last of his old tears. "I've been trying to achieve this my whole career," he says, attention fixed on wiping down the table. "This isn't novel; I'm only starting the first human trial a few months early." And—Hayden bites down hard on his lip, unwilling to give the last thought breath. And if it works, he'll have his father back. He will. Even if only for a moment.

Horatio can probably feel it, this bone-deep ache. The wanting.

Hayden grabs the body's arm before he can think better of it. The flesh refuses to yield when he touches two fingertips to the skin, so he presses down harder until it does give. And then it's much too soft, too much without structure. Hayden rubs his thumbs over and into the muscle, inch by inch working some tenderness back into the body. With some effort, he manages to roll it so that it lies face-up.

The entire left side of its face is caved in, a weeping wound crawling across the crumpled remains of its cheekbone. Hayden's hands are still where they're curled around the body's neck, fingers lightly grazing both greying skin and the cool pad of the neuromapper embedded in the spine.

The eyes are still gaping open, dried tear tracks trailing out from their corners.

"*It's not him anymore.*" For a second, it sounds like Hayden's own voice, whispering from the dark corners of his brain, but then he registers that it's Horatio, so close he could've been speaking from inside instead of outside.

Hayden bows his head. "I know."

He takes the other arm, still as gentle as he can, and lays it out flat. Dull numbness falls like a blanket over his head. The table feels miles away. But as long as he can still think, he can still work.

Reaching back, he unspools coils of tubing from the ECMO and lays it over the body.

Taking the catheter needles and cotton swabs, he wipes down the unturned forearm. A tendon stretches taut from wrist to elbow. Hayden pushes the tip of the needle against one still-swollen vein. It slides in easily—barely a dribble of blood escapes. He tapes it down.

The other catheter is for the neck, but the jugular is still split wide open.

He forces his hands to stop trembling to pick up the scalpel.

It is surprisingly easy to cut the damaged skin. Easier still to identify the rubbery artery slithering between the exposed edges of the dermis. Hayden rips the suture kit open, plucking the needled wire up with the forceps. Under his guidance, the needle pierces the broken epithelium, sinks deep into the flesh. The wire follows, sharp, quick. What leaks out of the artery is pale, tinged yellow, not nearly the rich red it should be. When it's done, he slides the other catheter into the lumen. Hayden grits his teeth and finishes the stitching. His knots are sloppy, but there's no one around to care.

Staring now, his eyes refuse to blink. All he sees is the shattered mosaic of his father's cheekbone. There is no fixing this puzzle; there is too much bone, too many shards. But the ugly break helps him remember this is not the same face that lingers too brightly in his memories.

His father—no, there is nothing of his father left here. Hayden squeezes his parched eyes shut, reaches out blindly for the ECMO, and flicks the machine on.

For a long time, nothing happens. The dull whir of the centrifugal pump drones on. Thick red liquid moves through the tubes, disappearing into the mess of machinery and winding back out, but the body is still. There is, mercifully, no leakage. His own pulse pounds in his ears, discrete against the rush of the machine, a steady beat to its unstable roar.

The ECMO was built to pump blood in lieu of a heartbeat. Can a body be called a corpse anymore, when life is forced to course through its veins?

Blood is easy. It's the brain, what makes up a person beyond the prison of their body—that's the hard part.

That's the point of the neuromapper. Hayden slides the neurotopographer gently over the corpse's head. The thin band of metal rests like a crown on his father's brow, gleaming a polished silver. As the magnet snaps into place over the embedded device in the spine, the whole circlet hums. The corpse's skin has taken on something of a flush. There is something moving inside it now, rushing, quick.

Hayden brings out the last piece of the puzzle: the vial of Sisyphus Formula. Trapped behind glass, the yellowing liquid inside bubbles. It shimmers, little ribbons of precipitation rippling like something alive. Innocuous on the surface, but this vial houses a miracle.

He loads it into the applicator.

This time, his hands do not shake.

Two fingers to the corpse's intact cheek, he pushes to turn the head to expose the suboccipital, where he aims the applicator. He doesn't close his eyes as he presses down on the trigger. The drill bit whirrs, slicing through the bone, then a shuddering recoil thuds up his arm as the needle slides in. As he pushes the syringe down to unload the formula, the neurotopographer beeps a rapid trill, recognizing the influx of neurotrophins flooding his father's cranial space, past the dura, past the arachnoid, piercing the pia and cutting through all the natural barriers the body has evolved to protect the secrets lying in the folds of white and grey matter.

When the vial is emptied, he pulls the applicator out. The skin gives a wet gasp, and Hayden pales as he smooths over the damp edges of the wound with a bandage.

"*Is that it?*" Horatio asks. He sounds, despite himself, as fascinated as Hayden is.

"Yeah," he says. "Normally we'd start with reconstructive procedures or something—I don't know, I'm not a surgeon and we hadn't worked out our plans for the trials, but there's no time for that, and—"

"*You're not trying to keep him alive.*"

The applicator clatters from his fingers. He stares hard at his own still shaking hands, traitorous things that they are. "No," he whispers, and he should be drowning in the guilt, but there is only an empty, sucking cavern behind his sternum. "I'm not."

All that's left now is to wait.[6]

The corpse's face is blank. Hayden wonders when it will cease being a corpse, if he will ever see it as anything but. He wonders if the carefully cultivated serum of mitogens and stem cells are working, signalling growth pathways to speed up, finding what few living cells exist and amplifying

---

6 *In vitro,* cell cultures showed near complete recovery in as little as thirty minutes.

them beyond what they were ever capable of in life. And even if it did work, would they follow the course laid out by the neuromap? Could they relink the topography of his father's brain, synapse by synapse? He wonders if there is anything left of his father in this corpse.

But no matter.

Hayden does not need his father back; he needs answers.

Before he can look away from the broken, terrified visage that he doesn't recognize, a previously dark screen in the cold room flickers to life.

Hayden whirls around.

The lone console at the back of the room glows.

"Hello?"

It is, impossibly, his father's voice. Not from the corpse—but through the speakers on the console.

"This is a bit odd, I confess," the voice continues. *"To be talking about one's death before it happens, that is."*

A shadow fills the screen, the flash of a white lab coat surrounding it. Hayden is frozen. From here, the video is grainy, the details hard to make out. His father's face is dim and blurred, but it's still obvious when he reaches up to adjust his glasses. *"I have been dreaming of dying of late,"* he says, tone wry. *"Perhaps this is presumptuous of me, but if you are hearing this, Hayden, it means you've linked up my neuromap."*

Behind, the corpse lets out a low wheeze. Hayden stands stock-still, trapped between the body and the video[7], both shadows of the man his father used to be.

"Needless to say," the man in the video says with a wide,

---

7 Proof of Graham Lichfield's last video and testament has never been properly uncovered. Contemporary accounts describe his voice as perpetually hoarse, a smoker's tone, though he never seemed to tire of speaking when he became heated.

pearly smile, "*I hope it works. And I'm proud of you, for trying.*"

Hayden's throat is suddenly thick. He presses his knuckles into the surface of the table to keep himself from swaying on his feet, eyes burning as he looks into the screen.

"*To get down to business, if indeed I've gotten myself killed, you need to know how Elsinore works.*" His father rolls out a map, smoothing it over the desk he is sitting at. The camera shakes as he angles it downward. It's more of a blueprint than anything, and Hayden understands that he is looking at Elsinore's insides.[8]

He takes a step closer.

The blueprint is utterly strange to him—disconcertingly so. As his father keeps talking, fingers gliding over the spidering lines that make up the floorplans, he realizes that he's never seen some of these rooms before. Phantom halls, stretching out into what he once thought was empty space. An entire room on the third floor never before known to him. Hayden stares wild-eyed around him, trying to find Horatio's cameras as if that will resolve Elsinore back into familiarity.

But Horatio is uncharacteristically silent.

"*Tread lightly,*" his father warns. "*Some rooms are more dangerous than others.*"

By the end of it, Elsinore sounds more like a prison than a lab. Worse, a prison he doesn't know the way out of. Hayden's earliest and fondest memories are of the soft white glow, moments spent cradled in a reading nook, Horatio's voice at his back, before he was ever Horatio. Giving the Elsinore Labs Operating System his own name had felt like

---

8 As above, nothing remains of the original Elsinore floor plans. We only have approximations created out of Hayden's memory.

something meaningful, when Hayden was eight years old and too desperate for a friend. Horatio feels as familiar to him as ever. Hayden wonders if Elsinore has always been bigger than Horatio[9], if Horatio has been as trapped as the rest of them, his consciousness held by the building's concrete shell.

How much of this place did Hayden ever know? How much did *any* of them ever know?

"*And,*" his father says, "*one last thing.*" On the screen, he folds the map away. Neat, pristine corners. "*There's a lab, in the basement. I've kept it entirely private; it's not on any of the maps. There should be samples of the Sisyphus Formula in there—make sure they don't fall into the wrong hands. The room is passcode locked, labelled Supply Closet P28. Now, listen closely,*" he says, leaning in. "*The wrong code will fill the room with nerve gas. So—*" his father shrugs good-naturedly, the corner of his mouth twitching in slight mirth—"*I'm sure you don't want to accidentally stumble into that. Everything I want to protect is in that lab. The code is five-eight-eight-two. It's yours now, Hayden.*"

His now, but never before.

Hayden's fingernails dig into his palms, anger thrumming in the line of tension running from wrist to elbow. What else had his father hid? He wants to turn the console off; he doesn't want to know.

But on the screen, his father falls still in the way that has always demanded Hayden's attention. He settles his gloved hands on the table, then leans in close enough to the camera

---

9 As per the operative theme as everything else thus far: not many records of the Elsinore Labs Operating System from prior to this night remain—what little exists is perfunctory and professional, largely scraps of thoughts recorded in conjunction with Graham Lichfield's research notes. What we understand of Horatio is inextricably entangled in what we understand of Hayden.

that the dim light finally illuminates his face. It looks the same as it always does—*did*. The wide eyes Hayden never inherited, the hard jaw he did, smiling like it's the easiest thing in the world. From his slightly shaggy hair, pressed down by his glasses, Hayden guesses he filmed this months ago.

"*I have one last request,*" his father says, solemn. "*If this was malicious, once you're sure the research is safe, find who did it.*

"*And I hate to ask this of you, Hayden, but…*" He blinks once, backlit. Mouth still curved in a soft smile. "*Help me return the favour.*"

The video ends.

In the sudden silence, impotence leaks into Hayden's veins like sedative. Around him, the glass walls of the cold room warp his vision. He's standing in a glowing box, held up on display. And for whom? To what end? What other things lurk in that bright light?

A wild impulse screams through him, loud enough that he feels it in his skull: to replay the video, press his face up to the screen, drink all his father's secrets in before he disappears again—but before he can lunge forward, there is a clatter.

This time, Hayden spins slowly. The corpse's arm has fallen off the table.

For an agonizing moment, there is nothing, and then the body seizes. The trolley shakes as his father jerks. Jaw dropping, mouth opening and closing in a silent gasp, still trying to draw air into collapsed lungs. Hayden scrambles to grab an oxygen mask, fitting it sloppily to his father's face. He squeezes once, twice, trying to keep a steady rhythm against the desperate choking. His father's eyes roll.

"No, no," he finds himself mumbling, sensation bleeding back into his hands. Finally, they start to tremble. "No, stop."

A sour odour floods his nostrils, overwhelming the crisp smell of alcohol. Air hisses out from between his father's teeth.

He looks alive.

Hayden thinks: is this what he looked like before he died? Is he reliving it? How much awareness is left? How much does he see?

Does it hurt? *Did* it hurt?

His knees buckle, and he falls heavily down over the table. The oxygen bag still in his hands, he squeezes. His father's face is mere inches away. Hayden is close enough to see the minute twitches in his cheeks, close enough to hear the guttural groan that the oxygen has birthed, escaping his throat. Close enough for his father to extend a hand and grasp onto Hayden's sleeve.

He flinches so hard his elbow collides with the table with a splitting pain. The guilt of doing so is a palpable second hit, quick and furious. But no matter—his father's arm jerks inward again, and Hayden loses his balance, crushed down into a macabre embrace against his chest. He struggles to push himself back upright, but there is an inexplicable strength in the rigid lock of his father's muscles. The oxygen mask falls to the ground. Hayden can barely hold his head above his lab coat. Against his cheek, his father's chest rises and falls, shallow breaths, too tachypneic to draw in anything useful, but he feels strong and solid and here.

"Dad," Hayden manages to gasp, "please, let go." Tears blur his vision, suddenly. They are hot and burning, sliding down his cheeks in the cold, deadened air. "Dad, please, let me up. I can't breathe, Dad—"

His father's grip draws even tighter, draining the last of his breath.

A harsh choke escapes the gaping mouth as his father's lips move, smacking together as if to get words out. Hayden tightens his grip on the side of the table and drags himself forward, straining towards the long column of his father's throat.

"Dad." He chokes, too, as he manages to spit the word out. "What is it? You have to—you have to tell me."

Noises, indistinguishable.

"Dad, please. I need to know. I need to know who did this to you—I need to—that's what you wanted, remember?" His teeth grind against each other. "That's what you wanted me to do, right?"

His father closes his mouth. His spinning eyes finally stop flitting and focus, bloodshot irises fixed directly on Hayden's face. His hair is short, now. It doesn't curl. "Chhhhhhhh—shhh—Chhhhhhhhhharles," he half hisses, half mouths.

"Charles?" Hayden repeats desperately. "My uncle?"

His father's eyes remain wide and open. "Hhhhhch—Haaay—Hhhhuh."

"Dad," Hayden tries. But something thick in his throat overwhelms the rest of his words.

He repeats the horrible attempt at Hayden's name, over and over, wheezing when the air finally runs out of his lungs. Hayden wants to say something, *Dad, I'm here, Dad, please, I'm right here, tell me what you wanted me to do,* but he can't find a gap in his wracking sobbing to get any of it out. All he can do is mouth around the questions: *What do I do now? How do I fix this? Dad, did you really want me to kill for you?* He shudders and buries his face deeper into the crumpled lab coat. He hasn't held his father this close in years, this tight, desperate way like in his fleeting memories of childhood. All he can remember is stumbling into a lab for the first time, standing on tiptoes to peek into the microscope, his father's warm presence at his back to guide him through it all. His soothing voice whispering instructions—*open the light, brighter, brighter, yes, that's it!* Now, his world is the dark, and his own hot tears, and something warm underneath that feels like his father, still alive.

Hayden tightens his grip on his father's shoulder and waits for it all to stop.

Eventually, it does.

Hayden comes back to himself in a daze, still half bent and pinned down. The chest his face is resting against isn't moving anymore. His own quiet sniffles have ceased, and when he works his jaw open, breath comes back to him, soft but almost steadied. The world is a blurred mess, streaked with flashes and smears of colour and not much else.

Slowly, he extricates himself from the body. Sweat slips down his back, sticking his shirt to the skin. It's cold. Everything is cold.

The ECMO came undone sometime during the resurrection, and a growing pool of blood is streaming from the tubing's end. He thinks dully of cleaning it up, but only manages to summon the motivation to take a step back before it hits his shoes.

"*Well,*" says Horatio. "*Fuck.*"

The laugh that's been lodged in Hayden's throat finally makes its way out. Hayden rubs at his wrist, the phantom of his father's fingers still bruising the skin, and slumps against the glass wall. "Yeah," he says. "But it worked."

"*Did it?*"

On the table, the body is still again, though one arm remains locked in a half-embrace.

But *he was alive.* For the briefest of moments, he was here, Hayden believes that with everything he has. "Yes," he says.

"It did. It worked. I did it."

"*Are you sure he... understood what you were asking?*"

"Of course—he said my *name*, Horatio." Hayden's jaw trembles. He presses his hand to his mouth and draws a slow, stinging breath. "He knew I was here."

"*He also said your uncle's name.*"

And like that, the numbness slams down again. "He did, didn't he? Do you think it was an accusation?"

"*Do you?*"

Hayden looks down. His vision clears, only enough to better see the mess he's made of the cold-room. "I don't know."

"*He was saying your uncle's name for a reason.*"

"What if he was calling for help?"

"*Do you think he was asking for someone to come?*"

Two truths loom before him. Either his uncle is the murderer, or his father was calling out to him and Hayden both in those last moments, and neither came.

"I don't know," Hayden says. He wants to put his father to rest and wash his hands of the whole day, go get that drink with Rasmussen after all and drown himself in easy normalcy and seaside spirits. But nothing is that simple anymore.

Horatio doesn't answer. Hayden wonders if he's come to his own conclusions and wants to spare him of them. His hand comes up to touch his own neuromapper, chilled and smooth. It's infuriatingly blank, something that's meant to link them both, but the human mind is stubbornly small, unable to hold the complexities Horatio exists in. It renders Horatio as unknowable to him as Elsinore, and that, for some reason, is the realization that makes Hayden's knees weak all over again.

"Did you know?" Hayden asks.

"*About the hidden rooms? No.*"

"So you can't see what's there."

Irritation sparks brightly enough through Horatio's interface that Hayden can feel it, a spike of pain at the back of his neck. "*No.*"

The lights in the room flicker, only once, but the split second of darkness blooming back to light imprints a splintered chiaroscuro on Hayden's eyelids. For a moment, Hayden is suspended within Horatio—he's here and he's everywhere—his senses shift, tilt—and he's—

Your body is not a body, except you feel all of it, all at once. The footsteps in Charles's office a steady thrum, pacing an even rhythm that fades into a metronomic background tone—*tap* tap *tap* tap—and elsewhere, the great bellows of the emergency generators heave energy into the building's gulping maw, a rush of sensation, like a cold flood in your veins, if it felt like you had any veins at all. You have no lungs, so there is no breath, but you draw yourself together nonetheless. Charles is still pacing, like the marker of time that would be a heartbeat. You shudder, and then you are Hayden again, and Hayden stands quiet in the middle of the room, alone in his own body.

"*Sorry,*" Horatio says. "*I'm trying to run maintenance. I don't know what that was.*"

Hayden taps his temple. "Neuromap."

"*I... didn't know that could happen.*"

There's a shocking loneliness to being stuck inside himself. Hayden wraps his arms around his torso, briefly embodied properly, thinking only of his own senses, what it's like to stand here, the sore burn of his chest when he breathes, nothing else. "Me neither," he says quietly.

"*I'll... try to control it.*"

"You sound more shaken up than me."

A quiet huff, inside Hayden's head this time. *Maybe I am.*

Hayden wants to smile, and then he hates himself for even having the impulse. *It's not so hard,* he thinks towards Horatio, *having someone else in your mind.*

You don't think it's strange? Too revealing?

I think it's comforting, to not be alone.

Quiet. Hayden thinks, briefly, that he sees the enormity of Horatio—all of him, the thinking parts, the parts keeping Elsinore alive—hovering against his own mind, a behemoth of information brushing up against his meagre existence.[10] Then, the pressure eases.

The lights flicker again, and Hayden can imagine the frustration that comes with it, Horatio's circuits fritzing like his own synapses sparking in emotion. *"I can't access those rooms,"* Horatio says aloud. *"It's like they don't even exist."*

Maybe he's admitting something, his own limitations. Hayden lets his head fall back, condensation mingling in his hair over the chilled glass, and hates his father for forcing him to come back to reality. "Fuck him," he mumbles.

"You don't mean that."

Some twitching thing shifts under Hayden's skin, buried deep in the dermis, an emotion that can't be named unless he rips it out. "Fuck him," he enunciates, "but fuck *me,* I'm going to do it, Horatio."

"Do what?" Horatio asks, but the edge in his voice tells Hayden he already knows.

"I need to be sure about who killed him," Hayden says.

"Yes," says Horatio, *"and then?"*

---

10 A network of minds—of any number—was unheard of at the time, and certainly there was little understanding of the impact of entanglement on the psyche even in the short term, let alone lasting ramifications. Needless to say, safe practices were not known.

In the answering quiet, Horatio sighs, the sound like air hissing through the vents. Hayden chews on the inside of his cheek and looks upward again, comforted by the white noise. Wishes he could think the thought only and have it be understood, but he wants to give this his voice. It's what a decision like this deserves. Dedication, full-hearted, full-blooded. His knees unlock, and he lets the wall cradle him as he looks towards the darkened console screen. *Return the favour,* his father said, and Hayden can hear it now in his soft-spoken voice, echoing in his head.

Kill, he'd meant.

Such a small word. It sounds easy.

"I need to design a test," he says, instead of voicing it plain. Doesn't know who's listening, even now. "I want to know how Charles'll react to my father's voice." The words come out easily, too. His father's gurgle of his name hangs in the air. "Can you set up a voice emulator?"

"*Of Dr Lichfield?*"

"Yeah."

"*Of course.*"

"Thank you," Hayden whispers.

"*Please don't thank me,*" Horatio says.

"Okay," Hayden agrees. "Okay. I'll just—" He jerks his head over his shoulder, knowing his time here is up. He can't afford to linger. Anyone looking at the security cameras could see. All he can hope for is that his fellow prisoners in Elsinore are good enough to give him some sense of privacy, here, with his father's corpse.

He starts to pile the instruments on the metal table for something to do, ready to toss in the trash, but his hand hits the suture kit, and he remembers that he still has the data card resting in his pocket. Regardless of what he has to do to find the murderer, Hayden has one priority: keep the data safe.

And he can think of only one place to hide it that no one would dare look.

He glances at his father's body and clenches his jaw tight enough to hear the teeth creak.

"Horatio," he says. "I need a few more moments."

"To do what?"

"Keep it safe," Hayden says, like a mantra. Keep it safe. Keep it away from prying hands. He pulls the lapel of his father's lab coat back. Dragging down the shirt collar exposes a harsh mosaic of bruises, stippled against the ribs and blotching across his sternum.

He picks up the scalpel.

INTERLUDE

>playing/HORATIO/security/
camera_233B::08/12/2047::23:02.078

Lights dim. Minute drips of a thin fluid fall from the edge of the table, no pattern discernible. The room is otherwise pristine, shining white. Hayden Lichfield leans over a body, shirt torn partway open. Large, serrated scars line the torso; an empty suture kit lies beside it. Hayden Lichfield pulls the fabric up and arranges the arms across the exposed chest. Pigment covers his fingers. The colour profile and splatter patterning are consistent with fresh blood plasma. Under the red tint, his knuckles are white.

Hayden Lichfield's face is tilted downward. His features are washed in too much shadow to distinguish his expression. The body's face is exposed. Its eyes are wide open, as is its mouth. One side of its face is caved in, the discolored skin sagging, pulling the cheek down. A pale yellow crust dots the corners of its lips.

The drips slow.

Hayden Lichfield flexes his hand, then wipes away the puddle of fluid that has gathered on the side of the table. His tendons are taut. His shoulders tense, then rise, and fall.

He flicks his hand, then looks to the left, face still obscured. The same red pigment is present in inconsistent blots across his right cheek. He folds himself briefly over the body and smooths the front of its coat down. He takes both hands and cups the body's face, thumb overlapping the wound on the left. He wipes a hand over its eyes, sliding the eyelids down. His lips move.

Hayden Lichfield straightens. He runs a hand through his hair, pushing most of the light brown locks away from his face. The pigment from his fingers, still stained a bright red, streaks across his brow bone. He drops both hands back on the table. Rise. Fall.

Hayden Lichfield looks up into camera 233b. His hair has fallen back in his face, over the red. His pupils dilate.

He smiles.

Suresh: Switching gears, a little, then: does your personal account give more of an insight into your relationship with Hayden Lichfield?

Xia: Oh, are we calling it a relationship, now?

Suresh: Would you call it something else?

Xia: I think that's for another interview, for another day, don't you agree?

—An Interview with Felicia Xia

CHAPTER FIVE
Excerpted from *Tell Me A Tragedy*

I DON'T NEED to tell you what he did in there.

You've seen his statement in all its gruesome glory. There is nothing I need to repeat here.

But I didn't know what he did, not then. All I knew was that Hayden emerged from the cold-room shaken, but not broken. I could see cracks, here and there—in the twitch of his lips and the tight, stiff way he held his hands—but he seemed stable.

Enough to give me a small smile as the door swung open ahead of him. It clicked shut in his absence, the soft swish of the building itself following on his heels. He was so pale, he seemed a part of the walls himself. "Let's go," he said, tugging at one sleeve. His hands lingered, fingers digging into the folds of the fabric. They were scrubbed clean, but traces of pink lingered on his knuckles, stark against stretched white skin. I was curious, but I couldn't bring myself to ask.

I was thoroughly convinced at that point that somebody

was lurking in the bleached white labyrinth of a lab, a foreign killer. I didn't suspect any of them, then: not Hayden, not Charles.

I swept the halls one more time, turning to peer down both sides.

"Anybody?" Hayden asked.

"Not that I can see."

"Anything happen while I was... gone?"

I shook my head, not wanting to admit that a modicum of relief had settled in my chest when he'd emerged from the room unscathed. "We should get back, anyway," I said. "Just in case."

"Right."

"Well?" he said. "Lead the way."

I did. Our footsteps echoed. Hayden walked close enough for me to hear the steady rhythm of his breathing.

He must've felt the stifling emptiness, too, because after a long stretch of hall, he spoke up. "I think it was for the research," he mused. His voice was small. I could barely hear it behind me.

"Did your father have enemies I didn't know about?" I asked. I remembered the stricken look on Charles's face—but also that his face had crumpled in devastation and not surprise. "Did anyone have a reason to want to hurt him?"

Hayden let out a small huff that must've been an attempt at a chuckle. "Not too many people like the work we do," he said. "Fringe stuff, they say. Everyone in the field told us it was insanity, and then the first test trials showed promise, and suddenly they were afraid. A lot of them told us to stop. It got... aggressive. But... I never thought that anybody would..." Somehow, his voice grew even smaller, scratchier, jagged in the silence of the halls.

I slowed. "We still don't know what happened," I said.

"Right." Hayden cleared his throat. "It could've been anyone. My father never told me who'd taken umbrage anyway."

Anyone.

I shook my head. "Well, you shouldn't dwell on it anymore. What's done is done." Let it be known that I am not the most comforting person.

We'd stopped, only a few paces away from the office door, but I was already moving too sluggishly, and Hayden had drawn further and further away from me. White spaces will always grow enormous when you stand in them for too long—Elsinore was hardly an exception. I spun in a slow circle, still searching for an intruder who was never there.

Hayden reached out and tried to catch my hand. I started, wrenching my whole body aside.

He winced. "I didn't mean to startle you."

"What is it?"

He scratched at his wrist, his hands dangling in front of him awkwardly. We were standing close enough for me to see the rise of his chest as he breathed, the subtle bob of his throat as he turned his face away from me.

"What are you doing here, Felicia?" he asked.

Of all the questions he could've asked, I wasn't equipped to answer this one.

When I stared for too long, Hayden pulled away. He rocked back on his heels and rubbed a hand up over the back of his head, messing his already ruffled hair. "I mean," he said, "why did you want to come with me?"

"Are we still talking about tonight?"

Hayden sighed, a defeated thing. "No."

Thus far, we'd talked to each other like allies. But now, the veneer of neutrality between us threatened to crumble under the weight of one word from him.

"This is the worst time to be having this conversation," I told him firmly.

"I know," he said. "I just… I want to know if I can trust you."

I frowned. "Excuse me?"

Hayden shook his head. "Why are you *here?* You broke up with me over this lab, and maybe you were right. Maybe I did love this place more than you. But then you take the internship. You keep working with Charles. You learn all the things of Elsinore we have to give. I didn't say anything, because I don't want to fight anymore. But I still can't figure out what reason you have to come with your father here so late tonight. And then you volunteer to come with me to put a body to rest. We're alone. There's no one watching except for—There's no one watching." The corner of his mouth twitched, like he was holding something back. "Tell me I'm wrong, Felicia. Please."

Anger twisted up my chest. "Is this an accusation?"

Hayden shrugged. "It's a question," he said. "I just want to know if I can trust you."

The thought of having to stand in front of him, *his* hands bloodied, and prove my innocence incensed me. I stepped forward, crowded his space. I wanted to force him to look at me properly, at least. "Is it so hard to believe that I might've still cared enough for you to help?" I managed to say.

"Well," Hayden said, then laughed a little. He tilted his head up and blinked at the ceiling. Shrugged again, still kept his eyes safe from my scrutiny. "Yes," he said, and there it was again, one quiet word from Hayden, enough to break apart all my blustering rage and leave me with the quiet devastation of guilt.

Perhaps this is where I provide some better context:

Ours was a naïve romance—stupid, stumbling, uncertain. Too young and too eager. I think we fell apart because we'd been on the cusp of adolescence when it started, and then afterwards, we'd grown up into different people. But Hayden had grown up in and around and within Elsinore; it was stamped onto his genes. And I knew—I *know*—that I never wanted to be trapped with him. So it fell on me to do the cruel thing and break us apart instead.

My first taste of Elsinore was two summers ago, when the lab was but a name on my application page, a long list of potential internships. I had no idea my father knew anyone here, let alone was planning on taking a job here, when he said, *Pack your bags, bǎobèi'r, we're going to Helsingør.* And when I went, a whole world opened up before my eyes. Hayden was just a small part of that.

Undergrad, third year, puttering away at a biochemistry degree I didn't know what I was going to do with afterwards. I had some vague idea of what I wanted to do with my life, but it's hard to see anything when you're trapped in the grind of academia. I know better now. The first day of our arrival, my father introduced me to the Lichfields, and then Hayden was there. I kept him up all night in the hotel room, until we were both sleepy and dizzy and our walls were broken down a little. I kissed him in the gentle blue bioluminescence of the streetlights. We fell asleep together tangled under the sheets, soothed by the wash of the ocean.

The next morning, Hayden was a rumpled mess, bleary eyes, but he wanted to go for a walk by the pier, and he kept talking, kept spinning me stories with the grandeur of ambition all students have, and I wanted him.

"It's brilliant," he said offhand, eyelashes speckled with sea spray, and he meant the ocean, but I thought, *You're brilliant; I want to explore you.*

That same harbour was where I broke his heart, a year later.

Even as I write this, the memory of that night blooms again in my mind. The sky so dark it was like staring up into a void. The gentle lapping waves, a rush of noise in my ears. Stars hanging like pinprick daggers in the distant void. Hayden out on the edge of the pier, stretching his arms up over his head, the edge of his shirt lifting to reveal a sliver of moon-bright skin. I tossed little rocks into the drink, skin heated with the lingering buzz of spirits we'd grabbed on our way.

"Ever think about what happens when we die, Felicia?" He balanced on the edge of the drop, nothing but black water ahead. He didn't sway, but a spike of dread shot through me at the sight of it.

I frowned, growing tired. "That's depressing."

Hayden turned away from me. "Or just an inevitability."

I was scared, that night. Of all the things Hayden wasn't telling me. He spent more time in the lab than not. He slept there, sometimes, and I brought him blankets and coffee instead of asking him to leave. I kissed him there. I slept there, sometimes, too. He had the same look in his eye as he did those mornings, driven by something, hooked. Brilliant, I might've thought once. *Haunted* might've fit better. In those waking hours, he worked, and his face thinned, and in the rare times he emerged, all he wanted to do was ask me questions about our fragile mortality.

But I didn't say any of that, and maybe that was my fault. "I don't want to talk about it," I said instead, still trying to pull the conversation back to familiar places. "Let's get back to yours. It's getting cold."

Hayden shrugged, skimming the toe of his shoe over the

ocean's mirror-still surface. "That doesn't mean you can avoid it," he said, and he sounded defeated. It irritated me, then, when maybe it should've scared me. By then I knew enough of Hayden's moods, enough of how hard it was to pull him back when he didn't want to be pulled back.

But I was insistent.

I grabbed his hand, tugged until he finally acquiesced and stepped a bit away from the ledge. We sat cross-legged, face to face, just like the night we first met. This time, Hayden's eyes were dimmed, bags haggard under them, his right hand locked around his left wrist, like he was searching for a pulse. His gaze trailed off, back out to the stretch of water. "Mesmerizing, isn't it?" he asked, his mouth pressed in the barest of smiles.

I joined my gaze with his, drank in all that darkness. I didn't know what he saw out there. All I could see was a grey-tinged horizon, wavering.

Once, I thought that if I could just understand this obsessive melancholy, I could reach out. Pull him back.

But that night, as the salt breeze made my eyes water, I realize how deep it went. Elsinore was across the bay, a glowing white box set on the shoreline. As wind rippled at the water, Hayden listed forward, squinting at the lab like he would've jumped in and swum to it if he could.

I did love him. I never doubted that. But I didn't know how to fix him.

"Hayden," I said, as gently as I could. "I think you need to get help."

He finally turned, his dark eyes made opaque by reflected moonlight. "What?"

Carefully, I pried his fingers away from his own pulse. Cradled his face with my hands so he couldn't let his gaze wander again. "What are you working for, Hayden?" I asked. "It can't be worth this."

Hayden blinked, childlike. "Death is an inevitability," he said again, like a broken recording, and my heart clenched. But then he smiled. It split his face open, crinkled the corners of his eyes. It was full and bright, and he was brilliant again when he said, "See, I intend to do something about it."

It was my turn to be breathless. "What?"

He leaned in, still beaming. "I'm going to live forever, Felicia," he said.

And when he leaned in to kiss me, I realized what lit him up wasn't brilliance, not anymore. It was madness, fever-bright.

Hayden kissed me with a promise of the impossible; I kissed him with a goodbye.

I smoothed my thumbs over the curve of his cheeks, leaned our foreheads together, and I let him go.

"I'm sorry," I said.

"I can't do this," I said.

Hayden was mute, his face blank, shadowed by the clouds. And I left him sitting on the shore without another word, giving myself one look back when I was far enough away and hidden in the night. He was standing. A lone figure, silhouetted against the rolling ocean. I watched, and waited, and eventually he turned and started walking along the shore. He was headed to the lab. I knew I'd made the right decision.

And that was it. We spoke, the next morning, and I offered him something stumbling and halting, the opposite of how sure I was when I first kissed him, touched him, asked him to stay. He said he understood. I don't think he did.

But then at the end of the year, Charles pulled me aside, and offered me that internship I thought I would be horribly unsuited for, after all that. His own project—not Graham's, not Hayden's, his—and it could be mine if I wanted it. I won't bore you with the technical details here, but he wanted Elsinore to stand for something other than theoretical maxims and chasing the inevitable; he wanted something more concrete, to take what Dr Lichfield had done and bring it to some sort of public use. And despite it all, I wanted to find it for myself, that thrill of discovery. I wanted that ocean for myself.

So I said yes.

"Don't pretend you're the only one who cares about this place," I told him now. We'd exchanged more words in a few minutes than we had in the entire year since, all because of a murder.

Hayden scoffed. "Enough to risk your life? I'm sorry, but I don't believe you," he said, his smile curving up some more.

I grit my teeth. "I'm at Elsinore because I believe in the work we're doing. You're here because you want to please your father and because you're so afraid of who you are outside of this lab that you can't stop working. I'm here with you right now because I still care, and if you don't believe that about me, at least have the decency to believe that I'm not a murderer."

Hayden's eyes flashed. There was more red, high on his forehead, half-hidden by his limp fringe. "I am not *afraid*," he practically hissed, his mouth splitting, teeth bared. "We're doing something revolutionary here."

I stilled, wanting suddenly to push him away from me. The distance I'd already put between us wasn't enough. "Are you still doing it?" I asked. "Do you still think you can do the impossible?"

Any remaining warmth bled out of his face. Hayden tipped his head back and looked at me down the straight line of his nose. That bright dash of red made his skin look like a death mask, blanched. "Of course," he told me. "It's just like I said, Felicia. I'm going to live forever." And when he smiled again, his skin stretched over his skull like something brittle, sharp with that same madness from the pier. Only now, it was fiercer, brighter, so much worse.

So you see: that's how deep it ran.

He was still drowned in Elsinore, even now.

I turned around and headed to the office, steadying myself with a slow breath.

CHAPTER SIX
HORATIO

HAYDEN AND FELICIA Xia return unscathed, and Horatio tracks them until the door to Charles's office clicks shut and they are once again on the inside.

Spine curled against the wall, Hayden settles behind his uncle's desk. He has his hands pushed together, fingertips touching. Horatio experimentally dips 2% of his consciousness into the neuromap path and lets the beat of Hayden's faint pulse colour the room, an easy 1.4 Hertz pace that overlays the offset irregularity of Charles Lichfield's footsteps. His memory remains dull and useless; Horatio wishes there was some way for guilt to linger on a person like radio waves, something there for him to analyze, dissect, take apart and give to Hayden instead of the stupid plan that Horatio can sense brewing at the back of his mind.

But Charles Lichfield is pristine, suit shoulders sharp. The look of a man who had the business sense to build Elsinore from an idea when Dr Lichfield might've been content to play chemistry in a dusty basement forever. "I trust that nothing went wrong?" he asks, halted by the door.

"No," says Hayden, not looking at him.

Charles's face softens. No one else is looking at him, either. Horatio is left with the peculiar sensation of being the only one to witness this unperformative gentleness. He holds his hands out as if he doesn't know what to do with them.

His knobbly knuckles are free of lacerations, or any trace chemicals other than unscented hand cream.

"Paul and I have been discussing the situation," he says.

Hayden shrinks tighter against the wall. He digs his nails into his skin—twin pinprick rows of dull pain. Enough to draw him into his body. He closes his eyes, and Horatio sees the shuttered darkness through their link. It shades the room, the lines of the walls like pencil on draft paper.

Charles resumes his pacing. "You didn't see anything at all unusual on your way back?"

"No," Hayden says.

"Nobody suspicious in the halls?"

"No."

"Nothing weird in the lab itself?"

"No."

A pause. "Are you alright?"

"N—yeah. Yeah, I'm fine."

Hayden breathes shallowly, cheek pressed against the wall, nose prongs of his glasses pushed askew. A double rhythm echoes out to Horatio—Charles's footsteps picking up speed as Hayden's heart pounds harder, syncopated beats against each other. "This isn't over," Charles says as he pries Hayden away from the wall. It's a gentle touch. "Hayden," he says. "This isn't over."

Hayden lets himself be moved. Horatio sees reluctance in his stubbornly closed eyes, but his muscles are pliant. He's tired. He comes upright as his uncle guides him.

"I know," Hayden says.

"This won't be over until we fix it."

"I *know*."

"Hayden, look at me."

Light leaks back into the room. For Hayden, the world is first black, then hazy colours as he blinks his eyes open. What he sees layers over Horatio's understanding. Horatio sees the whole of the room and then in perspective: Hayden's uncle crouched in front of him, brows stitched together in concern. Horatio studies the bend of Charles Lichfield's spine, the way his hands on Hayden's shoulders elicits an involuntary little sigh from Hayden's lips. "So long as you're here," he says, "you're under my protection, and I intend to get to the bottom of this."

Through the link, Horatio catches sight of a flitting memory, so powerful it suddenly overpowers him. Only a flash: red slashed report cards, Hayden seventeen and teary, his uncle prying his hands off a glinting kitchen knife, sitting him down on the couch. Hayden's hands clutching his uncle's; bruises, the next day, dotting the pristine line of Charles's knuckles.

When the image fades, Hayden is pulling back from his uncle's embrace. "Thanks," he says, his lips twitching into a smile. "I'm okay, really."

Charles nods once, curt. He turns out towards the rest of the room, and Horatio does a quick catalogue: Paul Xia, wiping at his forehead with a handkerchief; Felicia Xia, a foot propped up on the doorframe; Rasmussen, standing quietly by Charles's desk.

"Paul," Charles says, "you had a thought earlier, didn't you?"

Paul Xia's nose twitches. "I did, yes," he says. "We've already established there is no security footage available from the time of 9:01pm to 11:45pm." Even his finger twitches, but he hides that better with gesticulation, widely sweeping as he explains, "If we can establish whether the cameras were disabled prior to this time or erased at some point afterwards, we may have an idea of whether or not the murder was premeditated."

"Wouldn't it have to be?" Felicia speaks up.

Hayden's heartrate spikes at the sound of her voice.

"If there was an intruder, they'd have to have planned this, right?" she says, pushing herself off the doorframe and forming a small circle with her father and Charles.

Paul Xia pulls at his collar. Standing side by side, Horatio can see the resemblance between the two of them, the striking dark eyes and angled jaws, though there is nothing of Felicia's steel in her father's spine. Paul clears his throat. "That's a good point," he says, "but we're not ruling out... a crime of passion."

Nestled behind the small huddle, Hayden rolls his eyes.

Still, there's truth to the statement. Horatio wonders if Charles feels any of it, the tightening of spaces in the room, the gazes of everyone around him. If it was really him, was any of it planned? It wouldn't be difficult. The tableau laid out underneath Horatio's cameras looks something like a stage, Charles guiding it along like he was reading from the script and waiting for them all to fall in line.

It seemed real, when he told Hayden he would fix it. Horatio senses the lingering emotion in Hayden's body, rosy as dawn. Hayden certainly believed it, even if only for a moment.

"Horatio?" Charles suddenly calls, breaking the sullen silence.

"*Yes, sir?*" Horatio calls, purging his voice of everything except superficial politeness. "*What can I do for you?*"

"Was Graham in his lab all of tonight?"

Horatio does a quick scan of the footage he does have access to, mapping Dr Lichfield's biometrics against the steady background hum of the recorded atmosphere in the room as he goes.

"*Oh,*" he says. "*No, sir.*"

Everyone in the room catches their breath almost at once. The temperature rises by a fraction of a degree.

Charles puts his hand to his mouth, obscuring his features. "When did he leave?"

"*My system says the front door was opened with his ID a little before nine.*"

"And when did he come back?"

"*I don't know.*" Horatio starts up his scan again, but it cuts out into frustrating, impenetrable black before anything can become clear. "*That was when the system was down.*"

Charles swivels immediately over to Hayden. "And where were you?"

Hayden works his jaw. He looks small, barely a smear of colour against the white walls. "In a storage closet," he says, "looking for supplies."

Paul Xia frowns. "It took that long? And why didn't you notice your father leaving?"

"I did," Hayden says, scowling. "He told me he was meeting someone. I left for supplies around 11:30. The whole thing didn't take very long."

"Well," says Charles with a contemplative hum, "regardless of what Graham was doing, the culprit has to have interacted with the system, too. Horatio, did someone access the cameras for lab room 233 earlier tonight?"

Horatio doesn't know if it's his own suspicions that seep into the tone of Charles's voice, so casually demanding in a way that Dr Lichfield had never been. He rests with his own sullenness and zooms in on the ticks in Charles's face, tries to find any fault in the smooth lines of him. "*Yes, sir,*" he says obediently.

"What time?"

"*8:49pm.*"

In the ensuing quiet, Paul Xia clears his throat again, rough and ragged. He presses his already-wet handkerchief to his forehead.

Still hunched in his little corner, Hayden is massaging his fingers. Horatio keeps most of his cameras focused tightly on Charles, trying to find him from all angles as if the rustle of fabric at the back of his suit will give away something of his motivations, but he notes Hayden through the link, a creeping frost spreading down his spine and out to his hands.

The only thing Horatio cannot see is the line of Charles's mouth, tucked carefully behind his hand. Whether it is a grimace, a troubled frown, or a secretive and triumphant smile is as much a mystery as whoever it was that violated Horatio's interface. Horatio's frustration blends with Hayden's panicked fear, gritty like grinding gears, something cold and foul.

"There has to be some way to know who accessed the system," Felicia says, marching valiantly forward. "Even if it was hacked into. There should at least be some trace, right?" She scans the room, then her gaze drifts upwards. "Horatio?" she asks, tentative.

"*Yes?*" Horatio replies, on as unsure a footing as she seems to be.

"Could you check the logs?" Felicia asks.

"*I need permission from someone with executive level access,*" Horatio says, and if the trace of bitterness makes it into his voice, he's at his splintering end. The infuriating protocol that keeps him from accessing the whole of Elsinore at once did not die with its progenitor. Horatio's probing slides off some parts of his own mind like soaped metal, precise but slick, unable to grasp onto what he wants to find.

"And who has that?" Felicia asks sharply, matching his tone.

Charles clears his throat. His hand drops, revealing his blankly neutral line of a mouth. "I do. Check the logs for me, Horatio," he says, and Horatio tries not to feel overwhelmingly impotent.

"*Just a moment,*" he says, scanning his systems for what he still can. Something catches his attention, an entry that seemed innocuous at first, but flares bright now. "*Well, it appears my controls were accessed by a user already registered in the building.*[11]" Horatio starts slow, monitors the room for changes in breathing patterns, keeps track of the steady contractive pull and release of everyone's diaphragms as he doles out more information. "*Records indicate,*" he says, "*that it was an account with executive level access.*"

This time, it is Charles's turn to be pierced with a glare. Felicia turns on her heel, her mouth falling open in mild disbelief as she scours Charles's face.

The man himself breathes as usual. His heart rate picks up, but not by much; in the grand scheme of it all, it's insignificant, only more noise complicating the profile that is

---

11 Whether a log that was maintained by a being who, for all intents and purposes, was an independent, sentient personality on his own, could serve as court evidence would later become a key point in trial.

Charles Lichfield. His eyes are red-rimmed, his usually neat hair is loosening in the grip of its wax.

"I'm not the only one with that designation, am I?" he asks. In the right tone, those words could be accusatory, a desperate attempt to shift the blame. But curiously, he sounds defeated.

Realization comes to Hayden and Horatio at the same time. Hayden jolts out of his seat, the line of his spine straightening. Horatio scatters his cameras, stops scrutinizing Charles's every move. Because the truth is that it doesn't matter how guilty Charles looks.

The only other person in the room who looks guiltier is Hayden.

A quick, desperate burst of thought from the link, *no, please, don't say anything,* Hayden practically begs, but Charles Lichfield has asked Horatio a question, and his programming demands he answer.

He could fight it, but Horatio is certain that Charles would find some other way around, ask over and over again until Horatio is overwhelmed.

"*The only three users who've had executive access are you, sir,*" says Horatio, trying to delay the inevitable anyway, "*and the late Dr Lichfield.*" Charles inclines his head. "*And,*" says Horatio, regret catching his voice in a digital whine, "*Hayden Lichfield.*"

CHAPTER SEVEN
HAYDEN

THE ROOM EXPLODES into chaos. Rasmussen shouts something, then Paul Xia barks something back, but all the words are swallowed by the sudden roar in Hayden's ears. He keeps his back straight and still, too aware that anything and everything he does now can be suspect. He curls forward, scapula jutting back and edged against the wall uncomfortably, but he can't stand the thought of pulling his shoulders back in front of them all.

Instead, he bites down hard on the inside of his cheek and finds Felicia's eyes from across the room.

She doesn't look away, but there's clear fury in the twist of her mouth. *You fucking hypocrite*, he can imagine her saying. Or maybe that's just his own mind, recoiling from his own spineless paranoia, the fucking naivety of thinking he could get away with this bereaved and blame-free, all this childish short-sighted arrogance he's never quite shed.

But before Hayden can do anything but drop his gaze in shame, Rasmussen slams his hands against the desk with a loud crack, shearing the tension. Everyone halts. Rasmussen is a wiry bundle of nerves.

"Well, it has to be one of *them*," he says, eyes blown wide and lips trembling. "That's the only explanation. They're the only ones who could've changed the camera." As he turns, he looks towards Hayden's uncle—does he suspect him? And if so, does he have a good reason? There's none of his usual ease left over, and he appears gaunt in the wake of panic, hair astray, lanky form twitching. He doesn't look at Hayden, but there's no way to know if that's a deliberate choice.

Xia tucks his handkerchief back into his pocket. "Well—"

"There isn't a 'well'," Rasmussen snaps. "Call the police. Case closed."

Charles raises a finger.

Hayden finds himself on the edge of his seat, still hanging on his every word.

"The research," he says, "is still missing."

For a moment, Rasmussen stays locked, arms braced against the table. He grits his teeth with an audible *click*. "The research?" he half barks, a muscle in his jaw spasming. "Is that what you're worried about?"

"Yes," his uncle says, and he sounds calm. He's pacing again, a perpetual motion that keeps the room as loose as his strides, a well-lubricated joint. "You must understand," he says, "Graham wasn't working on some common curiosity here."

"Oh, *I* know what he was doing," Rasmussen says. "Considering I'm the one who clocked all his supplies and did all the menial work."

His uncle's smile thins. "Then you'll know how important it was. His research was going to change the world."

Rasmussen flings his arms up, as if searching for something

to grasp onto. "And that's more important than keeping us all safe?"

"Gabriel," his uncle says, somehow gentle and condescending all at once. When he approaches, Rasmussen flinches back, like all his bravado is nothing but a flimsy front. He looks wiry, held together by sinews and tight skin, nothing like the confidence in his uncle's silhouette. "You'll be adequately compensated, of course. Consider yourself on the clock."

"You think I care about that?"

"I think you do."

Rasmussen is quiet.[12]

His uncle watches Rasmussen like a conductor, like he was the one jerking Rasmussen's arms about, one corner of his lips raised in a slight smile. "Besides, Graham's research was important to him," he says, and it makes Hayden's blood boil, makes Hayden want to crack the answers out of him, to say out loud that he wasn't lying, even if his word can't be trusted now, not ever again. But suddenly he's nodding towards Hayden, his eyes catching the light like pale glass.

"And Hayden," he says. "It's important to Hayden. Neither of us want to lose the last thing Graham ever worked on."

That's true.

Hayden's eyes burn.

He wants the rest of it to be true, so he hasn't lost his uncle and father both in one night.

"We were going to change the world," Hayden echoes, and it sounds pathetic even to himself.

---

12 Gabriel Rasmussen was providing for a brother on his way to obtaining a Master of Fine Arts at the Royal Danish Academy of Fine Arts. They had been each other's support since childhood, and much of Valdemar's oeuvre is on display across the world, notably with a gallery exhibition in the new SFMOMA.

"You did," his uncle says plainly. "And someone killed him for it."

Rasmussen barks out a high-strung laugh. He sweeps his hand towards the both of them, nephew and uncle. "Yeah. That 'someone' being one of you."

"Let's not jump to any conclusions," his uncle says. "No one's committing any more crimes today—we can all agree on that, can't we?"

"What then?" Rasmussen demands. "Are we supposed to just sit tight here and wait for you to find your precious research?"

"That's what I was hoping, yes."

"Convince me it wasn't you."

"And how am I supposed to do that?"

"What were you doing between nine and eleven?"

"Talking to Paul," his uncle says smoothly.

Rasmussen spins to lean into Paul Xia's face and raises an eyebrow.

Spluttering, Paul Xia leans back and puts his hands up like he's the one on trial. "We were here!"

"The whole time?"

"Of course."

"I want to hear you say it," Rasmussen says. "Tell us you didn't do it."

His uncle returns his stare evenly. "I didn't do it."

Rasmussen's nostrils flare. He drops his hands back on the tabletop, breathing deep. Hayden thinks he hears fear in that shaky exhale. He doesn't look like he wants to cooperate, but Hayden would do anything not to involve the authorities. Not before he can find the murderer. And not before he can cut the data card back out, keep it safe.

But there's nothing he can do to make Rasmussen believe him, *or* his uncle. Guilty men look guiltiest denying it.

So, when Felicia, thorough in her scan of the room, finally looks at him again through a curtain of choppy bangs, Hayden doesn't peel away from her accusatory glare. She tilts her head, jaw tight. Your move, her eyes say.

Hayden brings his hands to rest lightly on the desk. He lets them unfurl, palms up, fingers loose and open and inviting. Look at this, he wants her to know, my hands are clean now. It's true enough. Clean of murder. Is there a crime for the opposite?

Felicia sweeps her gaze away. He barely has time to contemplate what that means before she's clearing her throat, cutting the whispered conversation between his uncle and her father short.

"Felicia?" Charles asks, looking pleased for some reason. "Is there something wrong?"

"Surely it's possible someone cracked one of our accounts to wipe the camera," she says bluntly.

Paul Xia rushes to Felicia's side, pulling her forward by the elbow. He leans in, head bent towards her as if to share a secret. But there is no privacy here, not from Elsinore. Hayden only has to tap a finger to the neuromapper, and Horatio understands what he wants, amplifies every word of the furtive conversation in the back of Hayden's mind.

"You don't have to worry about this," Paul Xia says, low and urgent.

Felicia shrugs him off. "I'm not worrying," she says. "I'm trying to figure out what's going on."

Her father's tight smile wavers. "You don't have to."

"I *want* to. Please answer my question."

Her father looks at a loss.

Hayden's uncle heaves a small sigh, eyes flicking up to the ceiling. "Horatio?" he asks. "Is it possible your system was hacked?"

"*All I know is that I'm missing time,*" Horatio says. Hayden feels the gnaw of displeasure needling at his nape, and forces himself to relax his tensed muscles, and when Horatio speaks next, it's softer, like he felt it. "*I've been tampered with. It isn't fun. But of course, it could've been an intruder. I just wouldn't know.*"

"You said the door was opened with Dr Lichfield's ID," Felicia says. "What if that was someone breaking in?"

"Then where would they have gone?" Paul Xia challenges. He squints at the ceiling. "...Horatio...?"

"*Yes?*"

"Have you seen any intruders in the building?"

"*Not currently.*"

Rasmussen sinks back, scoffing.

"*But the late Dr Lichfield insisted on keeping some areas of Elsinore unmonitored.*"

Hayden nearly rolls his eyes at Horatio's typical penchant for dramatic timing. He receives a quick rebuff through the link, a strange little shock of static fizzling to his temples, and looks up, incredulous. *I'm helping you here,* Horatio whispers to Hayden and Hayden alone. *That hurt,* Hayden thinks back petulantly.[13]

"Are you absolutely certain?" Paul Xia asks, and Horatio's consciousness pulls back as he's addressed.

"*Yes,*" he responds to the room at large. "*There are a number of blind spots in the building.*"

"Alright," Felicia announces. "Then I want to investigate."

Flushed hope rises in Hayden's cheeks. In his mind, the prison bars of this situation ease a little wider, enough for opportunity to slip through the cracks.

---

13 My analysis of the neuromap logs shows that they acclimated to the networking fairly quickly, certainly a feat given the lack of blueprint to follow.

"Felicia, I'm not doubting you," Xia says, folding and unfolding the handkerchief like it's a lifeline. "I'm terrified you're right. What happens if you go out there and encounter the intruder?"

"An intruder who went to all these lengths just to frame one of us," Hayden's uncle chimes in, voice silky smooth.

Felicia raises an eyebrow. "In that case, we're all sitting ducks anyway," she says.

"Is there a schematic of the lab?" her father asks a little desperately. "Something that lays the blind spots out?"

"*No*," Horatio says with an amused little flicker. "*Dr Lichfield did not grant me access.*"

"You see?" Xia wheedles. "You can't possibly know where to even start looking."

"I'm sure if we go through all the rooms we can map out where the surveillance tapes don't match," Felicia counters.

"Felicia!" Xia finally barks. "I'm not willing to let you put yourself in danger for something you don't have to involve yourself in. Please, just behave and listen to me."

The line of Felicia's mouth wavers, barely, but enough for panic to grip Hayden's throat again.

"Hey," Rasmussen cuts in, "if she wants to go out and find what the hell's going on here, I don't see why we should stop her."

Xia takes a step towards him. For once, he looks stormy, hardened. "That's not for you to decide."

"I'm just saying," Rasmussen says with a shrug. "What, you afraid of what she's going to find? Why exactly did you show up this late out of nowhere, again? You been hiding something from us, Xia?"

"Are you insinuating—?"

"That you might be guilty? I am."

"I could say the same about you."

Rasmussen jerks a shoulder at Hayden. "He and I found the body together. What, you think I'd have had time to kill the man, get myself all cleaned up, then run back to the supply room before Hayden had time to get back to the room?"

Xia is in his face now, and Rasmussen is returning the glower, all his earlier aggression returned. Faced with anyone other than Charles Lichfield, he's all boxy shoulders and bravado.

"All I want," Xia says, a harsh, guttural undertone catching on his voice, "is for my daughter to be *safe*."

"*None* of us are safe."

"He's right," Felicia says. She touches a hand to her father's shoulder, and it sags as if he can't quite hold himself up anymore. "We're not getting out of this without finding the truth, baba."

"But—"

"I know where the hidden rooms are."

Hayden doesn't realize he's spoken until everyone's eyes fall on him, but as soon as he does, the world slides into bright clarity again. He sees his father's map, sharp in his mind. Rapping his knuckles on the desk, he steps out from behind it.

His uncle doesn't move, but he does frown. "Since when did you know that?"

Hayden wonders if Charles tasted it then, the brittleness of trusting his father. Did he know secrets were kept from them both?

"Is it so unbelievable that Dad would share with me?" he asks, tipping his chin up.

To that, his uncle has no retort.

"Hayden," Xia says, almost gentle. "You're still a suspect."

92

"So is my uncle. And the rest of us all, if someone cracked the system."

"Your uncle isn't leaving this room."

The door is agonizingly close. He could reach out and touch it, push it open with the heel of his palm. "What could I possibly get up to?" Hayden asks. "I'll be with Felicia."

"That's the problem."

Felicia mutters something under her breath he can't make out, but as he leans in, her hand snaps out to grab his wrist. Before he can jerk back, she laces their fingers together and clasps something cold and heavy around it. The loud click of a hard, black shell locks around both their wrists. "Look," Felicia says, raising their joined hands. "I'm not letting him out of my sight. Stop worrying so much about me."

A strange pull settles around Hayden's wrist. When Felicia drops it and he instinctively tries to snatch it back, he can barely move half an inch, stopped by some invisible force. Another experimental swing doesn't budge the gap either.

Paul Xia pats his pockets, looking scandalized. "You swiped my magcuffs."

"Yeah," Felicia says, unabashed.

"They're still *prototypes*."

Felicia shrugs. "I know how to use them."

Xia looks like he wants to say something—perhaps something to do with his daughter handcuffing herself to a suspected murderer—but Felicia turns away and he falls silent. "I'll be fine," she says to the door. "You don't have to worry about me. Just keep an eye on everyone else and mind your own job, okay?"

The way Xia sighs speaks to something that goes deeper than this night. He tucks his handkerchief away and nods, stepping aside.

Without even looking back, Felicia tugs on the cuffs. Her face a smooth, impassive neutrality, she mutters, "Let's go," quietly enough that Hayden knows it's only for him, the space between them small enough now for that. It stirs a strange resentment in Hayden's gut—and as they step out of the room, he can't help but think of stepping out of one trap directly into the path of another. The tension at his wrist pinches with every step. He doesn't know whether to thank her, and eventually, when they're far enough from the office and unmoored amongst the blank halls again, it's too late to say much of anything at all.

Transcript of recording taken from
Felicia Xia's phone, 11:58pm, 08/12/2047[14]

(Scuffling. Scratching sounds, as of a microphone rubbing on fabric. Footsteps, distinct and rapid.)

FELICIA: Where to first?

HAYDEN: My father's private lab.

FELICIA: It's in the basement?

HAYDEN: Of course.

FELICIA: I thought your father's lab was up here. In the room where you found him.

HAYDEN: Blunt as ever, I see.

FELICIA: You know I don't like to mince words.

(Silence, 8 seconds.)

FELICIA: The lab on the main floor seemed private enough.

---

14 This transcript, and all following such documents (transcripts, message logs, etc.) have been taken as-is from publicly available records from *Denmark v Lichfield*, 2049.

He never let any of us in there, only you.

HAYDEN: My father has—had? Has, I guess; they're still here, even if he—anyway. Many secrets. Due to the sensitive nature of his work.

FELICIA: I see. And did he let you into this even more secret one?

HAYDEN: I work in the lab up here.

(The footsteps slow. They start to echo, becoming steadily louder.)

FELICIA: That's not an answer.

HAYDEN: (quieter) He... he let me pursue my own research. My own goals. The Sisyphus Formula was <u>my</u> idea. I'm... grateful for that.

FELICIA: The Sisyphus Formula.

HAYDEN: You know what that is.

FELICIA: I don't, actually. Secretive man, your father was.

HAYDEN: Ah, I see.

FELICIA: What?

HAYDEN: You <u>want</u> to know.

(A short laugh, from a distance.)

FELICIA: Tell me you didn't do it.

HAYDEN: Don't change the subject.

FELICIA: Tell me.

HAYDEN: I—of course I didn't.

FELICIA: I don't believe you.

HAYDEN: Felicia...

FELICIA: This doesn't look good for you. You know that, right?

HAYDEN: Of course I do.

FELICIA: Then say something to convince me you didn't do it.

HAYDEN: Are you enjoying this? That I was wrong? Is that why you dragged me out like this? You want to be the one to get me to confess?

FELICIA: I just want answers.

HAYDEN: Ask away.

FELICIA: Why did you want to put his body away? What were you doing in there? Why didn't you want anyone else to do it?

HAYDEN: Nothing. Cleaning up. Trying to say a proper goodbye. You didn't say anything then, why are you stuck on this now?

(White noise, source indistinguishable, 3 seconds. A scratching sound, like a nail against the edge of the microphone. Somewhere a heavy machine stops whirring—perhaps an air conditioner or filter.)

(Silence, 4 seconds.)

FELICIA: That was before.

HAYDEN: Just because someone might've used my name to break into Horatio's system doesn't make me guilty of my own father's murder.

FELICIA: Okay. Fine.

HAYDEN: I'm not a murderer.

FELICIA: I said okay. I believe you.

HAYDEN: Sure.

(Footsteps resume.)

FELICIA: Look, you accused me, I accused you, I'd say we're at an impasse here. If you believed me, I believe you. Good enough?

HAYDEN: Tell me one thing.

FELICIA: What do you want, Hayden?

HAYDEN: Do you want to see it?

FELICIA: See what?

HAYDEN: Don't play dumb with me.

(A sigh.)

FELICIA: Yes. Okay. Yes, I do.

HAYDEN: Why?

FELICIA: Do you know what it's like to care a lot about a place you don't fully understand? Charles wants grants, so I help him apply for them. I purify proteins, I don't even know what they're for. He lets me run my own projects for my degree, but everything else is classified. I stay so late I've been dreaming about the goddamn ocean when I manage to go home, and I don't know what's so secret behind all the doors that I'm not allowed to see.

(Silence, 2 seconds.)

HAYDEN: I might understand more than you'd think.

FELICIA: (quieter) Shut up. You don't.

HAYDEN: Quick to assume.

FELICIA: You have half a Bachelor's and a hot load of bullshit you're peddling around instead of real research. If you think you would've gotten

98

anywhere if your daddy didn't run this whole place, you're kidding yourself. And still I—

HAYDEN: You <u>what.</u>

FELICIA: It's impossible to talk to you about this, it's always been impossible—I give a shit, okay? I'm the first person in my family to go to university at all, and I am wasting my time here because I care.

(Rapid breathing, source uncertain.)

HAYDEN: I'll show you.

FELICIA: That's not—

HAYDEN: I know that's not the point, not anymore. But I'll show you, if you want it. Afterwards you can decide if I'm a murderer or not.

(The footsteps stop.)

FELICIA: Fine.

HAYDEN: Let's get to it, then. The stairs are over here.

(The footsteps resume.)

(A loud, long, high-pitched sound, as of a rusted door-hinge.)

FELICIA: It's cold.

HAYDEN: That's Elsinore.

(The echoes of their voices become louder and more sustained.)

FELICIA: How many floors down is it?

HAYDEN: Four from here. That's two floors into the

basement, if you're keeping track.

FELICIA: It's getting colder.

HAYDEN   That's Elsinore.

(A scoff.)

FELICIA: How's... your mom?

HAYDEN: What?

FELICIA: Is someone going to tell her?

HAYDEN: God, I don't know. We still don't talk.

FELICIA: Oh. I'm sorry.

HAYDEN: Don't be. It's my dad's own damn fault that...
             (sighs) Never mind.

FELICIA: Alright. Dropping the issue.

HAYDEN   I guess the only way we can have a proper
             conversation is if we're accusing each other of
             murder after all.

FELICIA: Maybe that just means I should've murdered you
             instead and saved us the awkwardness.

HAYDEN: Then you could've made conversation with my ghost.

FELICIA: Hilarious.

HAYDEN: I would haunt you very cautiously. Leave some
             vague messages alluding to my existential dread in
             your shower every morning. Nothing special.

FELICIA: Wouldn't coming back as a ghost alleviate most of
             that existential dread?

HAYDEN: You know, you might be right.

FELICIA: I just know you.

(Silence, 7 seconds).

(Their footsteps halt again.)

HAYDEN: In any case, we're here. Could you... not look at the keypad?

FELICIA: So many secrets.

HAYDEN: Look, he trusted me with this.

FELICIA: What happened to 'I'll show you'?

HAYDEN: I know, just— (sigh) You know that I took a break my second year of undergrad because I was dealing with some shit, but I never told you that he was actually kind of mad at me. He was out here, and I was back at school, and he told me to pack my stuff and get on the first plane to Helsingør I could find. And when I got here, he set me up in Elsinore and asked me if <u>this</u> was what I wanted to do with myself now, like it was a challenge or something. My father wasn't really the kind of person to say anything about how he felt. I don't think he ever told me he loved me, in so many words. But he let me—twenty and stupid—start this project, and he put his own name behind it. And I know that you know exactly how much that means. And I... <u>I</u> didn't know what the code was until I found it in his pocket, when I was tidying his corpse. I'm not hiding anything. I just want to let a dead man keep his secrets.

FELICIA: Alright... Fine. That's pitiable enough that I won't look.

**Message log, taken from
Felicia Xia's pager, 12:13am, 08/13/2047**

Dad
he lied
Charles. wasn't in his office when graham was killed
I went with it bc if he thought i was on his side i might get
smthing
not that i think its him
not yet

Felicia
when? How long?

Dad
half hour? btwn 9.30-10

Felicia
do you think it's him?

Dad
i don't know. Is it Hayden?

Felicia
dunno

Dad

let me know if ANYTHING happens

Felicia

im okay

don't trust anyone

going into lab now brb. report later.

The Sisyphus Formula wasn't enough. It was never enough.

—Elsinore's Legacy: A Retrospective

CHAPTER EIGHT

Excerpted from *Tell Me A Tragedy*

I THINK I have become obsessed with death. Some part of me can understand why it mesmerized Hayden so, why the promise of death hung so insistently over him. It hangs over me, too, now, but in writing this, I invited this ghost to haunt me. This is my own reckoning.

Inside the lab where Hayden introduced me to the Sisyphus Formula, the lights were on before we ever stepped foot within. They flooded the room with a blank whiteness, just like all the others here. That made it all the easier to see there was no one hiding in it. Hayden looked around, then tugged on our joined wrists, and I let him pull me into the centre of the room.

He squinted up into the ceiling. "No cameras," he said, neck craned back. He sounded surprised. For the first time, I wondered if even Hayden knew Elsinore as well as he claimed to.

"No intruder," I countered.

Hayden grimaced.

"Are there any other blind spots?" I asked.

"There's another room," he said, eyes still tracking something up in the ceiling. "Further up, top floor."

"Just one?"

"Just one."

The implication of what would happen if we found nothing there hung heavy between us. Hayden must've been thinking the same thing, and I wondered if it was worse for him if he were the killer or if his uncle were. Either way, I was too invested. Either way, I had stuck myself into this mess the moment I tied us together.

I couldn't bring myself to regret it. As soon as Hayden spoke up, I knew it: the only way to uncover Elsinore's secrets was through him.

"Okay," I told him, pulling him, half stumbling, towards the row of benches. "That means we have some time alone, right?"

Hayden nodded, craning his neck towards the shelves lining the bench as if he was trying to take in as much of the room as he could at once.

"So show me."

In the corner of the lab stood a bulky storage unit, half-rusted. That was where Hayden led me. He pulled the doors open. It all looked so innocuous, rows upon rows of clinking bottles tinted brown. A dull chill emanated from the unit—not quite as cold as a fridge, but enough to raise goosebumps on my arms.

Eventually, Hayden emerged with a vial. I leaned in to try and read the label, but what little I could see of the slanted handwriting was too faint. Hayden smoothed his thumb over it, once, twice, then again and again in a way that made me think he wasn't reading it at all. He set it down, then turned back, and I watched him move a whole shelf of the storage unit out over the counter. But instead of showing me more, when he was done there, Hayden stopped, hunched unmoving over the glassware on his benchtop.

"Are you looking for something?" I finally asked.

"No."

"Then..."

Hayden uncurled, standing straight, barely looking at the bench. He pressed his free hand over his eyes, throat bobbing as he visibly swallowed. "Sorry," he said, his voice faint but thick. "I just saw something I didn't expect to see."

"Is this not the Sisyphus Formula?"

"No, just—" Hayden's teeth clicked, his eyes watery as he tried to reach up with his cuffed hand to rub at his face, then stopped short with a growl of frustration. He put his other hand over the frames of his glasses instead, tipping his head back like he was trying to hold himself together by the touch of his fingers.

I peered down at the bench. The little vials were all lined up in a row. The labels were still undecipherable even though some of them were turned towards me—the cramped letters were Dr Lichfield's, I presumed. The writings of a dead man. Then placed far away from everything else, a dented red fountain pen.

The pen was heavy and cool. There wasn't anything especially notable about it, just a name etched into the steel. *Helen Lichfield.* A different Dr Lichfield, then—the one left behind. Hayden's mother.

Eventually, Hayden drooped, all at once. He pulled the pen out of my grasp, rolling it in his fingers. "I didn't think he kept it," he said by way of explanation. I thought about his fraught relationship with his mother, barely known to me. I thought about his words earlier—*it's my dad's own fault*—and carefully kept my mouth shut. I wanted to see what else he might say.

The barest sigh fell from his lips. "It was her favourite," he said. "She had a whole matching set of them. I guess she left this one behind."

And that was all he said on the topic.

I turned my attention back to the rest of the things on the bench. "Isn't this what Charles wants?" I asked. Despite myself, I had kept hope. That I could steal this opportunity to see it all for myself, and that would be all for tonight—we'd hand the formula over to Charles and he'd let me take over a branch of the project for real and I'd get to come into work next week with the murder solidly in the hands of the authorities.

Of course, it couldn't be that easy.

"My uncle wants the data," Hayden said. "This is just a prototype."

I looked back to the row of gleaming glass. A cloudy liquid swirled lazily inside each, giving off a faint yellow shimmer under the glaring lights, a thin film of something congealed at the top. It looked innocuous. I wondered who would kill for something like this, what was locked inside that was worth dying for. I wonder if knowing what it did would change my mind.

Hayden uncurled his fingers, jostling our linked hands, and I looked up, startled.

Hayden tapped one of the vials. "A prototype," he said, "but it still works."

*   *   *

THE SIMPLE ELEGANCE of the Sisyphus Formula is difficult to explain in words. I have tried and discarded half a dozen metaphors, but in the end, all I have left is my own sense of awe. And I mean that in the most primal sense: the kind of awe that leaves your eyes bulging, embeds wonder deep in your mind—but leaves behind fear, too, and a profound unsettlement. I was awed, at seeing cuts sealed in minutes. At watching skin stitch itself together, spurred on by Hayden's miracle. I thought: I am watching something that must never be seen. I thought: I want to see it again, over and over and over. I thought: I never want to forget.

In this field, we are often asked: why?

This is my only answer.

Since that night, I have tried to piece together my own research, tried to derive the formula's mechanics from what I'd seen. Admittedly, most of what I've accumulated through interviews and the stubborn scouring of scientific journals is too dense, too complicated, and, frankly, pointless for me to repeat here. It is one thing to know the biochemical components of this liquid miracle. It is another to witness it.

In the midst of it all, what struck me as most fascinating, especially given Hayden's demonstration, was how the Sisyphus Formula relied upon revitalizing what was already inside you. Earlier 21st century regenerative medicine often relied on computer technology and biotech. Replace an arm with metal and steel, replace a nerve with circuits and wires. In other words, they looked outward for solutions, they were additive in nature. They asked the questions: how can we replace what we have lost?

Hayden and his father's innovation had never been in the exact proteins they mixed together. It was in looking inward, finding mechanisms that had always lain dormant, deep within our cells, and unlocking them. In essence, they triggered the potential to grow and divide that was already there in all of us.[15]

But I didn't know all this, then.

All I had were my own guesses, my own greed.

Here is a warning: Hayden asked me, before we started, what it would take to put something back together. I didn't have an answer for him then, but I do now. To put something back together, you need to have something broken, and Hayden decided in that instance that to demonstrate, he would break himself. If depictions of self-harm are disturbing to you, you may want to skip this passage.

Hayden plucked the vial off the table and held it up to the light. He gave it a small shake. Bubbles pressed up against the glass, gleaming.

"What does it do?" I asked.

Hayden tilted his head. "It puts you back together." He held up our joined wrists. "I'm going to move around—do you mind?"

I let my arm go limp. "Go ahead."

Hayden's smile widened. Something in him lit up, right at that moment. He rolled his sleeves up. I thought it was to keep them away from whatever mess he might be making. Underneath the blinding white lab coat, he was wearing a soft green sweater, which he folded up to expose the long, faintly blue veins that ran up his wrist. The cuff was stark against his pale skin, resting just over the ridge of his wrist bone.

He snapped some gloves on and busied himself with gathering supplies on the tray: a syringe, a scalpel, some bandages.

---

15 Perhaps a simplistic understanding of Sisyphus and indeed all that it would come to represent—but I have left this explanation here unchanged from Felicia Xia's original publication as a testament to the thinking at the time.

The collection made me nervous, but I didn't want to interrupt. I wanted to see the miracle happen. I think I forgot why I was there. I think the lab, breathing in the steady, stale air, something about the fresh cold—I think it all made me forget what I was doing. I felt giddy, watching Hayden prep the syringe, levelling it into the vial, extracting that pale yellow liquid.

He flicked the body of the needle with some dramatic flair, then pushed some out the top. Yellow dribbled onto the tray. For a second, I thought I could see something swimming inside.

Hayden set the syringe down and uncoiled a length of bandages. With my hand limp and dragging along behind his, we nearly knocked over a vial, and I reached up to curl my fingers around his sweater instinctively. It was soft, fine-threaded cashmere.

"You always did have expensive taste," I murmured.

Hayden looked down distractedly, then scowled and tugged his lab coat over the slip of green. "It's comfortable," he said.

"Not afraid of ruining it?" I asked, because he had unspooled the whole bandage by now, and I was growing apprehensive at what he was going to do with the supplies.

Without another word, Hayden brought out a scalpel. He lay his forearm—the one I was still cuffed to—out on the bench, wrist turned up.

I didn't have a chance to wonder what that was for.

Hayden made a long cut straight down.

He followed a tendon.

His skin split like a melon rind, pulpy and fresh.

I flinched hard, but that only pulled at the cut, exposing a hint of beige tendon amidst slick pink flesh. Red started to pool, faster than I thought should've been possible—too fast to staunch, surely, and I had a sickening, sinking realization.

Had he been trying to trick me after all? Did he only bring me here so he could have a chance to hurt himself to—do what? Join his father?

No, I thought, and then, *how dare he?*

The words vanished unsaid.

But Hayden didn't look fazed, only a faint wince marring his face. He pulled the bandage over the wound, wrapping it around his wrist in quick, easy motions. What happens next is something of a blur. I try and remember, but I can only think of the panic rooting me in place, my own inaction glaring against all other memories. Hayden was calm, I think. Too calm, perhaps. But all I could think of was that I should've realized he was dangerous, that I didn't want his death on my hands.

Then he picked up the syringe and slid it under his skin, beneath the edge of the bandage. It was already soaked through. He pushed the stopper.

I stood. And watched. And that glimmering yellow disappeared, right into his veins.

I saw my free hand, white knuckled around his arm, clench— not with the cuff, but my panic—and I was angry. I don't know if I thought I could staunch the flow, or if I wanted him to hurt more. My nails dug into his arm, damaging what was already damaged.

Hayden looked up at me, his eyes blank. "Felicia," he said.

I must've looked wild.

"It's okay."

My mouth was dry.

"It's okay," he said again, a murmur, his head dipping towards his bared arm.

Bit by bit, Hayden unwound the bandage. Some forgotten instinct finally surged to life in me, and I lunged out, grabbing

Hayden lunged, but it was too late—we both watched as the miracle formula shattered on the ground.

My mind went blank.

Hayden bent his head. I could see the faint tremble at his shoulders, the hard line of his jaw, the bobble of his throat as he swallowed. I couldn't see his face. "Dammit," he whispered. His hands were clenched, joints stiff, so tight his knuckles cracked. The old instinct reared in me to ease his fingers loose, one by one, to slip mine in between. I'd gotten caught up, falling too close to old patterns, but I didn't want that for us, not anymore.

In the end, all I did was help him search, but we didn't find a single vial left intact in that lab room. Sometimes I wonder if I should've left it alone, declined to see a demonstration, but I can't find it within myself to regret.

"Why Sisyphus?" I finally asked.

Hayden's hand fell slack. "It was a stupid attempt at grandiosity," he said, cheeks flushing faintly pink. "And then the name stuck, so."

"But I mean, why him? Aren't you dooming yourself to failure with a name like that?" I thought of the mythic Sisyphus, perpetually pushing the same rock up the same hill, only to slip and fall at the last stretch. I didn't want to think about the parallels, the way Hayden wore exhaustion like a second lab coat, how he still didn't seem satisfied with the formula, sensational as it was.

Hayden shrugged. "Maybe," he said, "but Sisyphus was the first myth I'd heard where someone defied death. I think it stuck with me."

I stopped, my thumb frozen on a spool of bandage, thought about his words. "Are you saying...?"

"We're working—we *were* working on other things, too.

This was supposed to be just the beginning."

"What's next?"

Hayden was silent for a long time, even if we both knew he'd given it away. Eventually, he settled on, "I want to see how much damage is salvageable, how far we can push this."

"Meaning...?"

"Meaning inducing production past the point of irreversible cell damage. Meaning overcoming mass necrosis."

"Meaning transcending death."

Hayden gave me a half-smile. "Yes."

He didn't tell me then that he'd already succeeded, so of course I thought it was absurd. "That's impossible."

He turned his wrist over to expose the straight line of his newly gained scar. "This was impossible a year ago. And yet here I am, alive and whole."

I flinched away from it, nearly knocked the rest of the tray over, too.

Hayden looked at me out of the corner of his eye. "Are you afraid of me?" The corner of his mouth was loose, lax, and I suddenly remembered the shape of him in the dead hours of night, made vulnerable by exhaustion and the post-sex haze. A version of him I'd never seen anywhere else, without any of his edges.

"You're a murder suspect."

"And you leveraged yourself here, alone with me, just to see this. Are you afraid of me?"

"No," I said, and that was the truth. I have never been afraid of Hayden Lichfield. Only for him. "Just the things you can do."

"I could do so much. I could open doors that no one's ever even thought of entering before. I could change the world."

"For the better?"

"Of course."

I shrugged. Something sat uncomfortably in the pit of my stomach at the thought of it all. I still don't know how to parse any of it, but I am not writing this to cast judgment on the ethics of Hayden's research. I don't claim to be an arbiter over whether or not we should die[16]. That is not on me to decide—and the only other thing I was certain of, both in my capacity as a person of science and as a person with sense, was that it was not up to Hayden to decide either, no matter how afraid of the end he might've been. "Is this even testable?" I asked.

"Everything is testable."

"How many scars do you have under that sleeve?" I blurted.

Hayden turned sharply on me. His eyes were very wide, bloodshot, blank.

"How many times have you cut yourself open, over and over, trying to see if you could fix it? How many times did it fail? Your father was paranoid enough to poke blind spots into his own security system—don't tell me you performed a proper clinical trial."

Hayden looked at a loss for words for the first time. His mouth was slack, the lines around his eyes tired and confused. I was winding down to a question I didn't know if I wanted to

---

16 Again, I do want to highlight this as a commonly held belief at the time. Thanatologists argue the view was one born of impotence—we cannot be arbiters of death if we cannot control it, after all—but anthropological studies into modern radical naturalist communities suggests there may be a different underlying pathos at play. As activist R. de la Cruz of the Still Life Foundation said: "We've used power to control when people die since time immemorial—I don't have to get into all that bullshit. What's changed is that it's obvious, now. You're staring someone in the face and you're saying, 'I believe you deserve to live more than what God's given you.' That's too much responsibility for some folks to want to handle. I think that's a kind of moral cowardice, when the question isn't a hypothetical anymore. It's real."

ask but had been asking him this whole time, some variant of it hidden in all our arguments. *How far are you willing to go?*

"You say you want to turn back the clock on *death*," I said. "How are you going to test that?"

Would you die for this?

But of course, somebody already had.

Hayden didn't have an answer for me. The implications slid into the recesses of my mind, like needles, burrowing too deep for me to dislodge them. *Would you kill for this?*

Either way, Hayden meant to master death. He meant to chain it up like a prisoner, so that he could cheat it if he wanted, if he tried hard enough. I couldn't tell if he was doing it out of a deluded sense of grandeur, an overly ambitious belief in his own capabilities, or if he was doing it out of fear.

But he could tell me about exploring the undiscoverable all he wanted. His father's body cooling in Elsinore's makeshift morgue was proof enough that Hayden Lichfield was not the god-tricking king he thought himself.

Still, there was some part of me that understood.

The allure of it all, the miracle. And when everything else had burned away, the only thing I took with me was an anger so ferocious it could've swallowed me and Elsinore and the whole of Helsingør harbour alive. I wanted to reach out and shake sense into Hayden, to ask him why he would let his father's clear paranoia pollute something as world-shattering as this research. Without all the furtive secrets, things kept in the dark, no one would've had to die for this at all.

I promised myself, then, I would extricate this. I could be the one to untether death from the post Sisyphus had entangled it with.

I had hope. That was the difference. Right then, I still hoped there would be something gained once we'd passed the night.

**Message log, taken from
Felicia Xia's pager, 01:09am, 08/13/2047**

Felicia

dad don't let charles get the research

take it yourself if you have to just don't let him

Dad

You sure?

Why?

Felicia

I saw it

its hard to explain ill tell u when this is over

just don't let charles take it

Dad

ok

CHAPTER NINE
HORATIO

HAYDEN'S SKIN ITCHES. Furtively, Horatio traces the line of his scar, the prickle of lingering pain moving up the inside of his forearm, and follows the impulse shooting up Hayden's body: nociceptors, medial antebrachial cutaneous nerve, medial cord, inferior trunk, rooted in the spinal column just below cervical body seven—the one that's visible from above. All his cameras in the stairwell are grainy, but Horatio can still make out the lovely jut of Hayden's spinous process as he climbs. He holds his arm a little stiffly, the new scar still pulling at the fibres in his sweater. Horatio relishes the erythematous glow that must make Hayden's skin warm to the touch. It's tender, too, an ache down to the bones that resonates with the sternum-deep sense of anxiety that Hayden has always carried with him, and that Horatio has never quite understood until now. Descriptions like *pins and needles* and *jittery* and *it's like my stomach's dropped out from underneath me* are only words, but Horatio thinks now, yes, it's the skittering of static, it's the sudden shock of a short circuit, it's Hayden tucking his arm tight against him, the jolt of taut pain that pierces through layers of skin and fat and transcends the physical.

I'm okay, Hayden thinks to himself as he walks, and Horatio wants to echo it, would tell him that a thousand times if it meant he'd believed it just once.

Beside him, Felicia Xia seems shaken. Horatio has no access to her thoughts, her inner world, what she thinks of all this, Sisyphus Formula included, so maybe he's only projecting, in reading concern in the hunch of her shoulders, the sidelong glances Hayden's way when he's not paying attention.

"How many floors up?" she asks.

Hayden rubs his fingertips together. "Four," he says, and doesn't stop climbing.

"We never use the fourth floor," Felicia says.

Hayden only shrugs, a move that jolts the scar, another quick burst of pain splintering up his arm.

As much as Horatio wants to say something, Hayden's mind is a mess of *I'm okay, I'm okay,* in tandem with his heartbeat. Not the most receptive to soothing, and Horatio knows that Hayden's moods are fragile on his best days. He seems stable, for now. It's all Horatio can do to keep a metaphorical finger on Hayden's pulse, wishing he had the fine control to titrate enough acetylcholine to calm the racing pound of the beat.

Inevitably, they make it to the right floor.

"Afraid of what's up there?" Hayden asks, shouldering the door.

"Is it more mad science?"

Hayden laughs lightly enough that Horatio knows it's forced.

Then, soft enough that her voice scratches, Felicia mutters, "I think you're the one who should be afraid."

He is. But Hayden would never show it. He lingers in the doorway, face muddled with a frown. Dark grey concrete walls hem him in from either side, streaked occasionally with lighter bands. Cool air ruffles the edges of his coat. There are no windows, but rods of light line the walls, leading back down the way they came.

Horatio is afraid, too. There are so few spaces here unwatched. And yet Elsinore is already so contained within itself. He hates the idea of a whole hallway unknown to him.

Hayden ignores the jab and keeps moving forward.

Unlike the ground floor, the walls out here are not white. They are painted a dull grey, left unrenovated from when the building was first constructed. Horatio's systems are spottier, here, his wires not as deeply embedded in the walls. Posters litter the space from floor to ceiling: old diagrams, periodic tables long since outdated, a presentation board detailing the history of these walls, from when it was an academic centre to now. They curl at the corners, yellowed with age. It all makes Horatio feel young, the entire hall neatly preserved from half a century ago, on the cusp of discoveries yet to come. Decades before Dr Lichfield pieced him together. Horatio does not know what nostalgia feels like, his memories are easier to access than those coded with human circuitry, but he thinks it might be something a little like this, a dash of longing for whatever might've slipped through the cracks in the years between.

Hayden runs a hand along the wall, and it comes away black with grime. It seems years since anyone was here.

"Which way?" Felicia asks.

"Left." Then, "Horatio?"

"*I was wondering when you'd call,*" Horatio chimes in, trying, despite knowing the futility of it all, to restore some levity to the situation.

He's rewarded with a scowl. Horatio chooses to interpret it as fond. "Do you have the emulator?"

"*Yeah,*" Horatio says easily. "*I do.*"

"Thanks," Hayden says distractedly, then turns to Felicia with a wider, faker smile. "Sorry, checking to see if we have access." A blatant lie, but Felicia only raises an eyebrow and lets it slide.

"What room?" she asks.

"351."

Felicia stops. "The rooms only go up to 300 here."

Hayden shrugs, a sardonic smile hooking at his mouth. "I know."

He walks to the end of the hall, heedless of their still linked hands. The door at the very end is labeled *300*. Horatio knows Hayden has memorized the map his father showed him, can picture the invisible hallway stretching out to the right of that door. Even as Horatio thinks this, Hayden is reaching out, the pads of his fingers resting against the wall, dragging Felicia's along with him.

A jolt of surprise tingles through their link. "Oh," says Hayden.

"What is it?" Felicia asks.

"Feel it," Hayden says, hand still pressed against the yellowing wall.

Felicia's fingers are millimetres from his. "It's cold," she says.

Hayden cracks the knuckles of his free hand against the wall. The muffled thump echoes out between them all, and Horatio runs another scan of the floor, tries to find a camera, sensors, anything beyond the hollow ring. Every time, he's redirected, his efforts bouncing off a digital wall like magnets repelling each other.

Felicia curls a nail against the wall. "How do we get in?" Her voice is heavy with skepticism.

There is nothing, not even a keypad. Only the dead-end hallway, a door facing the wrong way.

Swallowing in a breath deep enough that Horatio sees the edge of his ribcage, Hayden leans forward and touches his free hand to the handle of door 300.

"*Shit,*" Horatio says. Twin-fold sensations feed into him— from Hayden, the simmer of electric heat at his skin; from the handle, the sear of a connection, conductance along the entire length of Hayden's touch. A starburst of information to his system, the sudden stretch of hallway blossoming before him, streams of data growing from Hayden's fingertip. "*It knows you,*" Horatio says, in wonder.[17] He watches the hallway take form, mould into something physical and real. Unlocked for Horatio by the treads of Hayden's fingerprint carving the information into reality.

The empty wall starts to slide open, inch by inch.

Hayden has his eyes closed, muscles tensed. The wall grinds, and an admixture of thick, musty odours billows out. Hayden's nose twitches at the scent.

Another loud click.

And then, stillness.

Hayden's eyes open. His mouth is slack, tongue darting out to wet his lips as he peers in. Horatio can see the whites of his eyes, gleaming in the dimness. Beside him, Felicia has a hand on the opened cavity, a dark blur crouched beside a darker void.

Horatio fumbles through the novel commands suddenly

---

17 Biometrics of a high enough complexity were a trustworthy authentication method in this time as they were still considered reliably personal and difficult to forge.

available to him. An air vent kicks up, droning, when he hits something without meaning to. But when he finds the right switch, the lights flare up in blocks down the hall.

"*After you,*" says Horatio.

THE WALLS GLOW, too. Hayden can't keep his hands off them, every trill of his fingers creating another shock of connection. The stark contrast of all that light only emphasizes the layer of dust coating the floor, motes floating around in the pure white.

There are no footprints.

Hayden doesn't say a word. Neither does Felicia. But it's obvious.

There is only one viable solution, here; there was only ever one way out. Horatio doesn't need to tell Hayden that he senses no intruder ahead of them.

His mind is unexpectedly still through the veil of their link, a silvered calmness as they reach the end of the hallway, and he pushes the door open with a quiet creak of the rusted hinges.

As soon as they step in, another memory nearly overwhelms Hayden, bright enough that Horatio can peek into it in its entirety and swim in the sensation, superimposed atop Hayden of the past. Shelves upon shelves of old data, paper files stacked on top of each other in boxes, languishing in a floor of history. The rest of the room constructs itself; Dad is there, ghostly, but that's only the quality of memory, his arms clasped behind his back and holding out a fistful of journal articles for you and him to go through. His encouraging smile, that you love so much. Your hand reaching out, still pudgy with middle school baby fat, already eager to learn what you can from him.

The door falls shut. The memory dies.

All that's left is an empty room.

"If there's anyone here," Felicia says, "they're invisible."

The mirrored calmness in Hayden shatters quietly. His throat is dry; pain rakes it as he swallows. He moves his lips wordlessly, groping for his wrist, digging his fingernails under the plastic edge of the cuff. Horatio feels it, the squeeze and shudder of his heart, but Hayden scrapes and scratches at himself with a desperate edge, tearing the skin with a ragged rip. It takes him too long to switch to his other wrist, and even then, the tension pulling his shoulders taut doesn't ease.

"*Hayden, you're okay. You have a plan, remember?*" Horatio murmurs to him.

Hayden's mind is busy with other remembrances. Here is where he spent an entire afternoon demanding his father draw out every step of meiosis. Here is where he riddled his fingers with paper cuts, digging out a paper on hypermethylation he was trying to find. Here is where they sat, him nestled in his father's lap, reading aloud from *Epigenetics & Our Future*. His uncle, walking in on them both with dinner. A lot of laughter.

Why did he seal this place off? Hayden asks, and the question isn't directed at Horatio, because Horatio didn't— doesn't—know, but it's the only thing in his mind loud enough for words.

Felicia is looking around, searching the shelves. Maybe she is still holding onto the idea that there might be someone else here. Hayden lets her pull him, limbs pliant as he stumbles along.

But then they emerge from a maze of bookshelves, and Horatio understands. Ahead of them stands a singular cabinet housing a scattering of memorabilia, and next to it, tossed over the ledge, rests a stained lab coat, the badge still pinned to the pocket. Hayden's mother stares up at them in preserved portraiture, old fashioned print film and a shiny frame. She looked caught in a moment, glancing up from her workbench, a pair of goggles perched over her dark hair.

Hayden's hand goes to his pocket, where her pen rests.

So Dr Lichfield was a man of emotions after all. Despite all his rationality, there were never any real secrets he wanted to seal off here, only the proof of his own weaknesses. Horatio doesn't often look at the truth of Dr Lichfield's mind, but he remembers the imprint of his failing marriage well enough, the weight of those memories sitting like lead in his circuitry somewhere.

It's obvious this room is empty, save for ghosts. Dr Lichfield, eternally haunting; the woman he loved, not yet dead but gone all the same; and the thing that sears Horatio the most to think about, proof of Hayden's younger, brighter self.

"There's no one here," Felicia says.

Hayden chews at the inside of his cheek, his hand coming up to rest at the nape of his neck again. *Horatio,* he thinks, *are you ready?*

I am, Horatio replies, and knows there is no coming back from this.

Thank you, Hayden thinks, rushed, like he knows Horatio doesn't want to hear how easily he'll comply to any one of Hayden's self-destructive impulses. Then, he pulls lightly on the cuffs tying him to Felicia and looks up at her through the curtain of his fringe. "Can we take another look around?" he asks.

Felicia presses her lips tightly together.

"Please," Hayden says, pitching his voice lower. "Just one."

You don't even feel bad, Horatio whispers to him.

Shut up, Hayden thinks, with a sudden fierceness that startles Horatio. *I do. I do.*

But you're going to go through with it anyway, Horatio says.

Hayden is saved from answering when Felicia acquiesces with a short nod, and they take a small tour of the room. There's no mystery intruder who shows their face. Nothing but more dust and suspicious stains on the ground. The important thing is that when they're done, they end up next to the door, and its flashing control panel.

"Horatio," Hayden says, out loud this time.

"Hayden, there's no one—"

He slams a palm on the panel and the door beeps in warning. "Please initiate override code Z-dash-five-oh-one and lock the door."

Felicia's eyes widen and she lunges forward, but Hayden stands his ground, and she catches on the cuff before she can reach the handle. She turns back to him, lips white with fury and hands curled into tight fists.

Hayden puts his hands up. "I'm sorry."

CHAPTER TEN

Excerpted from *Tell Me A Tragedy*

"I THINK," HE said, "it's about time I told you the truth."

"Shut up. Don't move."

Hayden kept his palm open and up, drawing his hand back from the door he had locked. "I know you have no reason to, but, please, trust me. I just want to explain."

The cuff on my wrist seemed to burn, and I wanted to divest myself of it as soon as I could, but I had been the one to do this. I wanted to know, and so I let Hayden lead me into the bowels of Elsinore; and now I was here, trapped with him. I didn't know what he was planning. I kept my hands carefully poised. I didn't know what I was capable of.

"What do you mean?" I bit out.

"I'm tired of lying."

"So you have been. This whole time. Lying to me."

Hayden had the decency to look chastised. He lowered his arm, tapped the tips of his fingers against each other like he didn't know what to do with them. "I had to."

Those words ignited the fury simmering in my chest. He was

still hunched over in front of me, pathetic, and all I wanted to do was rattle him, slam his head against the wall. I took a step forward and shoved his shoulder back, stepping up flush under his chin. "How dare you?" I snapped. "You asked me to trust you while you knew you were lying to me the whole time. How do I know you didn't do it? Am I supposed to still trust that you're not a murderer, and you're not about to make your second kill?"

Hayden flinched.

I didn't care.

I kept shoving, pushing until his back was flush against the wall, and I was glaring up at him.

"That's not what I meant," Hayden whispered, his head bowed.

"Then what the hell are you talking about? If you're going to confess, fucking do it!"

And then, he stiffened up.

My fingers dug deep into his shoulders. Our linked hands hung between the both of us—I didn't know who was trapped by whom anymore.

Hayden unfurled, straightening to his full height—not quite level with mine, but close enough. The light in the halls had always made him seem smaller, shoulders caving in. "Don't," he said, his voice scratching like metal on granite, "accuse me of something I didn't do. I didn't kill my father."

For a moment, I stood in disbelief, but the rage was naked on Hayden's face. It cut through all the layers of bloody deception and visceral lies, until I could see that underneath all of it he was only desperately angry, caught in a web of threads bigger than he knew how to untangle himself from.

"What's the plan, then?" I asked, gripping the back of his neck. "What do you want?"

Hayden swallowed, his pale throat bobbing in front of me. "I need your help," he finally admitted. The skin seen through his glasses was heavy, purple-bruised under the gleam on the lens. Weariness was etched in the line of his mouth, the blanched paleness of the rest of his face. I pitied him.

I decided, then and there, that he was no murderer. Could never.

Foolish, stupid me.

"Prove it to me," I said, because I still wanted to know. I wanted to know all of it. "Prove that you're not the murderer."

"I... How?"

"Do what you just said you wanted to: tell me the truth."

"Promise you won't hate me."

"I can *try*. Just tell me what happened."

"Okay."

And he did.

Transcript of recording taken from
Felicia Xia's phone, 2:24am, 08/13/2047[18]

(A click. Someone breathes, shallow but steady.)

HAYDEN: I brought him back.

FELICIA: Who?

HAYDEN: No, no, back up. I need context. I just... wanted to
          get that out.

FELICIA: Start with the murder, then.

HAYDEN: I have to go back further than that, actually.

FELICIA: This is sounding more and more like a real
          confession by the second.

HAYDEN: Shut up. Let me. Let me figure it out.

FELICIA: Okay. I'm patient.

HAYDEN: (inhales) So. We fought. Tonight, earlier, before.
          Whatever. (laughs) Over the research, of all
          things.

---

18 The claims made by Hayden Lichfield in this transcript are suspect; they were
hotly contested in court and most analysts were unable to determine which, if any,
are true.

FELICIA: That doesn't seem like a big deal, on top of the
            rest of tonight.

HAYDEN: I'm the one who wiped the files.

FELICIA: (pauses) And you still say you're innocent.

HAYDEN: <u>Yes</u>. Just—hear me out.

(Rustling.)

FELICIA: Keep talking.

HAYDEN: You know how this goes. We fought over the same
            thing we always do.

FELICIA: Say it for the recording.

HAYDEN: Fine. We fought because I wanted to reach out
            to my mother with the new project, and he didn't
            want me to share it with anyone. I was mad
            because it was <u>mine</u>, too, and he couldn't get over
            himself to give me this one thing, you know? I
            thought he only cared about what we were doing
            here in the lab. I... I don't know what to think
            anymore, but that's what he said. (inhale, then
            exhale) I don't know if he was talking to her. I just
            know he told me not to.

FELICIA: Why?

HAYDEN: You <u>know</u> all this already, Felicia, stop making
            me—I don't want to—

FELICIA: The recording, Hayden.

(A stretch of 5 seconds of silence.)

HAYDEN: My mother is the head scientist at Armstrong
            Labs.

FELICIA: And is Armstrong invested in all of this?

HAYDEN: Armstrong's been trying to buy us out for years. My parents fought for months when my mom took the job there, even if they were basically split by then.

FELICIA: And what does that have to do with anything?

HAYDEN: Well, I just wanted to talk to her, to let her know what I was working on, make her... proud, I guess? (scoffs) This is so fucking embarrassing. I miss her, I guess. My dad was convinced she would steal the formula.

FELICIA: And this translates to <u>you</u> stealing it, how?

HAYDEN: I'm getting there.

FELICIA: Get there faster.

HAYDEN: We ran a test on the Sisyphus Formula. It worked.

FELICIA: Y—you mean?

HAYDEN: Yes. It <u>worked</u>.

FELICIA: Who...

HAYDEN: On a mouse! Lab rats, standard procedure.

FELICIA: Oh. Okay. So, what then?

HAYDEN: I wanted to tell her. He said no. This was kind of a recurring argument, so I got worked up. I stormed out. I left for some air, I guess. Walked around a bit. Told him I was going to grab something from a supply closet and just wandered through the halls. By the time I got back, well...

FELICIA: Oh.

HAYDEN: Yeah.

FELICIA: I... I'm sorry.

HAYDEN: Are you?

FELICIA: Hayden, I—

HAYDEN: No, listen. I'm not done.

FELICIA: Alright.

HAYDEN: So I got back, and my father's dead, and what I'm

thinking is like, "Goddamn, he was right." There's someone out there who wants our research after all, even if it isn't Armstrong. He was right this whole time to be so paranoid. I see our files all opened, and there's nothing missing. Yet. What else was I supposed to do but grab all the files on a chip and wipe the system?

FELICIA: Call the police?

HAYDEN: I don't trust anyone with this. No one. My father died for this.

FELICIA: You don't know that.

HAYDEN: What other reason would there be?

(Silence, 2 seconds)

HAYDEN: Yeah, see? Either way, we're stuck here.

FELICIA: So who do you think did it? And what are you going to do about it?

HAYDEN: I don't know. I don't know.

FELICIA: Your uncle isn't going to rest until he finds that research again.

HAYDEN: He was always very passionate about it. It was... a family thing.

FELICIA: So...

HAYDEN: I have an idea. I don't want him to... I don't want him to know I was the one who took it.

FELICIA: So, what, are you going to drop it off like an anonymous gift? Leave a little bow on top?

HAYDEN: Something like that. Felicia, do you trust me?

FELICIA: I—

(A loud beep cuts her off.)

CHAPTER ELEVEN
HAYDEN

ALARMS BLARE.

"*Someone is trying to break in,*" Horatio announces to the whole room, not just him.

"Does this mean they've found us?" Hayden asks.

"*I think something alerted Charles when you locked the door.*"

"Dammit," Hayden says. "I thought we'd have more time. Okay. Do you still have the video?"

"*About half a minute of it.*"

"And the voice modulator?"

"*It's ready.*"

"There aren't any hidden cameras I don't know about in here, right?"

"*No.*"

"Okay. Thanks."

"*Stop thanking me,*" Horatio says, his words accompanied by another rattle at the back of Hayden's head, like a phantom flick. "*Just be careful.*"

Hayden fights the urge to stick his tongue out like a child. He cards a hand through his hair. Everything's in place, the plan, the bait, the trap. He should be ready. He's ready, but there's a nugget of doubt that he might call *hope* sitting in his chest still. The possibility that his uncle is innocent, that his father's death rattle wasn't an accusation.

Whatever the truth, his uncle's reaction to the plan will reveal it.

He taps on Felicia's still-recording phone. "I take it this is done, then?"

Felicia's lips are bleached with fury. "What's going on?" she demands.

"My uncle is trying to find out."

She reels back. She holds her stare for a minute, enough for the piercing tones to fade into the background, then taps the phone screen with perhaps more force than necessary and shoves it back into her pocket. "Aren't you going to let him in?"

"Of course not."

She raises an eyebrow. "I thought the plan was to return the research to him."

The thought of delivering the research directly into his uncle's hands makes his stomach turn. But that's what Felicia needs to believe is happening. Hayden nods.

"How?" she asks.

"I'm going to talk to him."

Felicia's lips curl in disbelief. For a moment, she looks like she's going to hit him again, demand more answers. But Hayden has nothing left to give, and maybe she senses that; eventually, she sighs, slumps back and slides down the wall, dragging Hayden with her. A brief impingement of guilt squeezes at his heart. An image flashes—the visage from a holiday spent visiting her at university that ended badly—Felicia with the same wrought tiredness lining her face, shoulders hunched as she slumped by the coils of her old radiator, Toronto streets outside the streaked window, her hair brushing over the bare skin of her shoulder. And just like then, when Hayden tries to reach out, she buries her face in her knees and turns away.

Hayden crosses his legs, keeps careful distance. Four layers of fabric separate him and her skin this time. He pitches his head back against the wall.

Tell me this will work, Horatio, he thinks blearily.

It will, Horatio says, with a conviction Hayden doesn't have in him.

Okay, he thinks back.

Together, they wait for his uncle to break down the security. Hayden pictures him pacing behind Rasmussen as they scan through the camera feed, looking for the missing one.

It's almost calm. He sucks in dusty air and scans the water stains on the ceiling, as if he can find a pattern in the brown smears, the winding cracks.

And then the speakers above them crackle.

"*He's trying to crack in,*" Horatio says. "*I'm going to let him.*"

"Alright," Hayden says, steeling himself. "Wait a minute, then play the clip."

"*Don't do anything too stupid.*"

"I think I'm long past that," Hayden mutters.

Horatio sighs. The sound of it washes through the room and then through Hayden's own ears, a rush of static that makes him wince. "*I know,*" he says, "*but I'm always worried about you.*"

"You should sit back and enjoy the show," Hayden says sardonically. "Make sure you watch for my uncle's reaction."

"*Right.*"

And then—it begins. His uncle's voice cuts into the broadcast, sharp and insistent.

"*It looks like we have a bit of a mess on our hands*," he says.

Hayden shoves his free hand deeper in his pocket to stop the shaking. "Depends on your definition of *mess*," he calls up cheerily.

"*So you haven't been murdered by an intruder.*"

"Judging by your tone, you wish I had been."

His uncle sighs in exasperation. "*What else was I supposed to think when we found the room wired shut?*"

"I don't know. What *did* you think?"

"*Please just tell me what's going on.*" He sounds like he cares, and Hayden hates it.

He drums his hand on the ground beside him. "I was looking for the research," he finally says, pretending reluctance to admit it.

Beside him, Felicia chews on her thumbnail and stares at him suspiciously.

"*Why initiate lockdown, then? We know it was you, Hayden.*"

"I didn't want anyone else to have it."

"*I can keep it safe, Hayden. You should've told me.*"

Hayden clenches my teeth so hard it hurts. "I know."

Before he has to conjure up any more falsehoods to present, they're interrupted.

"*Hello?*"

His father's voice echoes through the lab. There's no video feed this time, but Hayden can see it behind his eyelids. He still remembers the way his father moved, dreamlike, almost a shadow. "*This is a bit odd, I confess*," the voice continues. "*To be talking about one's own death.*"

"What?" his uncle says, more breath than words.

"*I have been dreaming of death of late,*" the video continues. And then a soft beep, and Hayden takes his last breath as himself for a little bit. He tries to cough surreptitiously around the sudden itch sinking its claws in his throat.

"It's a bit strange to be confronting the reality of it," he says, the modulator catching his voice and filtering it to sound exactly like his father's, the late Dr Graham Lichfield's, "but if I'm stuck talking to you like this, it means I'm dead."

Felicia snaps her head up. Her hand slides a few centimetres towards his, grabs onto one of his fingers with a grip so hard he knows it's meant to hurt, an accusation. But she doesn't say anything.

On the other side, his uncle is quiet.

"Well?" Hayden prods. "Aren't you even a little bit glad to hear from me, Charlie?"

"...*Graham?*" his uncle whispers, incredulous.

"In the flesh!" Hayden exclaims. "Well, technically in the artificial intelligence program, but that's details."

"*How is this possible? I... I saw your...*"

He doesn't finish the sentence. Hayden seethes. *Coward.*

"Mustn't have been pretty, huh?" Hayden asks, forcibly injecting more of his father's often-mistimed cheer in his tone. "But that's all done and over with, now. I'm still here."

"*How?*"

"It's simple, really." He starts to trace patterns in the ground as he speaks, protein backbones, alpha helices, beta sheets. "I've spent years mapping out the quirks of my neurological topography, logging it in, creating my own personal neuromap and all. The logical step following that was to fit that into an AI framework, train it to follow the same patterns, upload my memories every once in a while.[19]" Hayden pauses, trying to swallow the lump in his throat. Tries not to think about how many ways he might've saved his father, if they'd bothered to work on the tech. He stops drawing in the dust and brings his hand up to touch the neuromapper again. It glows warm under his touch, and Hayden finds himself unbearably grateful for Horatio in that moment.

His uncle sucks in a breath. "*So you're not* really *him?*"

"For all intents and purposes, Graham Lichfield and I are interchangeable. I have the same memories, same brain activity. Any differences are negligible.[20]" This *is* a lie, and it hurts most of all to say. The words stick in his throat, fighting to stay down.

But does his uncle believe it? And how is he reacting? If he's the murderer, he must be shaken, panicked somehow.

"What happened, Charlie?" Hayden asks, quieting.

There is a long stretch of silence. His uncle breaks it with a nervous chuckle. "*We think there was an intruder,*" he says.

"Did I get caught in the crossfire, or something?"

"*Something like that, yes.*"

His uncle's a good liar, after all.

But Hayden can be a better one.

"Is Hayden okay?"

"*He's fine.*"

"I don't have to ask, right?" he says. "You'd take care of him, right?"

"*Yes,*" his uncle says, much too quickly. "*Yes, of course I*

---

19 Another mere theory at the time.
20 Would that the philosophers of our time had this level of conviction!

would." Hayden doesn't know if he wants this one to be a lie, too.

"You sound stressed," Hayden cajoles instead of thinking about it, smiling sweetly even though Charles cannot see it. "You holding up okay?"

"*Yes,*" his uncle says faintly. Then, he laughs again, a choking disbelieving sound, and when he speaks next, his voice is thicker than usual. "*You're crazy, you know that? I can't believe you actually did this.*"

"Who do you take me for?" Hayden asks softly. "I always think of everything."

"*Yes,*" his uncle says, subdued. He inhales raggedly, and Hayden is horrified to hear a small sob slip through the speakers before it is muffled away. "*You really do,*" he whispers.

The truth slips away, muddied like silt running into a riverbank.

His uncle is the only one who had access to the cameras. There is no intruder. His uncle's name escaped his father's mouth. It has to be him. But—

"Anything else go wrong, then?" Hayden asks, to stall for time.

"*Whoever it was, they stole your research.*" His voice is smooth and almost cold. But not in a way that is unusual for Charles Lichfield. Hayden feels as if he is grasping at straws, trying to make the most minute of actions mean something bigger than they possibly can.

He has to pause to think about what his father would say in a situation like this. His anger was always chilling, the few times Hayden had managed to ignite it. When they argued, his father's voice lost all of its levity, its warmth.

"Pardon?" Hayden asks, bringing his voice down low.

His uncle coughs. He hems and haws for a while, then swallows. "*It's been wiped from the system. All of it.*"

"Have you found the intruder yet?"

"*No.*"

Hayden wonders if his uncle is wincing. He wonders how uncomfortable he is, lying through his fucking teeth. He runs the tip of his tongue against his cheek and tries to dip into his father's rage, but his own anger burns too brightly for him to understand his father's icy disdain.

He settles for something like a detached, disappointed tone, and hopes his uncle is too shaken up to question it. "Have you been searching?"

"*Of course,*" his uncle says again, breathless. "*I—I believe Hayden's been searching, too, but he's gone and locked himself in a room we can't unlock.*"

"He's done what now?"

"*Don't worry about it,*" his uncle says, voice clipped. "*I'll take care of it.*"

"Never mind about that. He'll be fine," Hayden says, hooking a hand over his glasses so he can set them on the ground, drape his arm properly over his eyes to block out all the light. "You need to recover my research. Charlie, please, you can't let it be lost. I'd rather die all over again." He lets a hot, stinging breath hiss out of his nose and waits for his uncle's response.

"*I—yes, alright. I'll keep looking.*"

Hayden still does not know what to do. Horatio has yet to come back with a reaction one way or another. He needs more time. More time to think, to dissect this moment. How sincere are his uncle's words? He's eager about the research—maybe *too* eager, but if he wanted it so badly, why didn't he just fucking ask? What does he want?

He presses his lips together, asks, "Is Paul with you?" to buy more time.

"*Yes. He's right here.*"

Paul Xia's voice comes in scratchier than his uncle's, with more of a nervous tremble. "*Graham?*"

"Paul," Hayden says, waiting for a response, trying to gauge what the man's motivations are.

"*Is it really you?*"

Hayden lowers his arm and tucks his hand under his chin. "Who else would it be?"

Felicia suddenly digs her nails in sharper at Hayden's wrist, the pain stinging at him. Her face contorts in a confused frown. Hayden shakes his head, once, and Felicia still does not interject, but she does lean in closer, her eyes like daggers.

"*How long have you had this technology?*" her father is saying above them. "*Is it ready for release? Does anyone else know you're working on this? And how thorough is it? Say, in a decade or so, how much does your... brain? program? ... er, I mean, regardless, how fast does it* develop?"

"I'll explain everything soon," Hayden says, blinking at the onslaught of questions.

"*Yes, yes, of course.*" Paul Xia clears his throat. "*I'm glad you're back, Graham. Truly, I am.*"

"Well," Hayden says wryly, floored by how deep Xia's voice is, how different from the usual reedy nervousness, "thank you. Me too. Obviously."

Paul Xia laughs, and for the first time, Hayden wonders how often his father had shared his research ideas with the man. Given the slew of Xia's questions, it must have been often. He wonders how his father acted around him, realizes he has no idea, no way of knowing. They'd been working together from the start. They built Elsinore together. How much of his father is locked inside of Paul Xia's brain? In memories he'll never see, much less understand?

But if Hayden doesn't know Xia, there's no way to fool him with this stupid charade.

Before he can worry about that particular snag, a piercing pain comes from the neuromapper. The equivalent of a panicked yell, screaming in Hayden's ears from Horatio. He closes his eyes and focuses on the shape of the echo, the demand so urgent there's no time to word it properly.

When it resolves into clarity, the message is crystal clear.

Hayden's blood freezes.

CHARLES. TOLD ME. TO ERASE. FILES OF. YOUR. FATHER'S NEUROMAP.

And there it is.

Over and above Horatio's repeating broadcast, the words echo and bounce in Hayden's head. Lodged there, like a rising wave encompassing all the rest of his thoughts.

Your uncle told me to erase your father's neuromap.

He tried to kill him all over again.

If that's not proof, he doesn't know what else is.

In the background, Hayden is hazily aware of Paul Xia calling out for him.

Well, for his father. But that's a wish no one can grant.

But there's no time to dwell on that. The only thing left to do now is to implement the rest of the plan.

"—*Graham? Dr Lichfield?*"

"Yeah," Hayden calls up, then winces. He's practically shouting, and his father wouldn't ever be that informal. "Yes," he amends, quieter. "I'm still here."

"*Oh, thank god,*" Paul says. "*I thought there was some sort of glitch.*"

"I'm still getting used to this, is all."

Paul laughs shortly. "*I figure there's a bit of a learning curve.*"

"You could say that. Say, Paul—I need to ask another favour of you." Beside him, Felicia tightens her grip enough to draw blood, her nails dragging at the already scratched skin at his wrist.

"*What is it?*"

"Keep an eye on the basement for me," he says. "If Charlie says there's an intruder, that's the most important part."

"*Alright,*" Paul says, no questions asked. "*I will.*"

Charles's voice crackles back into the conversation. "*What's in the basement?*"

"That's the next thing," Hayden says carefully. "My personal labs are in the basement."

Charles sucks in a breath. "*I—I didn't know that.*"

"Nobody did. That was the point."

"*The point of what?*"

"Protecting my research," Hayden says, smooth, with a hint of teasing laced in his words.

"*Shit, Graham. You've really thought of everything.*" Charles is practically breathless.

"I'm talking to you as a reanimated computer program designed to mimic the neural patterns of my original biological body; I think that's something of a given, isn't it? Come on, Charlie. Who do you take me for?"

Charles laughs. If Hayden didn't know better, he'd say it sounds loud, hard, joyful. But he knows the truth now. Hysteria spills from his uncle's mouth, colours it bloody red. He's desperate.

"*How do I get it?*"

"Room P28—it says storage closet over the door, but ignore that. There should be a keypad." Hayden pauses, drawing the silence out, fishing-wire-taut. "The code has to be kept secret."

"*I won't tell another soul.*"

"Remember this clearly: five-eight-two-seven."

"*Got it,*" Charles says. "*When do you want me to retrieve it?*"

"As soon as possible."

"*I can go now.*"

Hayden forces another laugh out, deep from his belly. So little to convince him. This is what he's always wanted, to steal the research. Make it his own. "That's my little brother."

"*What about Hayden?*"

"Tell him to stay put. I'll talk to him once things are settled. I don't think he's ready for... all this, yet."

"*Alright.*"

"From here on out," Hayden says, "it's all up to you, Charlie."

His uncle hums noncommittally.

Hayden wants to make it hurt. He wants his uncle to ache under the weight of his betrayal. He wants it to crush him. "Make me proud. I love you. We'll talk more later; we have all the time in the world, now." He barely manages to get the last word out before his jaw locks, as if someone has clamped a vice on his mouth. He breathes through his nose, nostrils flaring.

The line to Charles drops, but he's not done yet.

He forces his lips to move again, mandible clicking as he opens his mouth. "Uncle Charles?" He calls up. "Uncle Charles? What the hell? What's—"

"*Hayden,*" his uncle says, remarkably well composed. His voice is light, airy, and despite himself, Hayden still finds himself analyzing every syllable, looking for a crack, a break, anything that might signify the emotions he'd shown so freely earlier.

"What the hell happened?" Hayden snaps. "I've been sitting here in radio silence, wondering if you'd gotten hit by the intruder or something. Why'd you just drop the line like that?"

"*Then you know how I felt when Horatio said he'd lost contact with you,*" Charles says, and there is only sharpness in his voice. Hayden wants to laugh. From the side of this cavern, where the truth is evident, everything is tossed in sharp relief. Everything is a harsh reminder that this is nothing but a convincing show, a push-and-pull performance from them both, each trying to drag the story along a different path.

He scoffs. "Alright, alright, I'm sorry, okay? I wanted answers and you weren't giving me any. Besides, there was a blind spot up here."

"*Well, you'll have to sit tight again for a little while.*"

"What? Why?"

"*Please just listen to me for once, Hayden,*" his uncle says. He does sound exhausted.

For a moment, Hayden contemplates resisting. He wants to hear more of what it sounds like when his uncle is lying to him. He wants to drag this out until the guilt runs roots into Charles Lichfield's lungs and he chokes on it.

But Hayden has no guarantee he'll ever come around. He has no guarantee that Charles even cares at all. And Hayden is tired, too.

"Fine," he whispers.

"*Thank you,*" his uncle says.

"Yeah, yeah." He waves a hand in the air. "Go do whatever it is you have to do. Just don't forget me—"

Before he can ever finish the goddamn sentence, the lights flicker, and the room plunges into darkness.

Message log, taken from
Felicia Xia's pager, 2:57am, 08/13/2047

Felicia

basement room. Did u hear the code?

Dad

Yeah. Why?

Felicia

i don't trust any of this. I know
hayden wants him to have it but I don't think you
can let Charles get that research, dad.

Dad

I still don't know where he was
when the cameras were down
where he went

Felicia

hayden doesnt want to think its him
but i think...

Dad

who else could it have been

Felicia
right. Exactly.

Dad
What do u want me to do
he wants to go now
by himself

Felicia
you have to go instead of him
convince him somehow

Dad
ill try but no guarantees

Felicia
good enough
gtg

CHAPTER TWELVE
HAYDEN

THE ENSUING SILENCE is thick. Hayden fumbles for his glasses, but even with them back on his face the room is strangely washed out in the darkness—he knows this is because his rod cells are less attuned to colour, that grey bleeds into his vision because he needs only contrast when it is dark, but the slithering shadows that pool around the bookcases still make the back of his neck prickle. Evolutionary instinct pumps a rush of endorphins through his circulation, propping his tired mind awake. Hayden wants to shrink down, smaller than an atom, small enough to dissipate into the air like vapour. His hands have touched his father's body, stitched together the rubbery tubing of his vasculature, and yet this feels like the greatest violation of all.

"Horatio," he tries, but whatever Charles has done, the comms systems have all cut off with a hard stop and the speakers overhead stay silent as a grave. He bows his head, running a hand over the divots in the ridges of his spine. The neuromapper is still warm. *Please*, Hayden thinks, delirium creeping into his mind at the edges at the thought of losing this connection, too.

Agonizing silence, and then—

I'm here, Horatio whispers, *I'm here, I'm here.*

Hayden lets the breath rush out of his lungs.

A flash of imagery in his head—not quite diplopia, but everything before him blurry at the edges, like it's all layered over by a second film of visual input on his own. Hayden blinks, once, twice, and then he understands Horatio's sense of frustration—you're pushing against a dark, towering wall, and all you can do is bounce off it, curve away, never break it down or even so much as approach. *Did Charles lock you out of this area?* Hayden asks.

Yes, Horatio says, indignant.

Then you're seeing…

Through you, Horatio confirms.

Hayden can't help but smile. *Hey,* he thinks, *don't feel bad. What's the world like from my eyes?*

Felicia's mad at you, Horatio shoots back drily.

Hayden blinks again. There, in his periphery, he notices Felicia glowering, and winces. "Sorry," he mutters out loud.

Felicia's grip is still tight on his wrist, wet with his blood. "Something funny, there?"

Not for the first time, he doesn't know what else to say to her. "No," he mutters, opens his mouth to explain but thinks better of it. Doesn't want to get into—into the whole explanation, not with Horatio nestled right in his head then and there.

"Has there been a single time tonight when you weren't lying to me?"

"I didn't kill my father."

"Is that it?"

"I'm sorry to pull you into all this."

She rubs a hand across her temple. "Can you—tell me something first?"

"Anything you want to know."

"You're such a liar, Hayden."

"I'm sorry." He tries for another smile.

"How did you do that?" she asks. She drops her hand and sniffs, but her eyes are clear when she turns to face him full on. "How could you say those things, and pretend to *be* him, and not hate yourself for it?"

"I don't know," Hayden says. It is the only truth he has left. "I don't know if I hate myself for it yet."

She nods, slow. The pensive stare she gives him is worse than any angry glare. Her chin comes up, stray strands of hair falling down her cheeks as she cants her head to the side. The greywash lighting makes her eyes gleam. Like she's trying to see through to the truth of him.

As always, Hayden looks away first.

In the dark, the air is thicker. But as he sweeps the room to let his eyes rest on anything but Felicia's face, light gleams out at him, a soft green glow. There's something behind the shelf. Hayden climbs to his feet before he remembers that they're still tied together.

Felicia looks up, unmoving. "What are you doing now?" she asks.

"That light," he says, leaning around to see what it is. "There's no power in the room at all right now."

That's enough to grab her attention. She unfolds, coming up beside him. "That's not supposed to be on, then?"

"I don't know."

"Hm," she says, her lips twisting up. "Let's find out, then."

They both know this is nothing but a distraction, but Hayden manages to pick up his tired limbs enough to stride across the room until they find the source of the shimmering light: an ancient phone, blocky and embedded in the wall, a green bulb sticking out over a row of push buttons[21].

It looks worn, some of the numbers long since faded away.

"Is it on?" Felicia murmurs.

Hayden picks up the receiver and a long dial tone wails out into the room.

"There's no signal here," she says.

"It's old," Hayden murmurs, dragging a finger over the dust caked on the phone box. "I think this has a ground line." *Can you connect to this?* he asks Horatio, just to confirm.

No, says Horatio, and he sounds as confused as the rest of them.

Felicia stares at it for a while, shoulders hunched over. "Why do you need an old phone here?"

Why *did* his father need an old phone?

Secrets and more secrets. Once upon a time, Hayden thought that Elsinore housed everything fathomless and unknown, discoveries waiting to be made. But what if all these peeling walls were built to hide something rotten? A long dead core, the seeping decay edging towards them all.

There's a number, scrawled on the inside of the receiver. He thumbs over it, finding the edges of his father's spindly handwriting.

Before he can think better of it, he's dialling.

Felicia grabs onto his wrist. "Hayden."

"I just want to know," he hears himself murmur. "I want to know what he hid from me this whole time." And he doesn't care how much Felicia knows anymore. All he has is the

---

21 Landline telephones were considered nearly obsolete even in 2047, though the average person would have known how to operate one.

image of his father's face, wavering, slipping away like the dust of someone he never really knew anyway.

The phone dials. Rings. The sound of it echoing resonance, building in his chest until he's vibrating.

And then—

"*Hello?*" The voice is hoarse and worn, cracked with fatigue, and the sound of it hollows Hayden out. His limbs feel numb. He didn't know he ever had this much body to carry around, this much dull, heavy weight in his useless legs.

"Mom," he says, his own voice breaking.

There's a small intake of breath on the other side. "*Hayden,*" his mother says. "*What... why are you calling this late?*"

A twinge of guilt crawls into the empty space inside him when he realizes it is nearly 3am.

"I..."

"*Are you in trouble? Why are you at the lab?*"

So she knows this number. She knows where he is. Hayden feels like he's mourning his father twice over—the man he was, and the man Hayden thought he knew. His mother, too. The mother he could've had all these years. Tonight, he is made up of grief.

"Did he call you?" he asks, too tired to give context. "Before?"

His mother is quiet for a long time. "*Your father and I were in contact, yes,*" she says.

"Why didn't you...?"

"*It was me,*" his mother finally says. "*I didn't want to get your hopes up.*"

"What?"

"*Hayden,*" she says, and there's weight there. Heavy. Regret stitched into the gravelly sound of her voice. "*It was about the research. Nothing else.*"

"Oh. But you didn't…" He can't bring himself to finish the sentence, but the stupid, childishly entitled *But you didn't want to see me* bounces around his mind nonetheless.

"*Your father thought it was best that I stayed away,*" she says, voice just as tight. "*And I thought*"—she laughs, once, a little ragged and harsh—"*I thought you might listen to him over me, darling.*"

Hayden thinks of all his childhood memories, and all he can conjure is the image of the back of his father's lab coat. Nipping at his heels, hands all over his research. How Elsinore was the door he came knocking at instead of Armstrong. All this loyalty, and what did his father give back for it?

"Mom," he says again, and this time his voice cracks right down the word. He leans his head against the phone box, breathing harsh. "I'm sorry." And that can't be him, breathy and close to breaking. That can't be his voice. Hayden grips the receiver tight enough that the plastic creaks and nearly gives.

"*Oh, Hayden. You shouldn't be the one to apologize.*"

"Mom, he's dead."

The room swims.

"*What?*"

"He's dead. He was—it was murder. I—we're all stuck here now, and he's *dead*, Mom."

"*What happened?*" Her voice is floating from so far away. Whether she's quieter from the shock or if Hayden's mind is going numb again is unclear. He pulls his hand away from the receiver and digs his nails deep into his palms. The pain is supposed to bring him back. It doesn't. There's a dull ache that might be Horatio, calling, pressed at his neck, but his body is not a body anymore, only a collection of impulses and useless nerves, and it refuses to answer to him. His palm is coated in something slippery. He doesn't know if it's blood or sweat.

"An accident," he blurts. "I don't know, I—"

"*Were you there?*"

"No."

"*Did you see?*"

"*No*, I—I found him and…"

"*Oh*," his mother says again, something soft and sweet and trembling finally brimming out of her voice. "*Oh, honey.*"

"I don't know what I'm doing, Mom," Hayden gasps.

"Tell me what happened, slowly," his mother says. Her voice rattles, but it holds steady.

Obediently, Hayden explains, as best he can. The body, the research, the wretched resurrection. He whispers all the grimy details into the receiver, ever more aware of Felicia's heat at his back, ever listening. But his mother deserves this whole story; Felicia knowing will be the collateral damage, his repentance. He barely hears himself speak as it is, only the low vibration of his vocal cords at his throat telling him the words are audible. He swallows past the dryness in his throat to tell her about his uncle.

"I know who did it," he says.

"It was my uncle," he says.

"Yes," he says. "I'm sure."

His mother is quiet.

"Dad left me a video," he adds, too honest, now.

"*What did it say?*"

"He… he told me to get revenge. On whoever did this to him."

His mother takes in a breath, holds it, then lets it out in a steady thrum. "*Darling,*" she says, then she falters.

"I know you hate when I listen to him," Hayden says, "but I'm going to. I have a plan. I'm going to kill my uncle."

"*Oh, Hayden, you stupid boy,*" his mother whispers fiercely, and there's anger in her words now. Sharp and stabbing through the line as if she can traverse miles with will alone. "*Are you still so obstinate about his greatness that you're going to follow him into* this?"

"You don't understand."

"*I think I do. Your father asked you for something you can't possibly give, and you're going to ruin yourself trying to fulfil it. He's still the same man, even if he's dead now.*" She scoffs lightly, and the contempt in her voice hurts the most, drives the crack in Hayden's world deeper.

"It was the last fucking thing he wanted from me."

"*You don't have to do* anything *you don't want to, Hayden.*"

"But I *want* to make him—I want to do this for him."

"*What do you want me to say?*" his mother finally asks. It sounds like a condemnation.

Carefully, Hayden folds all the ugly, spilled emotions back into his chest. "I don't need you to say anything. It's already happening. Charles is going to die. You can't stop it, even if you call someone now."

"*Then why did you say anything at all? Why not hang up as soon as I answered?*"

Sometime during the conversation, his conviction has solidified into something cold that rests at the base of his throat. It feels like Horatio's reassurance, the understanding he's lent all this time. But he can still open his mouth around that steely core to admit, "I just wanted to hear your voice."

His mother blows out another shaky breath. "*I never wanted to lose you, darling.*"

"I know, Mom." The terrible, resentful part of Hayden's mind whispers that she lost him a long time ago. That he somehow chose, without meaning to, the damning day he stepped into Elsinore's halls.

"*Hayden*," his mother says, her tone softening, "*I love you.*"

"Me too, Mom."

She hangs up first.

The line goes silent. He stares down at the phone, the borrowed lifeline resting in his hand, and fights the urge to slam it to the ground. If it weren't attached to the wall, he would've. His eyes blur. He reaches up to swipe under them, but the sharp jerk at his wrist reminds him again that he is not alone. That he is not allowed to fall apart, not here, not yet. What's done is done. The rest of the night is yet to come. And Hayden is still to live up to his own hardened words.

He hangs the phone up. Felicia doesn't move.

"Felicia?"

Silence. Air whistles through the vents. He wiggles his fingers into the edge of his lab coat's hem, wondering if she believes him the worst kind of monster now. Her back is rigid against his. Everything is too loud and quiet at the same time, like the shimmer before a thunderstorm, like the white-hot flash of a blow—pressure and weight before the pain hits. The kind of silence Hayden knows he can't be the one to break.

She turns without warning. He catches the whites of her eyes, wide, glaring, before she grabs a handful of his collar and slams him against a bookshelf.

A shimmering wall of dust showers them both. In the dark, Hayden can see the contrast plainly on Felicia's dark hair. His teeth click as she shoves him harder into the shelf. His collar tightens around his neck. Her hands on him, so familiar. He could lean in. "What did I do?" he asks, wincing.

This close, her eyes are inky pools of black, fathomless, furious. Half her face is coated in shadows, the other gleaming a pale grey in the scant light. "Your plan," she says, "to kill your uncle. What is it?"

"I'm sorry," Hayden says. "I can't tell you that."

Her hands are shaking at his chest. "You have the research, don't you? You're still trying to hide it from everyone, your uncle included. You knew he was guilty this whole time. You were never planning on giving it to him; you were only trying to lure him out." Slow understanding dawns on her face as she talks. Her mouth goes slack. Stupidly, he wants her to know, to understand without needing another confession. Tonight, he is tired of confessions.

He keeps his face carefully blank.

"It's not in that lab room, is it?" she breathes. "You only want him to go there. I don't know what you have planned, but you put the research somewhere else, and you put on your father's face, all because you wanted your uncle to go there."

"Smart," Hayden murmurs, relief flooding the feeling back into his limbs. Pins and needles. "You figured it out."

A small furrow forms between Felicia's brows. Her eyes are round, impossibly bright in the darkness. "What's waiting for him there?"

"I told you my father was a very paranoid man," Hayden says. He takes her hand, gently, and pries her fingers apart, and she lets it happen. Carefully, he pulls back as far as the cuff will let him go, their linked hands hovering in the space between their bodies. They hold there as easily as any other position, eyes level. They're still less than an arm's length apart, but like this it's enough for him to admit more of his truths. "He left me certain safeguards he put in place, for cases like this. He wired the basement lab to only respond to the right code. If you put the wrong one in, the whole place floods with, well—" He cuts himself off with a distasteful frown, the gruesome details too difficult to give voice to. "It won't be pretty," he says instead.

"And you gave him the wrong code."

"Of course I did."

"Is it fatal?"

Is that disappointment he sees in her eyes? Felicia's face is lowered, shadowed by her hair. Tonight, he is a bundle of grief and guilt, a damned hypocrite. "I'd imagine it is," he murmurs.

"No," Felicia says, jerking her head up. "No, you're lying."

She grasps for something hooked onto her belt—not a phone, something smaller, older. A pager? Whatever it is, she presses at it frantically, clinging like a lifeline.

If she's calling her father to try and warn Charles off, it's too late.

"Why would I lie now? My uncle is going to die tonight because of me." Saying the words drags the act out of the dark recesses of his mind into firm reality. The darkness lays over them now like some hazy filter, distorting the reality he sees before him. Becoming a murderer is supposed to be a violent thing. All he is right now is still.

There's a clatter. Beside him, Felicia is shaking. Her pager lies on the ground, screen cracked.

The silence that falls again feels too fragile. Every breath dragged out of his chest sounds like a scream. Felicia has her head bowed, gaze locked tight on the pager.

Is Charles dying, now? That he doesn't *know* is the strangest thing of all.

He doesn't know what Felicia is thinking either, but it must be a violation to ask. She bends stiffly, moving slow as though through water to pick up the pager. Smooths a finger over the long crack and shoves it back in her pocket.

Her shoulders are turned down and away.

"Is the door locked?" she whispers, some emotion scraping through her voice, making it gravelly and low.

"I don't think so."

"Then we have to go," she hisses under her breath, and starts dragging him forward.

She's pulling him to the door and rattling the knob before he has the time to process. Harder than ever, the sharp tug on his wrist turning into a white pain as he trips over his feet after her. The door slams shut behind them. The sound stays with him, crashing against his ear drums over and over, a constant rocking boom that breaks him open every time. He wants to ask where they're going, but it almost seems fair for it to be her turn to do this. He tries to count his steps, but the ground blurs in front of him. They slide to a stop in front of the stairwell, and the door is there, but he can't help but think of the precipice beyond it. How they're standing right at the edge, the stairs swirling down on the other side. Felicia reaches out and pulls the door open in one swift movement, and then it's there for real, a hole opening up before them, dark and deep and surrounded only by narrowed and narrowing walls. She stands there, breathing hard.

"Why are we here?" Hayden asks, and it sounds like it's coming from somebody else.

"Did I ever tell you about how I managed to convince my dad I wanted to come work for Charles?" Felicia starts haltingly, gulping back something in her voice. Her hands clench and unclench at her sides, irregular, like broken pumps. "He didn't like the idea, said it wasn't good for me or my career, might've looked like nepotism if someone asked, because he already worked here. But I wanted to know so badly. I got a taste of what Charles and Dr Lichfield were doing and I needed—I needed to know if this was right for me. Needed Dad to know that it was worth it, everything he did to put me here. So I found a good time to talk, dragged him out to the pier because I know he gets all philosophical when he sees open waters—it's pathological or something, I swear—and we had this nice long conversation I don't remember anymore, and at the end of it I asked. And he agreed. Didn't even have to do much convincing, truth be told." Felicia finishes her speech with a gasp. Nearly doubles over, covering her mouth. The momentum pulls at them both, until they're suspended over the steps. She stares down into the blackness. "He knew what I wanted. He listened to me. He trusted me. Just like—before—I—"

Her jacket twists.

Hayden realizes she's holding onto something in her pocket. Likely the broken pager, and the buzzing in his head retreats long enough to wonder who she would've been paging all night.

He listened to me.

Felicia straightens.

Then, "I thought you didn't know your uncle was suspicious. I thought you were handing a murderer the most promising research I've ever seen on a silver platter. I decided to intervene."

"But you were here."

"Yeah," she says. "My dad wasn't. He was with your uncle. He—"

"Horatio," Hayden says like a prayer into the dark.

Charles turned all the fucking comms off—Horatio starts, and Hayden meets the missive with a frustrated hiss, his head light and weary, the whole world shaking.

Felicia turns to him, there in the doorway, and her face is

flat. All the earlier emotion is wiped away. Hayden feels the layers of him peeled back. They could tip over right now and fall into the gaping hole. The ground they're standing on might as well be a tripwire.

"How long, Hayden?" she asks. "How long does it take?"

"I don't know."

"Fuck you," Felicia spits. "Fuck *me*." Then she pulls him forward into the dark and he has no more excuses for himself, nothing left in him to fight her anymore.

Xia: You have to understand, the essay was in part
something I started to get me out of bed in the
mornings, something playing on repeat in the back
of my mind day to day. I really did think back on
that night tens of thousands of times.

—An Interview with Felicia Xia

CHAPTER THIRTEEN
Excerpted from *Tell Me A Tragedy*

I'M NOT SURE when I started breathing again.

There was the dark, and the realization that something was horribly wrong, and then more dark. We ran together in the dark, Hayden and I. I had reached for his hand. Twined our fingers together, because it made barreling down the stairwell faster.

And then the stairs ended, and there was only endless white hallway, and my fear lapping around my ankles like a stubborn ocean wave. There was a fierce heat in my lungs, but everything else was icy. Nothing felt real anymore. I was floating above all of it, looking down at us, zigzagging recklessly through the lab, colliding with the walls every time we made a turn.

I let that hope flare again. Again, and again, and again, so much that even now, writing this, something inside me wants to tell you I rushed forward, turned the next corner, and caught my father's stumbling body in my arms. Broken, but alive.

But the truth is that we dragged ourselves down to the basement door, and it was cold and locked before us.

Something dark leaked out from beneath the edge. I smelled burning. Bitter.

"Gas masks," Hayden gasped beside me. He had a sleeve pressed to his nose. "Hurry."

I let Hayden do the dragging this time, following him to a storage closet yielding a stack of sleek masks, only a strip of black cloth laced with nanoparticles to filter everything deadly out. Simple. Such a small barrier that could save a person. What I wanted to do the most, then, was crouch inside and stay there in the dark. I didn't want to go back to the door.

"Felicia, we have to hurry," Hayden murmured. "What if…?"

What if we were too late? What if we *weren't* too late? If we opened the door, could we save him? Could we get there in time?

I didn't know.

The uncertainty of it electrified me.

I pulled the mask on over my nose. Cotton filled my ears when it settled over my face; when we returned to the door, I had to ask Hayden to repeat the code three times before I understood.

The fabric was soft against my mouth. Breathing in as deeply as I could, I imagined everything focused down to the feeling of the keypad under my fingers—hard, tacky, cold—and that acrid stench.

Then I opened my eyes.

I punched in the code—the *right* code—and yanked the door open, too quickly to give time for regret.

There was a clatter, someone moving.

Again, fierce, drowning hope. Louder than the creak of the door.

Someone tumbled out, shivering and gasping in deep breaths.

I want to say I was a better person, but I stayed frozen. I want to say I wanted to help, but all I could hear was a cacophony of *no no no no* rumbling in my brain. I just stood there, waiting for Rasmussen to crawl out and collapse in a heap before us.

"Lichfield," Rasmussen groaned, pushing himself up. His arms quivered. "Hayden, help."

His mouth fell open and didn't close. Small bubbles of blood dotted the whites of his eyes, held into a thin film, like miniature snow globes. I watched, horrified, as his left eye twitched, blinking shut, squeezing blood down his face. A thin, milky film clung to his eyelashes, beading on his cheek.

Hayden took a step back.

Rasmussen lurched forward, his fingers twitching as they latched onto my ankle. They were cold, slimy somehow. With what, I didn't want to think about. "Don't go in there," he gasped. "Gas—door locked on us—I got out, but—" He broke off into a fit of coughs.

Hayden bent down to grip the back of Rasmussen's shoulders. The technician's arm shot out, too quick to be voluntary, and Hayden leaned back to avoid it. He nearly sent us all toppling into the room. Hayden did stumble, crashing awkwardly into the door, and Rasmussen spasmed as more of the gas spilled out. Good that Hayden was wearing the mask. With a dull grunt, he righted himself and pulled Rasmussen up behind him, head emerging from the fog.

Rasmussen blinked again, bursting more crimson bubbles, bloody tracks running down his face.

Hayden looked up at me, half-crouched, pinning Rasmussen's arms to his side. His eyes were bloodshot and wide, but whole and unmarred. He looked as scared as I was.

Under the bright fluorescent lights, he didn't have a shadow. I wasn't sure if he was solid anymore.

"Felicia?"

"Yes?"

"Don't look."

"Don't look at what?"

"Don't open the door," Hayden said, barely louder than a breath. "Don't look at what's inside."

I DID.

Good that I was wearing a mask, too. I never wanted Hayden to hear me cry.

INTERLUDE

> playing /HORATIO/security/
camera_012M::08/13/2047::03:33.078

The door closes in increments. Beams of light and tendrils of gas scatter over the floor. A small group of hazy figures move forward incrementally. Hayden Lichfield holds a gloved hand to the handle. Dark fluid spreads from a prone figure on the ground.

Felicia Xia takes a step back.

Hayden Lichfield leans on the door, and it shuts. The light dies. He bends to support a twitching body.

The other body lies unmoving on the ground.

The other body's arms extend over its head. Dark streaks roll down its cheeks. Its eyes are open, the sclera saturated with blood. Its mouth is open wide.

The door shakes. Felicia Xia has her back to it.

Very slowly, she slides down to sit on the ground.

Neither Hayden Lichfield nor Felicia Xia move.

Poor eye contact. Affect flat. Negative suicidal ideation, homicidal ideation. Alert, focused. Insight fair.

—Mental Status Exam, F. Xia
(MH0192832), 08/14/2047

CHAPTER FOURTEEN
Excerpted from *Tell Me A Tragedy*

I SPENT TWENTY-THREE minutes upstairs sitting with Hayden while my father was dying.

Most days, I manage not to remember that time.

The days I remember it, I lose my mind.

At least, it feels like it: like something shattering inside me, spinning out and pushing at my skull until I am about to burst. I trace my way down branching possibilities, wondering about all the what-ifs, all the things I am ignorant of. I think of those twenty-three minutes where I was oblivious, living on as if I still had a father. What if I'm oblivious to something else? Half-delirious, my mind spins reality out of nothing. What if between one sip of my coffee and the next, my brother died? An accident, maybe. Fatal collisions happen more often than we ever think they could. My brother is clumsy. He has more scars from banging himself on bathtub faucets than I can count, all overlapping on his back. He once flipped a bike off a hill and left long, jagged scars down the ridges of his spine.

My mind rips itself apart. I think about breathing the

same air as my father's murderer and I become quietly but stubbornly convinced that somewhere, without me knowing, my brother fell off his bike again, into the path of a trailer truck. It must've been early morning, I decide, long before I awoke. The scene unfolds in my mind, relentless, but hazy with blue. I imagine the flash-flare of headlights glinting off the wet slick of his blood on the pavement. I convince myself it was my mother arriving on scene, I imagine her sinking to her knees. I imagine his limp hand, palm open. I imagine the crunch, how much it must hurt, how long my mother screams afterwards. I imagine empty houses and long shadows, candlelight and bent heads. I wonder who has to clean it up. My traitorous brain conjures up a firehose, pressurized, kicking up little pebbles as it scrubs the ground clean of bits of my brother's bones.

I convince myself so thoroughly that when I break down in tears and call home, I don't recognize Art's voice, when he's the one who picks up. When I do, I think I am calling a ghost.

These days, I don't call home in a panic. These days, I take my wretched, fractured thoughts and write them down, so I know they are absurd, so I know I am mad. I will take madness if it means none of it is real.

As I said: to write this is always to think of death, but not writing it would be so much worse.

Either way, the story still spins out the same way, no matter how many times I write it: the door, slamming shut; Rasmussen on the ground, halfway to death himself; Hayden, the instigator of it all, unable to meet my eyes even once.

My father, dead.

On the worst days, I let myself wallow in the guilt of it. If I hadn't been here, would he have bided his time? Stuck with Charles?

Forgive me for lingering. I know you want the rest of the story, but let me have my grief.

My father took me to the pier at Helsingør first, long before Hayden and I fucked each other up there.

We took the maglev train down to the city and got a tub of fried noodles big enough to feed us for days. And then we crept into the old town[22], where there were no projected ads in the air, no sleek shining skyscrapers, where things were quiet. We walked ourselves down to where the old-fashioned gaslights overlooked the shoreline and we sat on a bench, watching the rolling waves. Dad picked out the peppers I hated from the noodles and told long, rambling stories about his work trips from Shanghai to Berlin. I told him I wanted to take the internship Charles was offering.

Right at that moment, I don't think he wanted me to go. He took out a handkerchief and wiped down his brow, his shoulders weary. But he told me he was proud of me.

"I want you to know," he told me, "that they will always see me when they look at you."

I knew what he meant. I saw the way Charles Lichfield dismissed him. A man who understood everything that went on in that lab, but who was never given the opportunity to prove it beyond his ability to guard the doors.

Some part of me was angry. Spiteful.

"I know," I said, and neither of us spoke anything else on the matter, because neither of us liked awful truths very much.

Dad used to sing opera[23]. He used to put on community centre plays in his spare time. Neither Art nor I understood him. All I remember from those shows were blazes of silk,

---

22 The old town, like all of Helsingør, was destroyed during the catastrophic storms of summer 2123.
23 Traditional Peking-style opera, from context.

raucous laughter, the way Dad's face broke apart onstage like it never had within the confines of our little apartment.

That night, after he kissed me on the forehead and told me he would support me no matter what I wanted to do, he handed me the tub of noodles, and began to sing. It was a song he sang often in my childhood, nothing like the ones he would perform on stage. Low and haunting, a slow serenade that spiralled out into the mist. When I was full of noodles, I tucked myself under his chin, ear pressed to his chest, listening to the deep vibrations of his voice as he sang, the wind ruffling his hair, his expression broken apart.

There is no point to this part of the story. There is no real reason I want you to remember it. Only that I wanted to show you my father as he was, rambling lectures and all, trying to protect me to the very end. Only that thinking about it makes me unbearably sad, the kind of melancholy I find impossible to put into words, except to recount it. Only that I think about it often, and that I do—I want you to remember it.

THAT DAY, WHEN my tired, stuttering brain finally quieted, Hayden and I were the only conscious bodies in the hall.

Horatio's voice filtered down from the speakers at us, firm and welcome. "*I'm calling Charles.*"

I supposed there was nothing around it.

Neither Hayden nor I responded, but it wasn't a request at any rate.

For a long time, I waited. Time didn't mean anything anymore.

"Felicia," Hayden said, his cheeks drained of colour under the black mask still plastered to his face, and my first wild thought was to push him into the fog.

"Don't," I said. "Don't."

"Okay," he whispered. "I'm sorry." Something plucked at the cords of my heart, then, at how easily the words slipped from his mouth, how real it sounded. It was the only thing he said that night that I still believe, with every breath left in me, but I hated him nonetheless.

There wasn't anything else left to do. The lab stuttered on around us. Charles was likely well on his way. My gaze fell on the cuff on my wrist. There was no need to tie myself to him, not anymore. I pulled the small remote out of my pocket and pressed the button.

There was a soft beep.

Hayden lifted his eyes. He watched me as I prised the cuff off my own wrist. We were still as close as the magnetic radius had dictated earlier, barely shoulder width apart.

I didn't have to ask; he gently lowered Rasmussen against the wall and held his other wrist out for me without another word.

His fingers were stiff and nearly blue. I could've snapped his wrist if I wanted to, when I closed the black cuff around it.

"Alright," I said. "That's good." The words tasted wrong in my mouth, but I triggered the remote again and the cuffs locked.

Hayden shrugged awkwardly, his cotton lab coat swishing softly.

More waiting. That's how, eventually, Charles found us.

I saw his shoes, first. I don't know why, but I remember the black polish, the shine, the stiff press of his slacks rising up. He seemed impossibly put together, looming down at our pathetic, paltry group, but his face was bone-white.

He swept his eyes across us, once, keen and quick.

"You were supposed to go," Hayden croaked from beside me. "You were the one who was supposed to go."

Charles's face was blank, but he still looked up. "Graham?" he asked the empty air.

Nothing.

"Well, then," Charles said, "I should've known it was too good to be true."

Hayden dropped his chin, his mouth hidden by the mask but his cheeks flushing with shame above the black fabric.

Charles stiffly drew a hand up to his temples, closed his eyes. I was sure he was hiding something beneath the clinical movement, some fount of anger or fear, or something more passionate.

"Let's go, then," he finally said, with the barest sigh. "At least we can clean up this mess you've made for us, Hayden."

CHARLES TOOK RASMUSSEN and swept him away somewhere else in the lab, presumably to treat the gas. He took Hayden and put him in some other room I don't remember. He locked the door. And then he swept me into his office. I'm sorry I don't have more details; I don't remember them anymore.

"You should rest," was the first thing he said to me.

Words were still too hard then. I think I stared at him dully, not understanding.

He gestured towards his desk. "I'm afraid I can't find any safer accommodations than my office for now, and it isn't particularly comfortable, but it is late. Given the current... circumstances, I thought you might want to rest your eyes."

I blinked.

My instincts shouted danger at me. Alone, with Charles, in his office. Bad idea to let my guard down.

But Charles said, "You must be tired," and it was like him speaking it aloud made the exhaustion real. Suddenly, it was all I could do to nod, and shuffle my way to the chair. I sank down into it, my shoulders sagging, sinking into the cracked leather.

"Try to get some sleep," Charles said.

I can't, I thought, but the room had been reduced to smears of bright light. I don't remember much else, just the brightness, loud taps as Charles walked away, and then blissful nothingness.

I slept for nearly an hour.

I don't dream very often, and when I don't, I close my eyes at night and blink them back open the next morning as if no time had passed at all.

That night, I floated in inky darkness.

Perhaps it was a dream after all. But not like any I've ever had since.

There was me, sitting, trapped. I didn't move. I was surrounded by nothing. Not the dark, not shadows, but a void: yawning, sucking. A gaping wound in my mind. Nothing.

Then, I blinked my eyes open, and Charles was there, and I felt a profound disappointment when I realized I was still here, that this was still happening.

I think some part of me will never leave. I think some part of me is still trapped there, swallowed by the soft leather, looking up at Charles through a curtain of white light, wishing desperately that I was still tucked away into nothingness.

"You're awake," Charles said.

Danger, danger.

"Am I?"

He smiled at me. "It seems so. How are you feeling?"

"Like crap."

"Well," he said. "That's to be expected."

"Where's Hayden?" Despite myself, I did wonder what Hayden was thinking. I wanted to know if it was different for him, to kill someone he hadn't meant to, if he felt worse for it, if I *wanted* him to feel worse for it.

Eventually, the thoughts tangled and crashed into each other so much in my mind that they felt like steel wool, scraping at me every time I moved.

Charles pressed a heavy hand into my shoulder. "You don't have to worry about Hayden anymore."

"Then…"

"You're in shock," Charles said. "Take as much time as you need to get back on your feet."

"No," I said, shaking my head, "I need to…"

"We're going to make this right."

"How?"

"You're going to help me, Felicia. We're going to fix this together."

A cold chill ran down my back. Charles perched himself on the side of the desk and leaned back just a bit, one leg stretching out long and languid in front of him. Fencing me in.

"Am I?" I asked.

"I'd like you to."

"You killed Dr Lichfield."

Charles put his other leg out, crossed his ankles. "Do you think I'm capable of murder, Felicia?"

"I don't know. I don't know you."

He inclined his head. "That's fair. Do you trust me, at all?"

"No," I said. "But it doesn't matter."

Charles raised an eyebrow.

I pushed myself halfway out of the chair. "Because I *know*

that Hayden is capable of murder. I don't need to trust you to know not to trust him anymore."

"That's good," Charles said. "Smart girl."

"What are you planning?"

"I need your help, Felicia," he said again, each word clipped. "If we're to make sure your father did not die in vain, I need your help to make it right."

"What do you need me to do?"

"Hayden still has his father's research."

"And you want me to get it from him."

Charles tucked his legs back, knocking them against the desk. He looked oddly vulnerable, younger. But then he stood swiftly, leaving the way open for me. "He owes you an unpayable debt," he said. "You have the most leverage over him."

"So you want me to convince him to give you the research."

"I want you to convince him to give *you* the research."

"And... after that? Who gets the research? What happens to Hayden?"

Charles smiled. He shrugged elegantly; the gesture was too careless to be casual. I knew what he wanted. I saw it in the glint in his eyes, how he leaned in conspiratorially. "I'll leave that to your discretion."

"Really."

"You know Hayden best," Charles said, and somehow, without me even realizing it, this conversation had left the realms of what normal people would do. Normal people would call the police. Normal people would lift this absurd lockdown. "And he hurt you the most. I think you're entitled to hurting him back."

"What are you trying to say, Charles?"

He held his hands up, ducking his chin in false contrition.

"Nothing, nothing. I only mean, once you get the research, Felicia, I'll turn my back. I don't need to know what you choose to do next."

I was, of course, acutely aware that I was sitting with a murderer.

Did that mean that Charles's moral compass was permanently broken? Once you kill one man, nothing matters anymore?

But I wanted it. The stupid thing was, I wanted to finish what I'd started. I wanted to make it all worth it.

The room shimmered, swimming before me. I blinked, and my nose was wet, so I pressed the heels of my palms to my eyes and squeezed until I saw a rainbow behind my eyelids.

I thought about Hayden. I wanted him to die. More accurately, I wanted him out of my life. I didn't want to be the one to kill him. I'd already heard him cry and break, I'd seen him smiling sleepily in the dull morning, I'd known him angry, screaming, desperate, but I wanted more. I wanted to peel back the layers of his flesh. I wanted to dig my fingernails under his skin like he'd dug his claws into my mind, because he'd given me this yearning for the impossible and left a void in me that wanted so badly to chase it.

Outside the void, the rest of me was mad.

In my mind's eye, I saw myself cutting him open with his own scalpel and cracking open the bars of his ribcage. I didn't feel good, but sick satisfaction slid deep into my belly when I imagined sinking my fingers between the bone, deep into his sweet, pulsing flesh. Then—triumphant—I pulled the data card out from the carnage, clutching it in my stained hands.

I swiped the useless tears away from my eyes and gripped the armrests of the chair. When I looked up, Charles straightened, inching back slightly. He must've seen something in me.

I know I felt something shift, rolling like an ocean of slick rage, heaving inside my chest.

"He killed my father," I said. "That's all I care about."

"I understand," Charles said. He came closer, then dropped his hands on my shoulders and drew me close. "I know it can't mean anything from me, but I am so sorry."

I leaned into his hug, and the bloody landscape of my mind didn't bother me. Because he said *I understand,* and I believed him. The ambient noise of Elsinore groaned in the background, some monstrous harmony of air hissing through vents and the low thrum of machinery. I tightened my fist in my lap, ready to consign myself to being trapped in the belly of the beast for however long it took to pry Hayden's secrets out, no matter where he hid them. My head pounded.

But I kept my eyes trained on the black and white grid of the office's floor, and I thought of Hayden's blood slicking it, and I imagined the tide rising over all of us.

CHAPTER FIFTEEN
HAYDEN

I DON'T WANT this.

I don't want this, I never wanted this, I don't—

I can't—

IT TAKES HIM nearly ten minutes to realize his uncle has locked him in that first room, the room he found his father's body in. It feels like days ago, not hours. Or, it feels like another reality ago, some time before everything shattered.

It is cold in here.

Nobody bothered to clean up the mess.

Involuntarily, he shivers.

The cuffs dig into his wrists. His paranoid mind is convinced they are tighter now than when he was bound to Felicia. He tries to tug his hands apart, but the magnetic field refuses to give, and the sharp pain only makes it more obvious there is nowhere to go.

Scanning the room only lets his eyes snag on the red smear

by the doorway. Looking away isn't enough. A screaming headache builds in the back of his mind, a livewire of thoughts. The pain is sharp like a needle, threaded into the base of his skull. Panicked, he brings a hand up, thinking of the worst, the neuromapper malfunctioning, short-circuiting, reduced to nothing but a lump of metal, leaving Hayden alone in his mind with only his own thoughts. The device feels the same from the outside, a nub of smooth metal. Hayden wants to claw it out, drag his spinal column out with it, break himself open and tease out every screaming nerve.

Every time he blinks, he sees a dead man behind his eyelids.

"*Hayden,*" Horatio says, his voice whisper thin.

What? snaps Hayden.

"*Please calm down.*"

I'm calm. Even if he can't open his own throat enough to give air to his words. He feels it. The tranquil surface of an ocean, smooth as glass. He can even crack a smile when he tries. *I'm okay.*

"No, you're not."

I'm fine.

"*Is there a reason you can't say that out loud, then?*" Underneath the edge of Horatio's typical dry sarcasm, there's something else, a disquieting break in the usual even tones he uses that hooks into Hayden's gut for some reason, burrows into him deep enough to destabilize. His fingers are shaking.

"You can't save me." It's only when it hurts that he realizes he's spoken aloud.

He blinks. Everything is too bright.

He tunes Horatio's protests out, can't bear to listen to that catch in his voice anymore. Turns a small, tight circle in the lab. The linoleum squeaks under his feet. It doesn't feel solid.

He's floating, not quite settled in his own limbs, everything moving a fraction of a second too slow.

Logic dictates that he should not feel this wretched. At least, he shouldn't feel this marrow-deep regret, threatening to crack his bones in two every time he moves, spilling out lipids and dying blood cells into his vessels.

He made his peace with becoming a murderer. Why does it matter which man he killed?

He wrenches again on the cuffs, hard enough to re-open the scratch wounds lining one wrist, to draw an edge of more blood on the other.

Eventually, he finds himself standing before a dark slab of a lab bench, closest to the mess on the ground. He bounces on the balls of his feet, his world jittering as he looks down on the scattered, jagged glass that he spilled. The ground is sticky. Anything that was in the samples has long since dried up, but all the shattered glass remains, coated in a pale yellow film.

He crouches.

Some stale, soured scent hits him when he leans down close enough. Hayden wonders how many dying cells are spread over the ground, how many times the guts of red blood cells had spilled out, scattering globules of hemoglobin and traces of hot iron over the ground. He maneuvers his hands towards the puddle, presses the pad of one finger to the stain.

Wet still, just a fine layer of liquid congealing over the rest.

He should pull away, but his arm doesn't listen. For a long time, he stays, fingers hovering over one piece of wicked glass.

Gingerly, so the sharp edges only graze the treads in his fingers, he plucks it out from the rest like candy.

STOP.

Horatio's voice bursts through the wall in Hayden's mind, a ray of light splitting into the weary fog.

Hayden laughs. "How do you know what I'm going to do, Horatio?"

"*I know you.*"

"Do you really?"

A brush like a gentle hand at his neck. Hayden leans his elbows against the table, turning the piece of glass over in his hands. Warmth spreads, trickling slowly into the collar of his shirt. If he stretches his mind, he can pretend there are fingers, softly threading into his hair.

I do, Horatio says, his voice in Hayden's ears and around him and shivering down his spine. *I've spent enough time watching you over the years that I have a pretty good idea.* Then, after a pause, he adds, *Besides, I'm here with you now, aren't I?*

"I don't understand how you do it," Hayden murmurs. He wants to shrug his lab coat tighter around himself, suck in all his leaking body heat. His eyes drift back to the glittering glass. He rubs his finger against it again, only enough for the most superficial layer of epidermis to flake. Enough for it to hurt. *How do you stand all this?* he thinks, not wanting to give it voice. *All my fucking—mess inside.*

He waits, as if pausing for long enough could make what he means bubble up from the recesses of his throat. But there is nothing, only the stale, unmoving air, the fading of all sounds into noise, the way the red looks more and more familiar. Something inside him thirsts for fresh blood. Not the drying, crusted mess on the ground beside him.

"*Don't say that,*" Horatio says. Hayden gasps when a gentle insistence trails down his neck, curls around his biceps, triceps, gently pulls at the muscles in his forearms until his grip loosens enough for the glass to clatter to the tabletop.

Hayden hisses and clutches at his arm. "What was that?"

"*I don't want to be anywhere else but with you, Hayden,*" Horatio says, ignoring him, soothing over the tingling shocks in Hayden's fingers. His muscles unwind at the touch—and there's no other word for it; Horatio is a careful presence surrounding him, pressure and heat, everything that a body is made of.

Hayden wants to relax into it, but Horatio's gaze is the same as his uncle's gaze, tangled up with each other, and having the comfort of one means the surveillance of another.

"*I'm not going anywhere,*" Horatio insists again.

"I know."

"*I'm sorry I can't do anything else,*" Horatio says, and for a lingering moment, Hayden senses the anger, a broiling thing that exists in Horatio, too.

"No," Hayden says, "no, no. It's okay. It's enough." *You're enough,* he thinks, this connection the only thing they have for themselves, untarnished but nearly obscene in its intimacy.

It was so easy, he admits into the private void, *God, so fucking easy.*

What was? Horatio asks without judgment.

Killing.

It shouldn't be.

But it was, Hayden thinks, *I'm—I'm still the same me. And I—*He looks at his hands, traces the same creased lines of his palms, the bony ridges of his knuckles, the tendons stretched under his paper skin.

Hayden…

I don't want to die, Horatio.

Does it sound convincing? In his mind's voice, there is no hiding.

Don't think I didn't notice you're still looking at the shard.

Blunt as always, Hayden thinks.

I can't afford to be anything else.

Sometimes I wonder. Felicia was right, you know; I've cut into myself so many times it's hard not to wonder what would happen if I didn't do anything to fix it. He holds up a finger before Horatio can reprimand him. *Thinking about it isn't the same as doing it.* It isn't. He still believes that much, at least.

It is, but I still don't like it.

I don't like it either. He drops his finger and the tendon flexes, strong and supple. *Doesn't mean I can stop myself.*

Tell me, then. Maybe letting it out will help. Horatio doesn't say it will make it better. They both know better than that by now. They've been here before, and this is what Hayden hates the most. Not like this, maybe, not this close, Horatio privy to every single ugly thought, but Hayden knows this trench, these demons, the same old fears and worries and raging ocean of self-loathing. The rumbling mantra of *I hate this I hate myself I hate this I hate myself*—nothing new. White noise.

The only difference is that he knew he didn't deserve it, before.

You don't deserve it now, Horatio cuts in, fierce, and Hayden hates himself all the more for how wearisome this is to carry, how fucking useless he is under the weight of it that he needs Horatio to help bear the burden.

Tell me anyway, Horatio says. *I want to hear it.*

Okay, says Hayden, *okay,* and does what he always does: spills out his insides for Horatio to see, splits himself open over and over so that they might find something precious in the mess.

"I want to," he says, the words unsticking from his mouth

like a weapon, leaving him raw-edged and exhausted. "I've wanted to so many times tonight I feel like I've forgotten how to breathe. Like the air is just more blood. But—"

He gulps back his voice because he can't hear it anymore. His pulse. He draws his hands in closer to his chest, presses his palms flat against his chest and waits. Waits. Where is it? His ears are plugged with static, useless, but suddenly a hot flux roars to life, the pound of his blood vessels amplified, thrumming with obvious life. "*I got you,*" Horatio says, coaxing it louder, "*keep going.*"

"I fell in the harbour a few months ago." Hayden is rambling now, the words floating to the forefront of his mind without real conscious thought. "Got pneumonia. I was stuck in bed for a week, coughing my lungs up. I remember pressing down here"—he brings his hands up from his chest to settle fingers around the base of his throat—"and feeling this dull ache, tingling down to my toes. I have all this information I know but can't see. That it's just my body trying to heal itself, cytokines, inflammation, all that shit. All the hurt was just collateral damage." He thinks about this body that is him, everything inside he doesn't understand, can't control. "Obviously, it wasn't me. I was just lying there, while hundreds of thousands of cells inside me were slipping into my bloodstream, rushing to where I needed them the most. Made me think of the idea behind the Sisyphus Formula."

"*That's still you,*" Horatio says.

"What?"

"*Maybe that's your own way of fighting,*" he says after a while. "*I don't... You know if something goes wrong, I'm programmed to shut down any unnecessary processes that might overwhelm my system, right?*"

"Right," he mumbles automatically, lips numb. "Typical override safety."

"Self-protection. Written into my code. You could say it's written to the core of who I am. Above all, protect yourself, right?"

"Sure."

"Isn't that the same? Sisyphus Formula, your own immune system, all of it is just circuits and pathways in-built to your body. On standby to protect yourself. You don't have to be aware of it for it to be working. But it's still all you."

Hayden shakes his head. "I'm not making any conscious decisions," he says. "It's—it's like an automated loop that doesn't mean anything, I still—"

"Are you afraid to die?"

Silence.

Then, "Yes," he whispers.

"Sisyphus Formula, right?" Horatio says.

Hayden almost laughs. "That's how I'm going to live forever," he mutters a little deliriously, squeezing his eyes against the imagined tide of darkness.

"That's a conscious decision," Horatio says. *"Everything you do for that project is a conscious choice to keep going. That's what you told me when we started."*

"Yeah," he says. "That was the point."

Can't be suicidal if you're working on defying death. It's too much of a contradiction. Paradoxical. The Sisyphus Project was a lifeline in more than one way. A transparent cry for help, an attempt to convince himself that it was possible to keep going. His father never called him out on it. Felicia never wanted to ask. Horatio's the only one who knows.

Can I ask you something? Horatio says into the tender space between them.

Hayden nods.

Do you want to live because you want to live, or because you're afraid to die?

The question cuts through his chest like a scalpel, drags down like a vivisection. Hayden leans against the table like he's been gutted for real.

"Goddamn, Horatio," he says, hands sliding down to his mouth. Then, *I don't know,* he admits, too true for real words.

Still staring down into the shard of glass, he sees hints of the ceiling in it, scattered, weak. Wires, tangled and distorted, hang in clumps. The hint of a prismatic camera lens. The lights flare. Or maybe it's his eyes. Maybe the exhaustion has eroded away at his optic nerve, swept away all the neurotransmitters and flickers of electricity. Certainly everything is blurred, now. The edges of the glass melt away, so all he sees is this bright, clear smear on the bench, so soft it couldn't hurt him even if he wanted it to.

Spots of dark dot the table, one by one. He touches a finger to his cheek and realize the blur is from seeing the world through a film of watery tears, and lets the laugh out.

"*Then be afraid,*" Horatio says, his voice a graze at Hayden's shoulder, smoothing down his back. "*I will take you afraid and alive over anything else.*"

Hayden bows his head. "I've been taking you for granted, haven't I," he says.

That, oddly, is what gives Horatio pause. His presence still hovers, draped over Hayden's back. "*What do you mean?*"

"I mean," says Hayden, "thank you, Horatio. And don't tell me not to say it this time."

Horatio hesitates.

"I'm grateful for you," Hayden says.

"*You don't have to say that,*" Horatio says.

"Yes, but I want to. I want you to know."

"*Oh,*" says Horatio, and doesn't say anything more. A flutter of heat burns at Hayden's neck, incandescent. Hayden's lips twitch, quirk into a genuine smile. He straightens, the ladder of his spine settling into place. It's easy enough to flick the shard of glass away and watch it shatter into some corner. Blinking brings the world back into focus.

This isn't the time to lose it.

If the Sisyphus Formula was his saving grace—the hand he reached out in the darkness hoping to find something to grab onto—he has to protect it. Hayden gathers his insides back up, braces himself for the night yet to come.

Revenge isn't enough. Not anymore.

He has to get the research back, and he has to escape.

Looking back at the footage, I see the viciousness
she describes, the flinty steel of her dark eyes. I think
I could be scared of Felicia Xia. I certainly wouldn't
want to be on the receiving end of her righteous ire.
—*An Interview with Felicia Xia*

CHAPTER SIXTEEN
Excepted from *Tell Me A Tragedy*

CHARLES LEFT.

He dragged murderous intent out of me, and then he left.

The biggest mistake Charles Lichfield made was believing in me.

But I almost didn't realize how much bigger the picture was than we'd thought at the beginning of the night.

For a while after he left, I sat in the plush leather chair, perched and fuming. I didn't want to sit in this fucking chair and wallow. But I wasn't ready to go anywhere near Hayden, not yet. There was a stack of papers on the desk, so fresh I could still smell the ink. I stared at the way the light glistened off dark letters, and that made me angry, for some reason. Too bright, too crisp, too clean.

I shoved the pile clean off the desk.

The pages spilled out onto the ground in a flood. I ground the back of my heel into one, feeling it rip underneath my shoe, crumple.

But I caught a glimpse of words.

Sisyphus Formula.

And for the first time that night, I started wondering what exactly it was that Charles wanted to do with the research.

When the murderer was still an anonymous intruder, there were a myriad of reasons. Stealing the research could turn a quick buck. Maybe they didn't even know what they were doing. But what reason would you have to murder your own brother in cold blood? All for his work? Why didn't Charles steal into the lab when no one was there, slink away with a stolen copy to sell on the black market?

I dropped to my knees and started rifling through the pages I'd spilled. He probably wasn't stupid enough to leave a paper trail, but the game had changed. I needed to know more.

—*Sisyphus Formula beta trial version 3A; biotinylation assay with Western blot for alpha repressor of potential signal cascade pathway*—my brain was too tired to parse the scientific jargon.

In the margins, Charles had scribbled, *ask Graham if he needs more HeLa cultures for other project—collab with Kang lab?* There must have been older documents stacked in with the newly printed stuff, because below that, there was a different note that could only belong to Graham Lichfield himself. *Don't worry, Charlie. I got it.*

I wondered why Charles had this out in the first place. It didn't seem important.

I don't know why, but something in my chest tightened at the thought. I brushed my hands over the page again, this time because I barely talked to Dr Lichfield the years I worked here, and I wanted to remember the trace of his handwriting, the subtle curve and flick in his t's, the little loop that formed his g's.[24]

---

24 One can view some scant samples of Dr Lichfield's writings in the Royal Ontario Museum.

The rest of the stack had nothing useful either.

I shuffled through all of it anyway, trying to parse the dense writing, until I'd scattered the last of it and uncovered the floor underneath.

I stood and turned a slow circle. The office was sleek and barren, save for the shelf behind the desk. But Charles was an old-fashioned man: I could only find field journals and old, dusty encyclopaedias.

It was starting to dawn on me that this was perhaps a stupid idea, thinking I could sleuth out answers on my own.

Charles hadn't said I had to stay.

I tucked my hands in my pockets and made for the door, chewing on the inside of my cheek. The old room we'd come from, and the landline. Maybe I could call someone, I thought. Maybe we didn't need to be in this wretched stalemate.

When my hand hit the door handle, my phone started ringing.

I started. After so long locked in, it didn't seem possible that my phone was anything but a dead lump of metal.

I plucked the thing out of my pocket with shaky fingers. Full bars, where there had been no signal when the lockdown started. Whatever was blocking our calls from earlier had let up its vice grip somehow. And now, there was a call from the outside.

Before I could think twice, I jabbed my thumb down and accepted it.

"Hello?" I rasped.

"*Hello?*" The voice on the other end was frantic. "*Oh, thank god, shit—is that you, Felicia? Hello?*" I was silent for too long. The voice descended into a short stream of curses, ending with a heartfelt, "*Please, is somebody there?*"

I nearly dropped the receiver. "Art?" I whispered, looking around the office with fresh eyes, as if I had uncovered something just by speaking to this voice from the outside—my brother.

"*Felicia,*" he hissed, with the same vivid ferocity.

"What the hell are you calling for?" I asked.

"*What do you mean, what the hell am I calling for?*" Art snapped back. "*I've been trying to get through for hours, fuck, Felicia, if you could've picked up the phone, why didn't you?*"

"What?" I asked, still confused.

Art blew out an exasperated sigh and it was like he was right there, glowering at me.

"What do you want?" I asked. "Is there—is there something wrong?"

As if anything else could've gone wrong.

"*Yeah,*" Art said, deadpan. "*I've just been worried shitless about you and Dad.*"

"Worried?" was all I managed before my voice failed me.

"*Yeah,*" Art repeated. He sounded mad, but I knew his voice. Beneath the caustic tones, all I could hear was the heavy weight of fear. "*Is Dad with you?*"

"I—he was."

"*You two safe?*"

"I'm fine."

Art snorted. Then, he took a shaky breath in and held it, as if there was a question resting under his tongue and he didn't want to send it through the line to me.

"What is it?" I asked—pushed.

"*You sick?*" he finally spit out.

I must've hesitated too long. Art sucked in another horrible, breaking breath. "*Felicia, please, tell me you're not sick.*"

"Why would I be sick?" I cut in.

Then there was another long pause. Long enough for me to tuck the phone between my ear and neck and walk deeper back into Charles's office. "Art?" I asked, when he still hadn't said anything.

"*Elsinore's under quarantine,*" he said. Then, in the silence of my shock, he huffed a little with laughter. "*But you didn't know that, did you?*"

"No," I said. "I had no idea."

"*Shit.*"

"What's going on?" I asked. The office felt smaller. Or maybe it was the desk, halving the room, hemming me in.

"*How am I supposed to know?*" Art laughed weakly. "*All we've heard so far is that Elsinore Labs is under quarantine, because someone died, and then someone else released some sort of experimental virus.*"

"I—*what?*"

"*No one knows anything. I've been calling you and the line to the labs every couple minutes because I just… I didn't know what else to do. Why the hell didn't you pick up earlier if you could've talked?*"

"Charles locked down the phones. I didn't have signal."

"*What? Charles Lichfield? Your boss?*"

"Yeah."

"*Why would he do that?*"

"He wants to recover Graham Lichfield's research, because that's what's gone missing. He doesn't want anyone to know."

"*Is—is that the virus?*"

"God, no. Nothing like that. I don't think they even studied viruses here[25], Art, what—?"

---

25 The truth was that the general public had little idea what went on within the walls of Elsinore Labs, as designed. This uncertainty, combined with an overall breakdown of trust in scientific institutions accelerated by the destabilizing, disease-ridden years of the early 21st century, was why Elsinore had a poor local reputation. The building itself had gained notoriety as a place of urban legend. Supposedly, the lights never went off because those inside never slept—the proverbial mad scientist, trading human life for inhuman secrets in the privacy of a locked down basement.

"*Then what the hell is Charles Lichfield playing at?*"

I gripped my phone. I kept my eyes locked on the thin sliver of light beneath Charles's door, alert for the shadows that would signify his coming back. "I don't know," I whispered. "But whatever he's trying to do, he's lying to all of you."

"*Someone died.*"

"Yeah. Someone."

"*Wasn't an accident.*"

"No."

"*Was it him?*"

"Maybe. I think so."

Something crashed on the other end of the line. I heard a scuffling, like something had been dropped, then heavy, ragged breathing.

"Art," I called. "Art, calm down."

His breathing was so loud when he picked the phone back up that I could almost sense the heat of it. "*I'm coming to get you.*"

"No."

"*I'm getting you out of there.*" Another loud crash, like Art was kicking a wall. Art had always been tempered by violence, more fury than boy. I thought of my brother, smile bright, anger brighter, and I couldn't stand the idea of Charles digging into him, like so much soft meat, like he had done with me, my father, Hayden, even.

"No," I said again. "I can handle myself. Don't come anywhere *near* here."

"*That doesn't sound like you're safe,*" Art insisted.

I opened my mouth to say something to keep my brother away from this mess, but that was when the door creaked.

No, I thought.

"Don't say anything about the quarantine, don't say

anything about what I told you," I said, my words running up against each other in the rush.

"*What*—?" Art's voice cut off as I spun around, faint smile readied.

"Charles," I called, as if surprised to hear the door swing open.

Charles looked up, and his gaze sharpened when he saw the phone so obviously pressed to my ear. "Who is that?" he asked, his voice light and calm, but I could hear the razor edge of something hiding underneath the innocuous question. I thought it might've been anger, but in retrospect, maybe it was fear.

"My brother called," I said, brandishing my phone with a sheepish smile. "He wanted to know how my father is doing."

From the speaker, Art said something muffled and indistinguishable.

"I didn't know we had cell signal," I said softly.

Charles rubbed at his shirt cuffs. "I needed to make a call," he said curtly, and nothing else.

I narrowed my eyes, but the line was still open. I didn't want to put Art in danger by having him hear me say too much.

"May I speak to your brother?" Charles asked. He learned up against the doorway, already holding out a hand for the phone.

"Of course."

I wanted to hiss a warning through the line. Art didn't know what he was getting into. But my brother was smarter than he looked: there was a hard centre of ingenuity wrapped up in that rage of his. I hoped with all my heart that he wouldn't give the game away.

"Arthur Xia, is it?" Charles asked. To whatever my brother said, he nodded at the phone, feigned concern in the furrow of his brow. "I thought it best that no one come in or out of Elsinore at the time being. The situation is rather... sensitive." Another nod. I couldn't hear even the faint tinny impression of my brother's voice through the phone, which meant he must've been keeping his temper to a simmer.

I didn't want to do it, but with a quick inhale, I reached out to pull on Charles's sleeve.

He looked up with a raised eyebrow.

I bit my lip. My brother was still saying something, or maybe he was waiting on an answer, but I knew there was a question he was going to ask, and I needed to be the one to answer it.

Don't tell him, I mouthed. I repeated it. Until Charles's eyes widened in understanding. Until he dipped his head in a polite nod. He turned away with a smile hooking his lips.

"Yes, everything is under control, Mr Xia," Charles said to my brother.

I worried at my lip.

"There's no need for you to come here," Charles said, still gentle. "We are unequipped to accommodate that at this time, and you have nothing to worry about. Felicia is safe. Your father entrusted me with keeping things that way." None of this was, technically, false. I hated how I'd used the same trick earlier, oblique references, vague allusions, anything to keep my brother from knowing the truth.

Afterwards, I asked Art if he would've broken down the doors if I'd asked him to.

'Course I would've, he said. *I just wish you did ask.*

"Thank you for your offer to help," Charles said, but I knew my brother hadn't been offering. Art never offered; he only demanded.

But the walls here were steel traps. Not even my stalwart

brother could tear them down. I didn't ask because I didn't want him ensnared.

"I think that will be all," Charles said, holding my phone far enough from his ear so we could both hear the cacophony of my brother's voice, yelling something incoherent through the line. "I'm returning you to Felicia now."

The speaker quieted.

Charles moved to hand me the phone, but he stopped a few inches before it was in my hand. I eyed the slim metal. Charles rubbed his thumb over the back, pursing his lips, and I should've just grabbed the damn thing out of his hand.

"Felicia," he said.

"Yeah?"

"Reassure him," Charles said with a bloodless smile.

"Of course," I murmured.

When I accepted the phone from his hands, it felt like I was accepting his lingering gaze, too. He hovered at my back, not close enough to touch, but enough that I sensed him there whenever I so much as shifted.

I didn't want to look suspicious.

So I swallowed and forced myself to stare straight forward.

I pushed the phone against my ear and it was still warm. I shuddered and curled inward as if I could protect my brother, even if he was miles away, and very clearly did not need protecting.

"*Felicia, what the hell is going on over there?*" Art asked, his voice strained.

"Everything's fine," I murmured. "Things are just a bit tense, that's all. I know what I'm doing."

For a moment, I worried Art was going to yell himself hoarse. I worried he would do something stupid and rash, barging out onto the streets in the dim night, trying to get into this prison of a lab. A part of me wondered what it would look like from the outside: the four of us stuck inside this glowing box, perched on the cliffside under a web of sky-wires feeding the city with electricity. Elsinore would be the only point of light shimmering against wet sidewalks— brighter than streetlights, illuminated as a warning. He needed to stay away.

But Art blew out a short breath, then snapped his mouth together, teeth clicking. "*Fine,*" he said. "*I trust you.*"

"That's it?"

"*What else do you want me to say, Felicia? You obviously don't want me there.*"

"I'm sorry."

Art scoffed.

"I just—"

"*Shout if you need me.*"

And then he hung up.

I stood, blinking blankly, the phone still propped up to my ear. My brother's voice was a comforting blanket around my shoulders, but it was heavy, too, weighing me down. I didn't want him to know I could be vulnerable. I think I wanted to cry.

Charles dropped his hand on my shoulder.

I jerked up.

"You're right, Felicia," he said, still smiling that closed-mouth smile, choosing his words so carefully, like he'd swallowed all our secrets and was trying not to let them escape. "Everything is alright."

He took my other shoulder, spun me around.

We walked over to the desk.

"Who else is there?" I hissed.

Charles didn't answer.

"Who were you calling?"

His touch was gentle, but I wanted to flinch away when he carefully pushed me to sit down in the chair. I perched on the very edge, and every time I shifted the springs squeaked.

"Nobody you know," he said.

"I thought protecting the research was imperative."

"It is."

"Then why did you call someone?" I nearly slammed my hand on the desk. I got as far as raising it, clenching my fingers into a fist, but I stopped just before I made contact. I don't know why. Maybe I didn't want Charles to see the full extent of my rage. Maybe I wasn't sure how deep that vein ran, yet, either, and I wanted to know first before I let any of it unspool out of me.

Charles raised an eyebrow. "Tell me why I should trust you, Felicia."

"I'm the one who's trying to get the research back for you."

"And are you going to speak to Hayden for me?"

"Of course."

"You never did tell me what you were willing to do to get it."

"You want me to kill Hayden."

"Hmm. Do I?"

I was done playing around.

"Yes," I hissed, baring my teeth. I looked up at Charles, so imperious and tall, and I got the sense that if I tried to stand up from the chair, he'd only push me back down. "Tell me the goddamn truth."

"I want you to admit that you want to kill Hayden. And that his death would make this all so much more convenient for the both of us when the fallout inevitably comes."

"Convenient to *you*, maybe, but I don't want to be facing murder charges."

"Maybe not convenient, then." Charles rubbed a finger across his lips. "Cathartic, maybe."

Something inside me crumpled. I don't know why. I felt misaligned, but I felt uncomfortably seen.

"Isn't this all being recorded?" I asked, belatedly. "Doesn't Horatio know everything that's happening right now anyway? What's this point of all this if you've already lost?"

Charles raised an amused brow. "Did you really think Graham was the only one here with secrets? My office has long been insulated from surveillance, I assure you."

"I hate this," I told him, because it was the truth, and I wanted to say something that was true for once. "But okay. Fine. I just have one request."

"Do tell."

"If—if you're planning to murder Hayden here, I want—" I thought of the dream again, I thought of slamming my hand down on the desk, I thought of wrenching Hayden apart. "I want to be the one to do it."

Charles leaned in. "Strange request," he said, though he seemed somewhat pleased with himself. He went around behind the chair and leaned his elbows on the back of it. With his weight dragging the chair back, it felt like he was leaning up against me, his hand a hairsbreadth from my cheek. "You can kill my nephew however you want," he said flippantly. "So long as you do it."

I stared at his hands—the hands that killed Graham Lichfield? There was no evidence of it, not even a scratch on his tapered fingers.

"Do you trust me now?" I asked.

"After that, how could I not?"

I sprang out of the chair, a wave of static following by my heels. "Then tell me who you called."

Charles put a hand up to his temple and shook his head. He chuckled, as if the whole thing was rather funny, a slight oversight on his part. "The person who wants the research," he said.

I nearly sat back down. "I thought *you* wanted the research."

Charles ducked his head, a little awkwardly, and I wondered if this was my glimpse underneath the perfect mask—or if it was what he wanted me to see. Vulnerability made a person easier to trust. Either way, he smiled a little ruefully. "Well, I do," he said. "She just wants it more."

She, I thought.

The night opened up, less a closed box mystery now and more like a sprawling thing, dark and endless. Proof of some invisible hand, directing the moves. Was Charles just as trapped as we were?

"And you're trying to steal it for her."

"Precisely."

Pieces were sliding into place, too fast. I whirled around, dragging a hand through my hair, anything to ground me. The room spun. I wanted to lie down somewhere, process everything.

"How long have you been trying?"

Another light chuckle. Charles pulled at the collar of his shirt, then cleared his throat. "A while."

I could see it all laid bare before me. The cameras turned off for plausible deniability, a planned theft that turned into an unplanned murder, and now this whole damned mess. And then whoever Charles's mystery woman was, I imagined she must've been sharp. Sharper than all of us, surely, to have set this all in motion and stepped back to watch the madness unfold. I admired her. Not grudgingly, but hungrily—I wanted to be privy to that sort of power, to be above all of this.

He'd *called her*. Which meant she knew what was happening. Which meant he had a line to the outside.

And the false quarantine meant—what, he had some connection with the police?

Everything was growing clearer. I felt like I had taken a step back, seen this whole place for what it was. Seen the flimsy set we were trapped in for what it was—a stage. And this mysterious *she* was the looming playwright.

But he could've kept all this information for himself.

"Why?" I asked.

Charles sighed, put his hands on his desk. A little smile took over his face, made it softer, the edge of his jaw limned in light instead of made harsh by the fluorescent glow. "Isn't it obvious?"

Whoever this woman was, Charles was willing to do anything for her. Like kill a brother.

That, I thought, made him human. Like the rest of us. Fallible.

"I see," I said faintly, nodding, everything hazy and haloed in white.

"You must think me foolish."

I tilted my head, imagined myself as sharp as she. "No," I said. "I think I understand you a little better now." And that much, at least, wasn't a lie.

"ALRIGHT," I SAID, after that.

I needed to get out of that office. I needed to move before the static in my legs settled in too much.

"I'm going to see Hayden."

"What are you going for?"

"I'm going to get that data card."

INTERLUDE

>playing/HORATIO/security/camera−
23J::<08/13/2047>::04:28.102

A long, empty hallway, with white walls.

A glowing sign, in neon red, labelled EXIT.

The wall is blank, but for a thin black line tracing the outline of a door.

The feed flickers, and a shadow appears on the right, edging into the screen and expanding.

Black lines criss-cross with growing speed until the shadows resolve into the shape of a person.

Felicia Xia runs into frame, alone. She stops before the outlined door, suddenly still. Her hands hang by her sides. She curls her fingers tightly into fists and uncurls them again.

With a sudden lurch, she launches herself at the wall.

She draws a fist back and beats it against the outline, three times.

The wall does not move.

She sets a foot against the wall at the base of the door frame and drags her boot back and forth. The wall does not move.

She runs her fingers along the crack. She digs her fingernails in, breaking them and leaving smears of blood on the whitewall. The wall does not move.

Felicia Xia stills.

Her hair falls back, parting in the middle of her forehead as she tilts her face up.

She takes a step back, then two. She turns, her feet moving in a tight circle, putting her back to the wall.

Her hair falls behind her shoulders as she tilts further back to look into camera 23J. Her mouth is drawn in a line.

Her eyes are black.

Felicia Xia turns and walks away.

CHAPTER SEVENTEEN
HORATIO

THE DOOR OPENS with a soft creak, delicate as the bend of a spine.

Hayden looks up from where he's crouched over contemplating a row of Bunsen burners, which, if Horatio is being honest, would have likely resulted in something of a disaster, so maybe the interruption of Felicia Xia striding into the room could be a welcome one.

"Fuck," Hayden mutters under his breath. He slams the cabinet shut, then nearly stumbles back with the force of it, hands flying to his head as he sways. "Fuck," he says again, falling then to the ground, cuffed arms pinned awkwardly.

"You look like a mess," Felicia says, looking down at him, feet planted and hands slung in her jacket pockets.

Hayden rolls his eyes. "Thanks for letting me know." He splays his legs out, head listing to one side, giving up on the pretense of being okay. It stretches out the hollows of his throat, his sinews and tendons a straight line down to the barest edge of clavicle buried in the curling collar of his sweater. On the edge of one wrist, a mottled bruise barely blossoms. "What do you want, Felicia?" he asks. "Did Charles send you?"

"No," Felicia says.

Hayden kicks his feet from side to side. "Come to see how far I've fallen, then?"

"You did all the falling before we even talked tonight," Felicia says.

"That's fair," says Hayden. He speaks with levity, but the knot in his gut twists every time his thoughts brush up against the memory of her father, the twisted, gnarled mess of his body. He lowers his gaze, eyes lidded, lashes like spun gold and lighter than the rest of him. "For the record," he manages to say, "I'm sorry."

"Look at me," Felicia snaps.

Hayden does not.

Deep in her pockets, her hands are shaking. Horatio wishes he knew her well enough to understand what the lines of her body are saying the way he does Hayden's. Slowly, she crouches before him until they are level. "Why did you do it?" she asks.

Hayden flinches. "He wasn't supposed to be there," he rasps.

"That doesn't make me feel better about it."

"I know."

"I hate you," she says, and there's no venom in it; Horatio can read the tone well enough to understand she's exhausted, as much as Hayden is, both of them hurting and wanting to hurt.

"You should," Hayden concedes, his chin dipping to his chest. "Tell me what you want, Felicia. And I'll do it, anything." And it sounds like the worst of his self-destructive impulses, the part of him that would cut himself open to make it stop hurting.

Felicia's mouth opens in shock. "Anything?"

One corner of Hayden's mouth rises. "Well, shy of offering my head to you on a silver platter, I'm not sure what else I can give."

"What if it's your head I want?"

Hayden swallows. "Then take it," he says, turning his wrists to show the feathery lines of his veins, caught under the black cuffs.

Brows furrowed, Felicia leans forward on her knees and places her lips next to the shell of Hayden's ear. A flash of shock widens Hayden's eyes. He tries to pull back, but he's pressed against the cabinet, and Felicia puts a hand on his chest to hold him still. "I need your help," she whispers. "I don't trust your uncle. He's talking to someone else on the outside."

She pulls back, but Hayden's heart is still pounding, a blotchy flush spreading over the bridge of his nose.

The mention of Charles Lichfield has Horatio on alert.

"*You want the research, don't you?*" he says to the room aloud and is faintly pleased when Felicia twitches in surprise when he makes his presence clear. "*Charles sent you to get the research.*"

Felicia's eyes flick up, once, and then she sits back and seems to understand.

Charles is listening. Charles is always listening. Impossible to escape him, not when the entire lab is a surveillance system, wires running through the walls like spider silk, too strong for any of them to break. And Charles himself is a black hole, locked away in his office where Horatio can't see him, can't hear him, can't find an ounce of his motivations in all this.

"He didn't promise me anything," Felicia says. "I'm here for me."

Hayden raises an eyebrow.

"I wanted…" She pauses, teeth tugging at her lips like she's searching for the precise way to get around a trap. She looks around again, her pupils hitting one of Horatio's cameras exactly, and presses a hand to the cabinet by Hayden's cheek, caging him in. "I wanted to see you," she says, and Horatio understands her plan.

"Ah," Hayden says. Maybe he understands, too. "I see."

"Is that so wrong?" she challenges.

"I don't think," says Hayden, measured, "that I'm the one who gets to decide that."

"Good," Felicia says. "You're right." And then she kisses him.

Hayden whimpers, eyes falling shut. His shoulders dig into the hard wood at his back, flexing helplessly. As soon as Felicia leans in, he lets his mouth fall open, sloppy, lips numb and lax under her. Horatio feels the shudder wrench through his body when Felicia threads her fingers through his hair and slams his head back against the cabinets, the pain of it a hazy ache against the press of her lips, her tongue curling against his. Hayden angles up, his body bared and open, and Felicia drags his head to the side and trails her lips over the pink spreading over his cheekbone, then lower, her teeth a shallow scrape over his pulse point.

"He asked," Felicia hisses into Hayden's ear when she's close enough, and Hayden's eyelids flutter, paper-thin lids lined with tiny streaks of veins.

"Who?" he pants.

"Charles," she snaps, then knocks his legs aside and rakes her hand harsh through his hair, brings their faces back together.

Hayden's body responds, flushed and taut, remembering the softness of her. Horatio, seeded with new sensation, weaves himself into the nerve ends, following the path of gooseflesh down Hayden's arms, the tensing muscles in his stomach, the curl of his toes in his shoes.

He brings his hands up together, finds the skin above her belt, shirt crumpled and riding up, and she shivers under his touch, too. Brings her hands down to his arms, tugs them away from her and circles his wrists.

Hayden surges up, lower lip smeared sideways to hers, barely a kiss. "Tell me what you want me to do, Felicia," he says, her name slurred wet in his mouth.

Felicia runs her hands slowly up his forearms, rucks up his sleeves and digs her nail hard into the seam of his scar. Hayden hisses; Horatio wants to mute the sparking pain for him, wants to keep it for himself, wants to memorize the exact pattern of Hayden's body, vessels constricting and pupils blown open in pain and want and the heady richness of another person's touch.

"Tell Charles you want a deal," she finally says, into the crook of his neck. From above, they're only whispered nothings, desperate words of two people who once loved each other. "We need to talk where he can't hear us," she murmurs in his ear.

Hayden shifts, his nose rubbing along the underneath of her jaw, still breathing hard. "What sort of deal?"

"Your freedom for the card. Tell him you want to negotiate with me. Only me."

"And then?"

"We'll think of the rest when we get to talk."

Hayden hooks a finger around a strand of her hair, long enough to dangle in his reach. "Okay," he says. "I can do that."

Felicia tips forward and presses another kiss to his lips.

Hayden's chest is tight in the way it is when his emotions overwhelm him. His throat is clogged, and the soft groan she drags out of him is wet with the threat of tears. This kiss is close-mouthed and tender, gentle, as Felicia carefully tugs her hair away from his fingers, and this is the kiss that has Horatio watching helplessly, a voyeur to the easy intimacy of the two of them, foreheads pressed together.

She lets his hands go, and he falls back against the cabinets again, eyes hooded. "Does this mean you still hate me?" he asks.

"Maybe," she says. "I don't know."

"Then why are you still here?"

Felicia barks a laugh, her face drawn. "I don't know why I bothered. Are you going to cooperate?"

Hayden shifts, and the set of his shoulders rises, changes him entirely. Less like someone on the cusp of breaking, more arrogance in the tilt of his chin, the slight curl of his upper lip. "Run back to my uncle," he says, flicking his fingers forward. "Tell him I'm not giving him anything."

Unfolding from between his legs, Felicia sits back on her haunches, face unreadable again. "You'll tell me eventually."

"Ask my uncle what he wants, Felicia," Hayden says, his fringe in his eyes and the smear of old blood high on his forehead. "Then make up your mind about whether or not you want to be his lackey."

"You want to know so badly, you should ask him yourself."

Hayden tilts his head forward, eyes bright with shared mirth. "I should," he says. "I want to see him."

And Felicia laughs, a barely audible huff through her nose. "Fine," she says. "I'll let him know."

And then she turns on her heel, and leaves without sparing him another glance.

As soon as they are alone again, Hayden slumps back down. His sleeves are still pulled up, exposing the angry mess of the marks Felicia left on his arm. He's pale, save for where blood has welled too close to the surface, the darkening bruise at his wrists, the flares of blush-touched skin trailing down his neck, knuckles painted in watercolour pink. "Horatio," he mumbles, lips kiss-swollen red.

Horatio, still half-immersed in the hot flush of Hayden's body, hums in acknowledgement.

"Do we trust her?" Hayden asks, chest rising and falling.

"*I don't know,*" Horatio says. "*She was with Charles.*"

Hayden bites his lower lip white. When he lets go, the pain of capillaries reopening is exquisite, plush warmth flooding his mouth. Unintentionally, Horatio lingers too long, presses into Hayden's mouth with exploratory curiosity, and Hayden's eyes snap open, a low moan dislodging from his throat. *Horatio?* he thinks, and even in his mind, his voice is edged roughly, hoarse from lack of breath and Horatio wants... He wants. He doesn't have the words for what he wants, but Hayden's mouth is parted and inviting, and he doesn't shudder away when Horatio pushes deeper, traces a sharp line across the sensitive skin of his inner lip, works at the clench of his jaw until his mouth is loose and open and spit-slicked with his own want.

Horatio, Hayden thinks again, his tongue curling. *Come closer. Please.*

"Okay," Horatio says. "*I'm here. I'm here. What do you want?*"

Touch me, Hayden thinks, and Horatio has nothing but his circuitry, the map of Hayden's body he's been building. He taps lightly at Hayden's eyelids, marvels at the delicacy, relishes in the hush of a sigh that whistles from between

Hayden's teeth. He ghosts down Hayden's sternum, a steady pressure that rakes all the way down until Hayden squirms underneath him, lungs squeezed tight, oxygen rushing fast as he pants. Each bloom of colour over Hayden's skin comes with a flourish of heat, a soft glow. Horatio encourages the vents to turn a little harder, nudges the temperature a little lower, triumphant when the cool air slithers under Hayden's shirt, teases at the pebbled peak of his nipples under his sweater as Hayden gasps and shivers.

Hayden's body responds to him guilelessly, muscles tensing and relaxing in tandem, the ripple of his thighs easy and supple under Horatio's control. His back arches clean off the cabinet. Horatio wants to dig into the divots of his spine, embed himself there entirely, carve out every nerve and ignite them. He wants more heat, a tongue to taste the salt of Hayden's skin, hands to ruck up his shirt. He nudges at Hayden's pulse instead, arteries compressing as his blood pounds through the narrowed fissure, pressure building until Hayden is starry-eyed and dizzy, panic and pain and pleasure all in a rush of endorphins that has him choking out a cry when Horatio lets go and he sucks in a lungful of grateful air.

Fuck, Hayden says.

Oh? Horatio asks.

And then Hayden laughs, the grin breaking over his face like waves against a cliff, sudden, vivid, tinged with relief. He breathes a little easier. Not so much harried tension pulling at his temples.

Sure, he thinks, the smile turning cheeky, *when all this is over, let's see what you can do with that.*

If there's any lingering heat, it's from Hayden alone. Horatio is grateful he has no spit to choke on, and then he's grateful for the relaxed ease in Hayden's limbs. He wants to shut the rest of the lab away, spread out this moment like gossamer floss, be useful enough to fix everything that's gone wrong tonight.

But as it stands, all Horatio can do is protect Hayden in this moment. He makes sure the door is shut, that everything is secure. The lights are dimmed, and Horatio wants to cut them entirely if it weren't for the fact that Hayden does not like the total uncertainty of the dark. He nudges the temperature back, warms the tiled floors. Nudges again against Hayden's lovely mouth, marvelling at how easily Hayden parts his lips for him, unveils the vulnerable parts of him, so much in contrast to the sharp point of his chin, the straight line of his nose. Horatio traces the planes of his face, taps little jolts over the fine freckles that blanch darker over paled skin. When he comes back to Hayden's waiting mouth, Horatio's careful insistence over his chapped lips is a kiss in every way but physical, a kiss boiled down to its visceral parts—plush and wet and beating with the red pulse of want.

Afterwards, Hayden blinks his eyes open tentatively, as if for the first time. *I need to talk to Charles,* he thinks, longing in his voice.

Yeah, Horatio agrees.

This isn't over, Hayden thinks.

I wish it was, Horatio says.

Then, *Again,* Hayden says, *until we run out of time,* and Horatio listens, follows his lead, tries not to think about the walls pressing in on them, the surety in Hayden's voice, so certain about the ticking clock running the night down.

CHAPTER EIGHTEEN
HAYDEN

THE BRIGHT LIGHT SLAMMING back into the room heralds his uncle's imminent arrival. Hayden nearly hits his head on the hard lip of the lab bench as he quickly straightens. He scrubs at his face, shoves his hands through his hair, then gives up halfway through when he realizes there's no way to make himself look anything close to presentable. He tugs the collar of his sweater up to hide the faint purpling starburst speckles from when Horatio misjudged the tenacity of his capillaries. The thought of... whatever to call what they were doing to break those capillaries in the first place makes Hayden want to tug the neck of his sweater all the way over his face, but the click of the door rings out loud in the room, so Hayden pushes it aside to analyze at a future time.

That is, if his future will allow him time.

When he licks his lips, there is a lingering salt of blood and sweat.

The tips of his uncle's shoes enter the room before he does, leather shining in the fluorescence.

He steps neatly around the mess in front of the door, mouth twisting in distaste.

"I thought it best not to ruin too many rooms in the facility," he says, adjusting the cuffs of his suit as he comes to a stop in front of Hayden. "Your father would've wanted us to keep this place well."

The look on Hayden's face must be skeptical, because he drops the icy mask. "Please, Hayden. You don't have to be afraid of me."

Hayden scoffs. "I wish I weren't."

His uncle presses his lips together. "I want to help you. I can't undo what you did, but there might be something salvageable in this mess."

"Is that what you think."

"I'm your uncle and I care about you," he says, and makes no move to come closer. "I have to believe there's something worth saving in you."

The words feel like a gust of wind, stripping him raw. Despite what he knows, he can't help but remember the quiet conviction in his uncle's voice from the beginning of the lockdown: *You're under my protection*. Felicia asked him how he had lied to Charles, took on his father's voice, but he wants to know how Charles had been lying to him all night. How *long* had Charles been lying? How long had he been planning all this?

Hayden's eyes burn. "I wasn't aware I needed saving," he bites out.

With one dismissive, weary sigh, his uncle tears the ground out from under him. "That's not what I meant," he says.

"That's what you *said*."

His uncle brings a hand up to massage his temple. "Don't try and turn this into something it's not, Hayden," he says. *You stupid boy.*

"What *is* this, then?" Hayden asks, hating the bared tremble in his voice.

"A cry for help. A misaimed attempt for you to earn some pity after you fucked up so badly. I don't know how I'm going to extricate any of us from the mess." His uncle shrugs, careless. "Please don't make this more difficult than it has to be."

"I'm not—" Hayden cuts himself off, shaking his head.

"Stop, Hayden," his uncle says.

Hayden shuts his mouth.

His uncle takes another step forward. Heel to toe, crisp and precise. Hayden barely manages to keep himself from flinching back.

And then there are hands, firm against his shoulders. Pulling him kindly but insistently to his feet. Hayden's legs buckle, unused to carrying the whole of his weight, but his uncle rights him like his bones are hollowed out, flutes of glass. And then they stare at each other, unfiltered.

Charles's face looks open, like he's not trying to hide anything. Though nothing of the light in the room has changed—painting everything in flat colours, dull and unreal—his uncle is close enough for Hayden to read the soft wrinkles in his face, the lines spidering out from the corners of his eyes, crinkling now as he frowns in a simulacrum of concern.

"I have to be honest with you now," he tells Hayden. "I should've tried harder to keep you out of this. I'm sorry."

The dam squeezing Hayden's heart like a second pericardium threatens to burst. He wraps a hand around his wrist, dangling trapped in front of him, the proof of all this mess, and has to hold fast to the ebb and flow of his pulse to make sure it hasn't run astray. He wants to laugh. Maybe there should be relief in the confession, but all Hayden feels is disconcertingly seen—as if the only truth left in his uncle's sorrowful eyes is searching for its twin in him. People have always said he looks like his father, but he blinks and sees the same face that greets him in mirrors: an unsmiling mouth, a nose too thin to be aristocratic, gaunt cheeks, opaque irises, honesty the very last resort.

"Did you really try?" Hayden finds himself asking.

"I never intended for you to get caught up with it all," his uncle says, and those words, most of all, have the taste of truth.

It makes Hayden laugh, the sound breaking out of him like bleeding a wound. "I've been in it from the start," he says. "I've been in it since I walked into a lab and found my father's dead body staring up at me." The truth is bubbling beneath his own lips, now, eager to escape, and he thinks, *Why not?* There's a crack in Charles's mask and he wants to wedge it open, excavate whatever fondness he might still have for their family, fucked up as they all are. All of them malignant, extending creeping veins into each other, leeching off the pain leaking out of the mass.

"I found him first," Hayden says. "Before Rasmussen. There was never an intruder, and I knew it all along. I just didn't want to believe it."

His uncle's face remains impassive. "Then you have the data."

"Of course I do."

"Where is it?"

"With my father," he spits. "Dead."

Charles's eyes flatten, catching the harsh lights like glass. "Hayden," he says with an attempt at command. "Tell me where it is."

"It's none of your fucking business," Hayden says. "I buried it when I buried my father."

His uncle lets out a slow breath through his teeth. He closes his eyes, and Hayden finally sees it, the wearing down of him at his limits, the aching exhaustion he's never let show before. His shoulders slump, and his hands run down the stained sleeves of Hayden's lab coat to gather his hands up. Carefully avoiding the cuffs, as if ignoring them is enough to undo anything. "Whatever happened tonight," he says slowly, eyes flicking up to the cameras periodically—because of course he's still aware of being watched—"I didn't mean for any of it. I promise."

Hayden hooks his fingers into his uncle's sleeves. "I don't believe you."

Charles's lips part in a soft breath. "Then I don't have anything else I can say."

"I brought him back," Hayden blurts.

The words drop between them like a stone in a pond, disappearing under the smooth surface of every emotion left unvoiced between them. It bleeds red, paint in water, a budding cloud of hurt muddling everything.

"The formula," Hayden continues. "It worked."

His uncle's voice is as faint as the grave when he asks, "What?"

"I found him first. I walked into the lab and he was there, and I didn't know what else to do but—but try. We were already on animal trials."

"So you—?"

"It didn't work all the way, okay?" Hayden snaps. "I brought him back; I opened his skull, I ripped open his veins to force his blood to run again, pushed air back into his lungs, just to hear him talk again, and when he said *your name* I—" His voice breaks, and he wants to wipe at his watery, no doubt red-rimmed eyes, but his uncle's grip around his wrists is firm. Hayden feels the pressure of his pulse mounting, pulsating, burning until it feels too hot for his skin to hold.

"—I didn't believe him," Hayden finishes, and then he's out of words, because there's nothing else to say.

He didn't believe his father's dying words.

He should've.

Charles opens his mouth, and Hayden decides he doesn't want to hear any more of his apologies, doesn't want to cut himself on the edges of his words anymore, to try and figure out the truth in them.

"I can't give you the data," Hayden tells him, clear-eyed and serious. "He told me to protect it with my life. But."

Charles waits.

"I'll talk to Felicia."

"Felicia," Charles repeats, her name cold and slithering on his tongue.

"Yes," Hayden gulps out. "Please, I just. I want to get out of here, too. And I know you well enough that I *know* you won't let any of us go without me giving up the only thing I fucking still care about, so—just—just let me negotiate with *her*."

He doesn't deny it.

Hayden's chest caves in, the tenuous hope that had kept his ribcage open collapsing all at once. He crumples, and all he has left is the memory of an uncle who loved him, once.

But Charles relents. "Okay," he says, letting Hayden's hands go and straightening his sleeves, like he's brushing himself clean of the whole ordeal. "That's fair."

He turns to leave, and Hayden lunges forward—

"Who's it for, Uncle Charles?"

He stills, the nape of his neck unblemished and bent, clean edges of his vertebrae tucked under his starched collar. "Myself, obviously."

"You wouldn't go this far, not for yourself. You're not stupid."

Charles straightens all the way. "It's best for you if you don't know."

"No," Hayden insists. "I think it's the least you owe me."

He shakes his head and starts to walk away.

Irrational guilt digs its hooks into Hayden's heart, prickling like needle points. How many times had they argued like this? How many times had they left the disagreement unspoken, so much silence to fill the gaps in place of outright accusation? Neither of them is an apologetic person, but before, it had always been with the caveat that there was something to come back to, a conversation left hanging, some tenuous relationship that could be mended.

This time, when Hayden draws in another breath, he feels the last thread unwinding, the whole damn tapestry being pulled apart.

"You did this to me," he calls after his uncle. "You made me—whatever happens."

He doesn't offer an answer, only the sound of his footsteps, loud at first, but then fading into the noise of Elsinore, nothing but sound.

**Transcript generated from
Operation System "Horatio"; 08/13/2047, 4:56am**

CHARLES: Horatio?

HORATIO: Yes, sir.

CHARLES: Could you connect me to Felicia Xia?

HORATIO: Of course, sir.

Connecting—Hall 2A, Camera 211; 4:57am

CHARLES: Hello? Felicia?

FELICIA: (over intercom) Charles? Yes.

CHARLES: Can you hear me?

FELICIA: (over intercom) Clearly.

CHARLES: Whatever you said, it worked.

FELICIA: (over intercom) So...

CHARLES: Are you in my office right now?

FELICIA: (over intercom) I just left.

CHARLES: Good. Meet him in the basement.

FELICIA: (over intercom) Basement where?

CHARLES: His father's private lab.

FELICIA: (over intercom) Why?

CHARLES: No cameras. I owe him that much, at least.

FELICIA: (over intercom) Do you really think he's just going to hand the data card over?

CHARLES: I don't know what he's going to do.

FELICIA: (over intercom) Then... why?

(Charles sighs.)

CHARLES: I don't want him to hate me.

FELICIA: (over intercom) Too late for that, isn't it? Besides, have you forgotten what you promised me?

CHARLES: No.

FELICIA: (over intercom) Then how's this going to work?

CHARLES: No cameras, Felicia. Do what you want.

FELICIA: (over intercom) You're just as confusing to me as he is.

CHARLES: Just go, Miss Xia. Please.

(Silence, 3 seconds.)

FELICIA: (over intercom) Fine. But not as a favour to you. I just want this to be over.

CHARLES: Of course.

Horatio
Felicia.

Felicia Xia
what the hell

Horatio
I have no access to the basement lab.

Felicia Xia
yeah that's the point

Horatio
Neither of us trusts Charles.

Felicia Xia
im not having this conversation with you
its not like i trust you any more than him

Horatio
I know you're planning to talk to Hayden.

Felicia Xia
you were there. you heard. im aware.
what do you want? i dont want charles to suspect
this sort of furtive texting thing? very high school you know

233

Horatio

Well, forgive me for not having an equivalent adolescence to reference.

I want you to promise me you're not going to hurt him.

Felicia Xia

and youd take my word for it?

Horatio

It's not like I have any other options.

Felicia Xia

sure, then

i can promise to be fair

Horatio

Fine.

I'll take it.

Felicia Xia

not going to thank me for it?

Horatio

I know you worry about him, too. I've seen enough.

Felicia Xia

thats the thing with you. you think you know everything because you see it all.

i worry for him, not about him.

theres a difference

Horatio

Consider it a favour, then.

Take care of him when I can't.

Felicia Xia

and what do i get out of it?

Horatio

Nothing.

My good will.

What else do you want?

CHAPTER NINETEEN
HAYDEN[26]

THE CONTOURS OF the basement have become familiar.

The winding stairs are the same: foreboding and terrible, worse to navigate without his hands. Horatio's missing presence at his nape feels like an unending void, a nonexistence so complete it feels like a weight dragging at him. Hayden

---

26 Forgive me, here, for this moment of fiction. As previously mentioned, everything you have read thus far has been a painstaking reconstruction derived from the neuromapper log captured from Hayden-and-Horatio from this night. I have done the work of separating their consciousnesses to the best of my ability and translating the thought-log into coherent narration. However, as will be evident, there are time gaps within this log, when recording was not done. I have done my best to include supplementary material where appropriate—primary excerpts from Felicia Xia's thorough account—but also included are other documents meant to convey the sequence of events. However, the ethos of my approach for this book is not to present a dry accounting of facts, but rather craft a narrative that will, in my hope, help you understand why such events transpired. In truth, I do not believe an objective account is at all possible, even with objective documentation. I have included, therefore, sections which are entirely fictional and of my own account. In my research, I have spent countless hours with Hayden, Horatio, and Felicia's voices—I have filled in encounters that I imagine may have occurred, that align with my interpretation of their motivations and actions, because I believe that a richer story arises as a result.

doesn't know how he's survived this long without it. His back feels exposed, jitters pooling on his neck and shivering down his spine with every step. Felicia's fingers are a steady weight on his elbow, guiding him, but Hayden has never felt so utterly alone. Although it's necessary, to hold something inside himself and only himself, to evade his uncle's all-seeing eye.

Now that they stand at the threshold to his father's secret lab, where he first let Felicia see what the Sisyphus Formula can do, where he healed his own arm and then, later, failed to save her father, the other all-consuming thing gnawing at him is the guilt. All he can think of is how freshly raw it must be for her.

Still, when she steps down from the concrete, her face is neutral.

"What did you say to Charles?" Felicia asks, halting pointedly before the door.

"Nothing," Hayden says, which is mostly the truth. "I told him I wanted to negotiate[27]."

Felicia tucks her hands into her pockets. "Okay," she says. "Sure. We can do that."

"Can I trust you?"

"Maybe. As much as I can trust you."

"I just thought—"

"If you think I care about your uncle's agenda, you're thinking about this the wrong way, Hayden." Felicia hunches her shoulders. The light above them flickers, a flash of darkness

---

27 Of course, the following conversation was paraphrased in terms of what was discussed and why, later in court, by both Hayden Lichfield and Felicia Xia. The raw transcript is included as an appendix to this book; I believe that for such a turning point of the night, this moment should be felt up close, as it would have happened, rather than with impersonal retrospect.

washed away by the illumination. She looks small against it, the white harsher, her jacket a smudge of coal. "I just want to leave, and I don't want any of this to follow me. And your uncle seems like the kind of person who holds a grudge."

"Yeah," Hayden agrees. "He is."

"So?"

"So," he repeats, and gestures with his cuffed hands to the handle.

Felicia scoffs and wrenches it open.

This time, the door is unlocked.

They step through together. Inside, the room is dim, but not black. There are a few straggling lightbulbs in the corners, casting streaking shadows over the floor. The light is yellow, here. It paints everything sepia, washed out in the gloom instead of cast in stark contrast like the fluorescent lights outside do. Felicia walks in a slow circle, as if trying to find lingering traces of death in the room. There is nothing. There aren't even any stains[28].

"Your uncle did a thorough job," she offers up.

He tries to banish the thought of his uncle on his knees, scrubbing away at the mess of his mistake.

"No cameras," he says. "We're properly alone now."

The side of Felicia's mouth quirks up into a thin smile. "Are we?"

"You can tell me what you found, now. And whatever my uncle wanted you to do."

She fiddles with something in her pocket, her eyes trained on the floor in front of her. "Your uncle wanted me to kill you."

What?

---

28 Later testimony from Hayden Lichfield in court about this conversation includes the scrubbed clean floors, which I found striking enough of a detail to highlight.

"No cameras. Easy."

"Shit," Hayden says, the word falling out of his mouth like a breath. His hand flies to his neck, then he remembers he is alone. He is alone. He is alone.

His heartbeat drains away from his ears, fainter and fainter. Panic clamps down on his muscle fibres one by one. It erodes at the edges of him, until everything is narrow, and the world is all a blur except for the cold, dark points of her eyes.

"He thinks it's easier this way." She drags her foot over the ground in an arc around her, as if she's trying to unearth something. All she finds is the tight squeak of her boots on linoleum, screeching and long. "I can't blame him. It would be an easier story for the police to swallow."

"Felicia."

She looks up at him through her lashes, a yawning, gaping thing peering out through her eyes. Something feral. For the first time that night, he doesn't recognize her anymore. "I think it would be easier for me, too. Or, at the very least, I deserve some sort of comeuppance, don't I? Some sort of vengeance? Isn't that what this was all about in the first place? Revenge?"

No, Hayden thinks, bleary with panic, his throat closing up. *No.*

Did he miscalculate?

Did she lure him here with fake information, only to—?

Cold trickles down his back. His lips move, but only a wheezing breath comes out, and there is no one to hear his racing thoughts, turn them intelligible.

No.

But then she scoffs, turns back around. "I can't believe you think I could kill you."

As soon as the feeling bleeds back into his limbs, he squeezes

238

hard on his wrist, but his fingers are shaking too hard to find the steady divot. He drags both hands up to his neck instead and presses his fingertips into the soft flesh, digging in until he's dizzied, feeling a steady, thrumming pulse under the pads of his fingers. He closes his eyes, lets the red waves wash over him, a steady reminder that he is *here*, goddammit, solid and real and alive and alive.

"Hayden," Felicia says.

"Mm?"

"I—I'm sorry, I just thought it would be better if you knew what your uncle was planning."

"Mm." He nods. The world shutters between thin red and yellow ambience as he blinks his eyes back open. "I know. I get it. I just—" He swallows, and there's a hoarse croak in his throat, tickling inside his neck, where his hands are still pressed too tight into his airway. Easing the pressure off brings more breath, lets him savour the raw scrape as words climb back up his throat.

"It's okay," he says. "I was just surprised, and also not. Is all." Then, "Dammit, I should be the one apologizing to you."

The upward crook of her lips drops, and they tremble. "Yeah," she says, reaching up to scrub viciously at her eyes. "This wasn't really what I had in mind. I just didn't think you'd freak."

"I'm sorry."

"I know."

"I killed your father."

She nods, once.

"I'm sorry."

She lets out a breathy exhale of a laugh. "I wasn't supposed to fucking pity you."

"Probably not."

"Let's just get to work," she mumbles.

Hayden nods.

"Charles is talking to someone outside the lab," she starts.

"Yeah," he says. "He wouldn't—at least I don't *think* he'd be doing this if it was just for himself."

"He lied to the police." Felicia flicks a hand through her hair, frizzing at the ends from the long night. "He was calling whoever this mystery benefactor is, so the signal lifted, and my brother got a call through to me. As far as the outside world knows, Elsinore Labs is under quarantine for the release of a mysterious virus you've been working on."

"That's—"

"A blatant lie?"

"Yeah."

"So, Charles is up to something sketchy." She drums her fingers on the edges of her jacket, looking more and more like the Felicia he knows again. He sees the flash of that jacket, remembers tugging it off her arms, the supple leather giving away under his fingers. The memory is interrupted by the rest of her words, and Hayden shakes his head, brings himself back to the present. "That's why I'm here. He promised me plausible deniability, but I don't trust that he won't betray me to the police once this is all done, to wipe his own hands of whatever mess he's going to make, and when I walk out of these doors, I want it to be for the last time."

Hayden whirls around, frustration hot on his heels. He paces over the scrubbed floor, chest aching with an unspeakable want. The ugly truth is that there is no leaving. The stains don't come out. The poison Elsinore sows stays, forever, but he's always accepted that part of him. Elsinore is still home and board, purpose; Elsinore is Horatio. Sometime over the course of the night, these walls have become the entirety of everything: eyes and ears and dulled white space, easy to touch.

It's not quite the same for Felicia.

Hayden marks the length of the room, ten strides, even.

"So, then, what do we do?" he asks as he turns the width. "What do you want?"

"We can try and expose him."

"But then whoever his mystery person is, won't they just try harder?"

Felicia worries at her lip. "Probably."

Hayden shifts his weight from foot to foot, then spins around the corner, stepping heel to toe to heel. "Then we need to make sure it ends with us, tonight. Fuck." His hands flutters to his throat, still sore.

"Exactly," Felicia says, then, "Hey, where are you going?"

"Dad always put mugs in his rooms," he says, reaching up awkwardly with both hands to pull open a cabinet. Finding nothing, he slams the door shut and moves on.

"What for?"

"In case we got thirsty and were too lazy to go to the canteen."

The next cabinet reveals a set of old drinking mugs, WELCOME TO ELSINORE stamped in dark blue on one side. Hayden reaches in and tries to reconcile how the familiar action is made unfamiliar by the room they stand in. *It's called jamais vu,* his father's voice chimes into the emptied-out space in the back of his mind, reminding him the way he used to do all the time: *Aren't you listening to me, Hayden?* He brushes it away with an irritated frown. *Stupid pretentious old man,* he whispers to the confines of himself, to nobody, *I don't want to think about you anymore.*

Felicia's footsteps are a whisper when she wants them to be. Without his even noticing it, she's here, by his side. "Do you have hot plates?"

"What?"

She rolls her eyes. "What kind of lab doesn't have hot plates?"

"*Why?*"

"Oh," she says, then tucks her hands into her pockets, smiling in a weak, empty way that tells him she is anything but happy. "It's just a thing my dad… used to say[29]. It's drafty in here. Hot water soothes the stomach. I guess it's kind of silly."

Hayden looks down at the mugs, his own dead father's lingering spectre, the twisted, grieving line of Felicia's lips. "It's not silly," he says, "but I wouldn't know where the hot plates are."

"Not going to pretend you know this lab inside out anymore?"

"No," Hayden admits. "I don't think I've *ever* known." It's a relief to admit it, but he's shedding the last vestiges of armour he has left, the illusion that he had any plans at all tonight.

She surveys the room again, like she, too, is seeing it in a new light.

"Thanks for the honesty, I guess," she says.

"I—sure."

Her lips twitch into a truer smile. "Cold water's fine by me," she says, and grabs the mugs.

---

29 "I wanted the soothing effect of a cup of steaming water in that lab, I'm not sure why. Maybe because it recalled to me the simplicity of childhood. Maybe I only missed my father. He used to nag at me about drinking water cold. [She laughs]" – Felicia Xia, *This American Life*, episode 1549 (2050)

When her back is turned, Hayden brings his hands up to cover his face, to lace them behind his neck. His fingers brush against the curling edges of his hair, the blemishes rising on his skin. He doesn't touch the perfect surface of the neuromapper, careful to avoid it, trying to feel less exposed. "My uncle needs to *think* he has the data," he ventures.

"Can you make something to fool him?" she asks over the splashing as she fills the mugs.

"I don't know."

"What if you destroyed the research?"

Hayden's hands slip. "*No.*"

"If the research is gone and we get enough to nail him for the murder, then he goes away. Mystery benefactor won't have a reason to come after either of us."

Felicia turns back around, and Hayden recoils.

"That's our best option, Hayden," she says, setting a mug before him.

He rests his forearms on the bench, flicking at the chipped rim. "I know," he says. "But I'm not willing to do it."

"Hayden—"

"We can make him think it's destroyed. It can stay with me. Whatever fallout comes with that, I'll make sure to make it clear you don't have it. I can shoulder whatever it is."

"It won't come back to me."

"No."

"Or my family."

"No."

She wants him to look at her. He can sense it, her searing gaze, the hairs on his neck standing up, a soft prickling itch at his temple. He gulps down fresh water instead of speaking. When he sets the mug down, his hands are flushed against the white ceramic. There is still a trace of dried blood under his fingernail, even after washing; there is still something lodged hard in his throat.

"You promise?" she asks, her voice cracking on the last word.

"Yeah," he finally says, looking up. "Yeah, I promise."

Felicia squares her jaw and gives a tight nod. The shadows shift as she takes a step closer. The orange backlit glow makes her a silhouette, her own shadow dragging across the floor and merging with his. "Okay," she acquiesces. "Thank you. That's good enough for me."

She curls her hand into the handle of her mug. Hooks onto it one at a time, index, middle, ring. Leaves her pinky out, the way she always does. "So how are we going to pull this off?" she asks.

"Might get messy," Hayden says, snippets of ideas floating in his mind, none of them easy.

She scrunches her nose up, kicking one leg into the cabinet with a loud *thunk*. "I'm not afraid of messy."

A few pieces of the puzzle coalesce in his mind, misshapen and ugly.

"I'll give him a fake hiding place," he says. "You can bring a fake data card and pretend you got it from there. We'll make a whole show out of handing it over—if I'm dramatic enough, he'll never suspect a thing—and then…"

"Then what?" Felicia whispers. "Where do you go after this?"

She turns her head towards him, and for a stupid, startling moment, he mistakes the reflection of fluorescence in her eyes for starlight, glancing off the harbour. For a moment, they're outside, standing in the fresh air, no misunderstandings or real-life mundanities between them, only an entire ocean spilled out. Dark as the void, but deep with possibility.

"I'll…"

"Your mom," she cuts in, almost desperate. "She said she loved you, even after you confessed to planning a murder. Surely she'll take you."

I never wanted to lose you, his mother says in his head, another voice in the slowly growing crowd there. But Felicia is right. Something of a future brightens amongst all the noise: feeble, but present.

"Okay," he says. "I can work with that."

"I'm going back to the office," Felicia says, "after this. I was nearly through all his papers before. I want to know who wants that research so badly."

"How do they even know about it?" Hayden mutters, mostly to himself.

But Felicia's head shoots up. "Did your father tell anyone? How top secret *was* this?"

He opens his mouth, thinks. "No one, I think," he says, slowly, in measured tones. "He always insisted on keeping a low profile. And he locked away all the evidence, so even if my uncle wanted to prove it, he couldn't."

"Maybe your dad told someone else," Felicia suggests gently.

Hayden shakes his head. The inconsistency is suddenly a thorn, burred in him with a relentless prickle. "He *wouldn't* have."

Possibilities flicker through his brain, ghosts come back to haunt him. What wires had his father run through these walls, hidden away from everyone else who lived and worked here? How much of all this did *he* ever understand? How much of the Sisyphus Project had been his, truly? How much of it had been promised elsewhere? "He wouldn't," he says again, tongue numb.

"Well," she says kindly. "I'll see if I can find something in Charles's office."

"Sure," he says, without believing it. "Thank you."

"Then all that's left is to get the card for real. Tell me where the research is."

"Well," he starts.

"Well *what?* This isn't the time to be hesitating."

"Like I said," he broaches, "it's messy."

Felicia pushes the mug away from her, water sloshing over the rim. Her shoulders pull up, drawing a straight line across her frame, metallic and fierce. "Tell me where you put the data card, Hayden."

"Alright," he says, and tries to gather up his own face the way he'd seen her do it, willing the corners of his mouth to stop trembling, his eyes to stop blinking. Until his expression is harder, less malleable—marble, instead of wet clay.

And then he tells her.

**Transcript generated from
Operation System "Horatio"; 08/13/2047, 5:33am**

Connecting to room 213...

FELICIA: (over intercom) He said yes.

CHARLES: Did he, now?

FELICIA: (over intercom) Well, he said he was willing to give the research to me.

CHARLES: And only you, I presume.

FELICIA: (over intercom) Yes.

CHARLES: Well? I'm assuming you want to get this over with.

FELICIA: (over intercom) He's going to pass me the location.

CHARLES: You don't have it now?

FELICIA: (over intercom) No. I wanted to make sure we were on the same page here first.

CHARLES: Fine. How is this going down, then?

FELICIA: (over intercom) Hayden will tell me where he put the data. I'll go retrieve it. You and I will rendezvous somewhere you have access to the controls. He'll stand by at the exit. We'll make the trade: I give you the data card; you open the door. Hayden leaves. I wash my hands of all this.

CHARLES: Thorough.

FELICIA: (over intercom) I want this to be over. How many times do I have to say it?

CHARLES: Fair point. Then I suppose you should go tell Hayden I agree. And we can get started.

FELICIA: (over intercom) ...One last thing, first.

CHARLES: (sighs) What?

FELICIA: (over intercom) I want to see my father one last time.

CHARLES: Pardon?

FELICIA: (over intercom) After—after we're done here, this place is going to be crawling with police and media and the morbidly curious. I want... I just want to see him, once, before that happens. That's all. Then I'll go to Hayden and get the card and it'll be the end of it.

CHARLES: That's fair, I suppose. Although...

FELICIA: (over intercom) What.

CHARLES: I'm... curious.

FELICIA: (over intercom) About?

CHARLES: Do you blame yourself?

FELICIA: (over intercom) Jesus Christ.

CHARLES: Humour me.

FELICIA: (over intercom) Of course I do. But that's neither here nor there. It's done.

CHARLES: Hm.

FELICIA: (over intercom) A question for you, then.

CHARLES: Of course.

FELICIA: (over intercom) Was it worth it?

CHARLES: For her? Anything.

Suresh: You mentioned not recognizing yourself—did you find yourself in the role of a spectator, then? I guess I'm wondering if reading it over gave you more of an objective view of the events, now that we're nearly half a year out.

—*On Reclaiming Stories: An Interview with Felicia Xia*

CHAPTER TWENTY
Excerpted from *Tell Me A Tragedy*

IF YOU ARE still reading this, I want to thank you.

It is not an easy thing, digging out the roots of my own ugly rage, dressing them up for the page, letting the truth of me out into the world. I don't regret anything I did that night. But I don't want to say there's no action I don't often wish hadn't come to be necessary.

Knowing where the data card was hidden was half the battle.

I stood over Graham Lichfield's body, poised with a scalpel, and couldn't stop shaking.

It was the cold, or else Graham Lichfield's half-open eyes—cloudy, now, a milky film congealed over the lens—or maybe how it was only half a lie I'd told, because my father's body was lying just a few feet away. But mostly, I thought about cutting into the body, prying open the stiffened skin, and I felt my own arms tingle with a phantom pain. Looking down at the grisly scene, the gap between Hayden and me grew. I wondered how he'd done it. I wondered how I could survive diving in myself.

His father's mouth was still open, thin purple lines trickling like lightning from the corners of his lips. His cheeks were slack. He looked like he'd died in the middle of a word, half choking for something to say. His skin was pale, but there was a thick layer of dried blood crusting his neck, brown and scaled like a mosaic. Swiping my hand across the metal table, I picked up a few flakes of brown rust with my finger.

It shouldn't have been so bad.

The man was already dead.

I will spare you the details. I'm sure whatever you can imagine is much worse than what I had to do. The truth is that eventually, I worked up the courage—and the cold was getting to me, my fingertips numbing, the sweat crystallizing into ice beneath the nape of my neck. The truth is that eventually, I sawed the scalpel across his chest and peeled his skin open, ignoring the deep fissures that broke into the frozen tissue. And I dug down into the layers of epidermis and fat and viscera, and I found the data card nestled between two ribs.

I didn't sew him back up. What was the point? Hayden had granted me permission to do whatever I needed to.

The truth is that it smelled, something chemical tainting the air, trying valiantly to mask the bitterness of decay. The truth is that afterwards, I couldn't get the ugly grit of blackened blood out from under my fingernails. The truth is that I put the card into my pocket and shuddered at the weight of it.

The truth is that I did it, and it was not glamorous, but it was not as horrific as one might think.

Like I said: the man was already dead.

The worst part of the night was standing over my own father, unable to look too closely at his face.

I tried.

I tried so hard to give him the respect he deserved, to give him his dues, apologize, hug him, kiss him, give him all sorts of last rites or whatever it was I could muster in that cold refrigerator morgue. But every time my eyes flicked down, something rose in me, bile coating my throat, and I had to turn in another direction. I inched my hand closer and closer on the table, but then I got too close, and my knees buckled. I fell down against the table, crouching under it, too low to see anything but a dark blur.

It was too cold. I wanted to say goodbye. I was supposed to have been able to say goodbye. I knew the drill. I was supposed to cry, fling myself over my dead father's body. I was supposed to kiss him on the forehead, carefully slide his eyes shut so he could rest.

All I could do was cry and kneel and press my forehead to the ground in a stupid, broken approximation of the respect he deserved.

What he looked like when we first found him, I don't remember anymore.

All I can recall is visceral disgust, a deep churning in my stomach. Death and decay clung to my hands—I had just excavated a dead man's chest—but the thought of even looking at my father's body turned me inside out. Saliva pooled in my mouth, bitter. My breathing came quick, panting, and I knew if I moved too quickly, I wouldn't be able to keep anything down; everything within me, all my disgust and fear, would come pouring out.

Now, sometimes, I close my eyes and try to remember my father's face. But as always, the living memory slips away. My mind can conjure nothing, only a blank darkness. In my imagination, his death mask is like wax. His eyes are sunken in, removed for an open casket funeral. One eyelid is turned slightly inward, exposing a little sliver of pink.

But I will never know for real. I never looked.

*   *   *

BEFORE I WENT to find Hayden, I stopped in the hallway, pushed on the intercom.

"*Are you done?*" was the first thing Charles asked me.

"Yeah," I said. Useless to be mad at him at this point. "You should head to the controls. I'll go get the information from Hayden."

"*Sounds good,*" he said. His voice was wry. He didn't insist on anything, on watching me go to Hayden's door, like I thought he might've. A small explosion of relief burst inside me, though some part of me wanted him to be alert. I wanted to see the sharp man hiding behind that bland smile, the one who started off the night killing his own brother and lying to the police about it, the one who tried to encourage *me* to kill.

What did it mean, if Charles was so mild now?

Did that mean the killing instinct—that it came from me?

I clenched my fist inside my pocket, closed around the data card. I could squeeze it now and shatter it into pieces. Charles would look up properly, then. Hayden would hate me.

"It'll be quick," I said, then hung up.

I still remember this moment when I close my eyes at night sometimes. Standing there, in the hallway, no one to tell me what to do, where to go. The loneliness of all those blank white halls stretching out ahead of me. Again, I imagined what Elsinore must've looked like from the outside that night. In the dark, glowing inside out, the black streets and black waters and black skies glazed with fluorescence. No stars. Floating like a planet against the endless void of space.

How was I supposed to do anything against this place? All I wanted to do was tear it down, but Elsinore was forever, would live on forever, entrenched like a weed in my head.[30] Even now, some days, I feel watched.

But I could look for things myself, too. If Elsinore was a fortress of spies and secrets, then I would become part of its subterfuge. Quickly, while Charles was on the move, I had a fleeting few moments unmonitored. I tucked the gun I had taken off my father's body, loaded and ready, into the depths of my jacket.

I hurried through the halls, headed for the office Charles had just vacated.

---

30 The long history of the Elsinore Laboratory building is a whole narrative in and of itself; suffice to say, the building stood excavated for a few years during the height of the trial proceedings, its value gutted overnight, before eventually being bought out by a pharmaceuticals company that had gotten its start mass producing what eventually turned out to be fraudulent needleless vaccines. Today, the building has been converted to a gallery space, run by non-profit company Edenite. As per the website: "Elsinore stands in its entirety untouched—we believe that by witnessing art within the walls of immortal space, we confer an eternality to each piece."

Horatio
Thank you.

                                                    Felicia
                                            Whats your intel

Horatio
Charles's office. There's a false back behind the bottom shelf.
I don't know what's inside, but he goes there often.

                                                    Felicia
                                            thanks, i guess

INTERLUDE

> reading /HORATIO/security/
camera_213A::<08.13.2047>::05:47.078
> ERROR–DO NOT RECORD

Charles Lichfield stands at the door, one foot in the office and one foot outside. He turns towards the room, makes a half turn, pauses, then steps out.

The door swings shut behind him.

Visible particles of dust float through the air, intermittently obscuring the camera lens.

[QUALITY–*Footage jitters twice in quick succession, creating image doubling and artefacts.*]

The door slams open, causing the camera image to shake and kicking up more dust motes as Felicia Xia steps into the room. She stands at the entrance, chest rising and falling. The door falls shut again.

Felicia Xia walks into the room.

She moves to the shelf in the back corner and runs a finger up the length of the wooden plank. Taps three times. Her shoulders slope as she turns her head from left to right, then crouches.

From the very bottom shelf, she pulls out a sheaf of papers, which she places at the edge of the desk, smoothing a hand over the top and flattening the stack.

She returns to the shelf.

Her hands disappear into the gap left by the papers, and a moment later, the whole shelf shudders. Felicia Xia removes a wooden panel and places it on the ground. Her arms disappear back within the shelf, apparently further than the visible depth of the bookshelf. She pulls out a box.

Felicia Xia turns her head towards the door as she stands and holds the box to her chest. She takes a step away from the shelf, pauses briefly, then takes two more.

The room is still.

Her shoulders fall as she turns back towards the desk. The papers on the desk flutter, possibly disturbed by an exhaled breath.

She sets the box down and removes the lid. The inside is not visible from the camera's position. She puts her hands in and removes several items: a stack of pages, a framed photo, a bright red pen. She takes one sheet of paper and holds it up to the ceiling with her right hand, closer to the light. Felicia Xia's eyes scan left to right as she reads.

Her left hand rises to her mouth, and her eyes widen.

Felicia Xia sets the lid back on the box. The lid visibly shakes as she does so. Her lips are pressed together in a tight line. The rest of her face is obscured from the camera by her hair.

Felicia Xia places a thin stack of pages into her pocket, then takes the rest of the paper, the framed photo, and the pen, and places them back inside the box. She draws her hands up to her brows and her chest expands as she inhales deeply. Then, she wraps her arms around the box and carries it back to the shelf, lowering her head as she slides it back in the cavity. She replaces the wooden panel.

Felicia Xia rubs her hand over her brow once. She places her hands back into her pockets.

She walks to the door, taking slow steps, then brisker ones. By the time she reaches the door, she is half-running, and she flings the door open hard enough it shakes the camera image again.

The door closes behind her.

Suresh: Do you regret anything?

Xia: That's a complicated question.

—On Reclaiming Stories:
An Interview with Felicia Xia

CHAPTER TWENTY-ONE

Excerpted from *Tell Me A Tragedy*

HAYDEN AND I made a show of handing over a small slip of paper, shielded from the cameras. He was back in the ruined lab, and therefore so was I—he'd come willingly, but I still resented the startling cruelty of forcing him to stand where his father had died. If it bothered Hayden, he didn't let it show. We didn't talk, much. Mostly worked in silence, knowing what was to come. That was when it sunk in properly: that after this, we wouldn't see each other. Possibly ever.

I wasn't sad. I wasn't happy. Mostly, I was numb, like someone had unspooled all the organs from inside me, leaving nothing but an empty husk.

He passed the slip of paper over, but his fingers lingered on mine, a voiceless question.

Was this the end?

I didn't know. His other hand traced over the contours of his own neck—something he had done often through the night, and I knew he was thinking of Elsinore, of himself, of all the things locked inside him that he never wanted to show me. But there were parts of me I didn't want to show him, either. The two of us, made new by this night, rendered strangers to each other.

Before I could think better of it, I slipped out the sheaf of papers I had stolen from Charles's office.

I didn't know how Hayden was going to react, but I thought he deserved to know. He, of all people, deserved to know. I couldn't have lived with myself if I sent him away, out into the wilderness of the world beyond Elsinore, without knowing.

But if Charles saw—if Charles saw, that would ruin the whole plan.

I thought: what worked last time must work again. I don't know if that was an excuse or not.

I grabbed Hayden's lapel and pulled him towards me. I crushed his lips to mine. It felt less intimate, somehow, than my fingers on his wrist, but I brought a hand up to his cheek and angled the kiss deep and harsh. Hayden made a soft whine, a surprised sound, but he leaned into me so easily. I swept a finger against the edge of his brow, barely touching his skin, and Hayden shivered. With my other hand, I slipped the pages and data card into his pocket.

Hayden was the one who pulled away first.

Not entirely. He touched his forehead to mine, eyes half-lidded, and I knew it. So, this was goodbye. In the quiet, both of us were breathing a little too heavily, a little too intimately. I dug my fingers into the soft underside of his jaw, where his pulse lived, and I pressed as hard as I dared, because I wanted him to know that I'd seen all of it. I did understand, to some degree. Maybe in another world, we could've made something from this place together, him and I.

He straightened. His gaze, for once, was bright and clear. His hair was matted halfway across his forehead, falling in his eyes, and the bridge of his nose was shadowed by a mottling bruise. But he looked like he could handle whatever came next.

I tucked my hands back into my pockets and nodded. I didn't wait for him to say anything before I turned away. It was almost over. We were almost done. After the exchange, after one split second of deceiving Charles, we could both walk away from this tangled web, this tangled love. And whatever else this night had to throw at Hayden, he could survive it. Which was everything I needed.

The last time I had left him behind, when we were both younger and stupider and all I knew was that *I* couldn't survive the festering thing that was growing between us, I wasn't as certain.

This time, it would be the end of it.

Letters: Dr. Helen Lichfield to Charles Lichfield

1. Notebook paper and fountain pen
[Estimated from May 2028]

Charles,

I find myself coming back to the photo of us from the graveyard in Vienna and how happy the three of us looked, despite being surrounded by the dead and decaying. Vienna was lovely—all those ancient tombstones worn away by the weather. Do you remember getting lost? It amazed me how far back the graves stretched, far enough that they stopped being rows, becoming clustered and irregular. Graham doesn't like it much, the photo. At least, I find it turned face down on the mantelpiece whenever I come down to the living room when he's asleep. You look content in it, which is more than I can say for when I last saw you.

How are you?

Something of a banal question, I know, but I worry. And I find myself wondering, these days. It's been so long, and I know last time we spoke it wasn't exactly friendly. I understand if you don't want to talk to me anymore, but we both miss your company.

Stupid way to put it, I know, but I don't know how to get us back on solid ground again.

I never got to tell you this before, but I appreciate you and everything you did for me. I'm sorry you felt like you couldn't stay.

Please, write back.

Best,

Helen

2. Notebook paper, torn, and ballpoint [Estimated from October–November 2031[31]]

Charles,

Thank you, for finally writing, for coming over, for hearing me out.

Graham is well, though he says you still refuse to be on speaking terms. I suppose I should apologize for that, too. I promise[32] I didn't choose him because you left.

Our son is turning five, soon. He can walk, imagine that!

Graham would like you to be in his life, I think.

I'd like that, too.

So—please. Consider it.

If you come in person, I can explain so much more to you.

All best,

Helen

---

31 Correlated with Hayden Lichfield's birthday of November 4, 2026.
32 Here the paper is nearly punctured, midway through the underline.

3. Commercial postcard, pencil
[Estimated from July 2033]

Charles,

Well, look at us, back to exchanging letters.

Graham doesn't know I still write to you. He doesn't even let me see Hayden anymore, most days. So I'd appreciate it if you keep it on the down-low.

I'm sorry it seems like I'm always asking you for favours, but I think we're getting so much closer to where we used to be, aren't we? I'd forgotten how intoxicating it can be with you, to feel so much like another person <u>sees</u> me, finally.

I'm glad that at the very least, Graham kept you in his life.

Take care of my son for me?

Big ask, but I know you love him as much as I do.

Let's see each other. No strings attached.

Cheers,

Helen

4. Notebook paper, fountain pen
[Estimated from sometime in 2040]

Charles—[33]

This is too embarrassing to say, and I want you to know, for real, in my writing, put down with my own two hands.

I still love you.

Now, take it and leave; I'll call you later.

---

[33] This page, in particular, is barely legible, the pencil faint and smudged, creased over so many times it was nearly destroyed in the archival process.

5. Printer paper, typewritten
[Estimated from February 2046[34]]

Charles,

Graham told me yesterday that Hayden has withdrawn from his undergraduate degree. Graham also told me that he indulged our wayward son and gave him a position at Elsinore. I would ask you to keep me in denial and tell me it isn't true, but I know Graham doesn't lie to me. Not about this, at least. I suppose all I have left to say is that if this was in any part your idea, I think it is foolish and stupid and a waste of all our time.

But I'm not above admitting that some part of me is hurt.

I sincerely hope none of it was your idea. I don't know what I would do with myself. I would visit, but I don't think Hayden wants to see me. I can only hope he doesn't try to follow in the footsteps of his father, so hungry for his work it starves him of everything else.

Though I can relate to that. There is something addictive about discovery, how it eats away at you every moment you're not standing before the lab bench, peering into the secret, minuscule world that makes up the foundation of us all. I started a new project last year—I don't know if I've told you that. Not over the phone, though I forget what we talk about too often. I've become fascinated by neurotrophins as of late, all the finicky ways our brains develop. Did you know how many inbuilt instincts and fears we have, wired into us from birth? I've become fascinated with breaking the circuits and seeing what happens. I've gotten myself

---

34 Reports from the University of Toronto records indicate that Hayden Lichfield's last semester was in the spring term of 2044, his first undergraduate year; however, there was no recorded contact between Graham and Helen Lichfield until two years following—it is possible therefore that news of Hayden's schooling was not known to Helen until this later juncture.

a little colony of lab mice. There is something addictive about solving the puzzle of a genome, piecing together disparate parts, looking for meaning amidst all that chaos—and something even more addictive about reaching in and changing it.

Don't tell Graham. But you know that already.

I suppose I'm writing this in part because I am worried about my son, and in part because I have had all these curiosities sitting in my own brain with no one to talk to. You haven't called me in too long.

Consider this a peace offering. A little glimpse into my own machinations to unlock some insight into Elsinore's sealed gates. What has Graham put forth that has my son so fascinated?

Don't write back unless you have some good news for me this time.

Best,

Helen

6. Notebook paper, pencil
[Estimated from February 2046]

Charles,

Please tell me you're joking.

Helen

7. Notebook paper, fountain pen
[Estimated from March 2046]

Charles,

I could've called, sure. But writing cannot be hallucinated. If you wrote back with the evidence, I'd know it was real.

I am a very practical woman, as I'm sure you know.

But...

I can barely bring myself to write down the words. What in the world is Graham thinking? Don't answer that question. I know Graham Lichfield just as well now as I did five years ago. He will stop at nothing to pursue what he loves. I suppose that's what he and I still have in common.

Tell me everything you know about this Sisyphus Formula. When did this start? Is this what Hayden was so fascinated with, that he dropped out of school?[35] I have a paper coming out soon, you know, about the mouse brains. There have been reporters doing dramatic write ups, calling my work 'remodelling the act of creation itself.' What irony, that my ex-husband would start on something as ambitious as mastering <u>death</u> at a time like this.

Please, Charles, write back. I want so desperately to know. I need it like Prometheus needed his fire. I would split myself open for this.

Love,

Helen

8. Notebook paper, fountain pen
[Estimated from March 2046]

Charles,

You can hardly call it a betrayal when you were never on his side to begin with, darling. That said, I understand your apprehension. Be that as it may, I still want you to consider my proposal with a bit more reason than you've given me. Think of what we could do, Charles. Graham is too much a scientist, not shrewd enough to take full advantage of this miracle. I know you're better than that.

I know you.

I <u>know</u> you.

---

35 The writing grows shaky here, lines crooked on the page.

And I know you trust me.

Tell me, how much time have you spent building Elsinore from the ground up? How much time has Graham spent locked in his lab, single-minded, lost to everything outside his own world?

As I said: I do understand. God knows I've spent too many days wasting away in my own lab. But I am a pragmatist. You and I are similar that way. I know what it is to create something truly magnificent, <u>and</u> I know what it is to put it to some actual use in the world.

If you still have doubts, ask him what he plans to do with the Sisyphus Formula.

If he answers with anything other than 'publish a paper' or 'run further studies,' feel free to ignore me.

Love,

Helen

9. Magazine paper, torn, the words are written on the flipside of a cover of *Nature*, fountain pen [Estimated from April 2046]

Dearest Charles,

I'm always thanking you, aren't I?

But thank you. Thank you a thousand times over; you could always see the world brighter than Graham ever did.

Come over tomorrow. Tell me when you plan to get me the data.

I'll tell you what I want to do with it.

It'll be spectacular.

Love,

Helen

CHAPTER TWENTY-TWO
HAYDEN[36]

HIS UNCLE SENDS Rasmussen to escort him to the exit point. Hayden hadn't thought he was well enough to walk; he thought he'd seen the last of Rasmussen after he stumbled out of that room, half broken. Clever of dear Uncle Charles. Makes it harder to escape when he's forced to stare down the proof of his own folly, should that be the goal. The sclera of Rasmussen's left eye is painted a brilliant scarlet. The scowling pallor of his face only makes this clearer, emphasizes the deep, darker crimson veins that run down blanched conjunctiva. He walks with a limp.

Rasmussen looks at him, dead on. Naked resentment he doesn't even try to hide.

There's a space in Hayden's chest where his guilt should be curdling, but—

It doesn't matter.

Nothing matters anymore.

---

36 Once again, the proceeding chapter is my own fictionalized account.

Can't escape if there's nowhere to escape *to*.

Everything he loves, he left back here. Even Horatio, nestled close as always. Horatio can't know the flurry of his mind, the crawling neurosis. Horatio can't know the plan, if Charles is to be kept in the dark, so Horatio can't be with him, now that Hayden needs him most. All he has is the data. But what could he do with data, without a lab? Without a safe place? Nowhere to go?

The letters sit in his pocket, red hot.

He wants to rip them to pieces, but that doesn't render what's written on them moot. It doesn't erase the truth.

He wanted to know—what had made Charles like this? What had made this so? What knife had twisted so deep in his uncle's gut to betray them all like this?

Now he knows. The betrayal had never been with him.

But instead of relief at finding the answer, all Hayden can see is the tightening grip of the future, black and unknowable.

"Come on, Lichfield," Rasmussen snaps, dragging Hayden's arm hard as he pulls him across the hall.

He nearly stumbles on his feet.

"Is this petty revenge?" he can't help but mutter vindictively. "You don't seem to have any signs of nerve damage. Far as I can see, you'll make a full recovery."

Rasmussen doesn't turn to glare.

"Come on," Hayden parrots, slowing his steps down a little deliberately. "Let's get this over with. I'm tired of this."

Rasmussen scoffs. "*You're* tired?"

"Of course I am. A lot has transpired tonight, Rasmussen. Don't you know?"

He stops dead in the centre of the hall.

Some hazy, grim satisfaction hangs over Hayden's head. Good. He doesn't want to continue to the exit. Not yet. He wants this kind of anger, easier to swallow. This kind of fight, petty words and taunting barbs he doesn't really mean.

"Are you fucking *hearing* yourself right now?"

Hayden raises an eyebrow.

"I'm escorting you to a cushy exit, where you can slip away into the night unscathed after you *killed a man* tonight— let alone what you did to me." Rasmussen's whole body trembles.

"I didn't do anything to you," Hayden says, flicking his fingers in dismissal. "Collateral damage."

"Fucking balls to stand there and pretend you weren't responsible for all of it."

Of course not. There are a million things he would do over. He could stay in this moment now, forever, if that was remotely possible. But regretting means never having to think about the nonexistent, nebulous future. Regret means living in the past, even if only in your mind.

And admitting that—his guilt, his regret—would mean admitting he doesn't want the trade to go through. Would mean discarding everything he's planned for tonight.

It's funny, and the humour of it closes on him like a trap, like the exquisite shock of an aneurysm twisting open; they'd all been sitting on this tragedy, building underneath them, the truth of it lodged up in the walls of Elsinore for years.

This is just the counterpoint. The fallout. The catharsis.

He smooths out the edges of his trembling mouth into a smirk. "I wasn't, though."

Rasmussen reels back. "Holy fuck, man. I thought your uncle was crazy."

Hayden snorts. "He is."

"You're all fucking crazy." And there it is, the shaking fear. Once, Hayden had thought he and Rasmussen were peers, but Rasmussen doesn't belong here, not really. He's scared. He's a goddamn coward, lured into the fray by people who had seen more of what was happening than he ever did.

"What did my uncle promise you?" Hayden sneers. "To help him out?"

Rasmussen gives Hayden's arm—still firmly in his grip—a hard shake. "None of your goddamn business."

"Did he offer to pay off your student debt? Bump your salary? A fancy publication, for your budding career? What did Paul Xia say to get you to let him into the basement? You blame yourself?"

With a rough snarl, Rasmussen backhands Hayden across the face.

For a moment, the world rings. Iron, bright on his tongue. Hayden's shoulder crashes against the wall. The already fragile infrastructure of his lip tears. An exploring tongue in the crevice feels out the vitreous tissue inside the epithelium, gelatinous and squirming. His incisors ache. His hands grope out along the walls as he spits out a glob of stringy spit laced with blood. When his vision clears, he realizes his glasses have been knocked to the ground, and he bends to pick them up.

"Satisfied?" he asks, not bothering to straighten.

Rasmussen stands, trembling. His hair has fallen out of the tie, spilled out over his shoulders. He looks like a fucking kid, spindly and in over his head, and Hayden laughs.

"You don't want to be here," Hayden says.

"Of course not," Rasmussen returns, voice raspy. There is still the flicker of—something, flashing across his face. Pity, perhaps. Or maybe regret of his own.

"But you're still doing it," Hayden says. "Letting him use you like a glorified manservant. Just because he's giving you empty promises."

Instead of an answer, Rasmussen reaches across the hall and wrenches Hayden back upright.

Hayden laughs again, dribbling more bloody spittle over his chin. "Is that it, then?" he asks, going pliant and letting Rasmussen drag him along.

They move faster down the hall, shuttling towards an inevitability.

"You're too ashamed now? You accuse me of everything, but you listen to him?" The anger mounts inside of him, like a tsunami, low and rolling at first, but suddenly fierce. "Is that all you have to say to me?"

Rasmussen is stubbornly silent.

"Is that what you think of me, now? Is that what you mean? Or have you *always* thought this way?" At some point, the questions have stopped being about Rasmussen. Hayden breathes in, sharp and stinging. "*Say something*," he snaps.

Rasmussen doesn't even turn his head.

Fuck, he thinks, then repeats it out loud for good measure. He's still angry.

He's still so angry it hurts just to walk. It hurts when his teeth clatter together. It hurts when he closes his eyes. It hurts when he tries to think about what happens now. It hurts when he wonders if anyone here ever loved him, like a keening wail stuck in his chest, trying to escape. Is there anyone left anymore? Is everyone going to betray him, or else leave him alone to blindly stumble through, inevitably fucking everything up? There's no refuge to retreat to. Nothing to show for tonight but spilled blood and ruined plans.

Unbidden, words from the letter float to his mind. Words his mother wrote, her hands steady and sure.

I would split myself open for this.

Hayden glances at Rasmussen's hardened face, turned away from him.

No, no, no, he thinks, a cacophony of thoughts spilling out, too fast and fierce, delirious with everything but the need to stop, to get out of this stupid plan, to escape somewhere dark and quiet so he can piece his mind back together. Panic clogs his throat, and he can't get at his own damn wrists to make sure his heart is steady and—*I need out of these fucking cuffs, I need everything to stop. I need to stop.*

He can't step out of this lab.

He can't let this spill out into the real world.

He can't—

Can't—

He shakes his head, a twitching reflex, a red cloud descending over his eyes. Breathing comes easier, now, though it feels like someone else's chest is rising and falling, somewhere far away from him. The only intelligible thing rattling through his overloading synapses is that he needs to leave, and that tonight, there will be blood to spill.

Perhaps, bloody thoughts are all he has left.

THEY STOP BEFORE a smooth white wall that once held an exit.

He finds the outline of it, fine and dark, like a ghost of a door. An imprint.

There's a speaker somewhere embedded in the ceiling. He pushes away the urge to look up for it and the cameras, stops his mouth from forming the shape of Horatio's name, doesn't want Horatio to know the truth of the writhing, madman's brain left over in his useless body.

"*Hayden?*" a voice crackles. Felicia's, not Charles[37].

His shoulders drop a fraction. "Yeah," he calls into the empty hall.

"*Are you ready?*"

"Is Charles there?"

A pause.

Then, "*I'm here. Did you want to tell me something?*" His uncle's voice is as cold as ever, but he can hear the strain like a violin string wound taut. Tight enough to cut. He's stressed. He's upset. And he doesn't want Hayden to know. He wonders if his mother told Charles not to tell.

He shifts his lab coat, slides his hands underneath.

"No," he says. "I want you to tell me something."

Charles sighs. "*What is it now, Hayden?*"

He wraps a hand around his left thumb, brushing up against the fluttering pulse just under the surface of his skin. "I want you to admit it to me," he says. Carefully, he presses down on the first joint. *Carpometacarpal,* he thinks, clinical clarity coming to him like a balm, *crucial to connect the thumb to the rest of the hand.*

"*Haven't we said enough by now?*" Charles asks.

He pushes down on his thumb experimentally, enough for it to ache.

"I just want to know one thing, then."

"*What is it?*"

"Did you know that it was mine more than it was his? The Sisyphus Formula," he says, his voice falling to a bare whisper.

"*...No. I didn't.*"

---

37 The following intercom conversation is as per the original transcript, altered only to eliminate repetition.

"Would you have tried to take it anyway, if you did?" *Would Mom still have wanted it that badly?*

His uncle's mouth must be close to the microphone, which transmits the halting, shaking breath. "*I would've, yes.*"

Hayden nods, slowly, realising Charles most likely hasn't even bothered to watch him.

That's enough, for some sort of confession. Which means it's time for the trade.

He pushes his thumb down harder, right into the divot between the bones.

"Thank you for being honest," he says.

"*Are you ready, then?*"

"Sure," he says. "Let's do it."

Then he sucks in a sharp breath and forces the joint all the way down. *Crack.* Biting down on his lip, he forces the cuff off over his hand as fast as he can. It doesn't feel broken. Dislocated, maybe. But he keeps the hand stiff and still anyway as he carefully holds the cuff—still magnetic, still drawn to the other—in his right hand.

Rasmussen gives him a suspicious look. "What was that?"

Hayden grits his teeth. "Nothing," he says, hoping he doesn't sound faint.

On the other end of the line, Felicia's voice comes back. "*Hayden, you have the data card, right?*"

Swiftly, he crouches. "I'm sorry, Felicia," he says.

Then he lunges, uses the cuff to whip hard metal across Rasmussen's face hard enough to stun him.

"*What the hell—?*"

Rasmussen wheels back with a cry. Before he can bring his hands up to guard himself, Hayden gathers his strength and uses the cuff to bludgeon him again. He cannot be certain, but he hits hard enough that he thinks bone cracks.

Rasmussen staggers. He's bigger and stronger, but Hayden has surprise.

And he has a weapon.

"Wait—" Rasmussen chokes out, and Hayden slams into his face yet again, catching cheekbone and sending a light spray of blood spitting out of Rasmussen's mouth. He uses his momentum to twine his fingers into Rasmussen's hair and bashes his face into the white, sterile wall, grinding down.

A weak breath wheezes out of Rasmussen's lungs. Hayden gulps down the bile trying to crawl up his throat and reaches into his pocket. He hooks an arm around Rasmussen's neck, and he pulls out the heavy red fountain pen that is still engraved with his traitorous mother's name.

It's quick. Stab, drag. The wet slick of blood and tissue separating. Rasmussen's wheeze. Hayden breaks cartilage, trachea. Pulls his arm back. Stabs again, finds the carotid.

Rasmussen himself only has enough time to choke, for his eyes to bulge. A flailing elbow catches Hayden in the ribs, strikes hard enough for pain to skitter over the whole of his left as Rasmussen crashes them both hard to the ground. Hayden grunts, tightening his grip. Rasmussen is weakening, one hand pressed tight to the wound. Slowly, the pressure against Hayden's chest eases as the whole of Rasmussen's body goes limp. Hayden braces again him, rolls them both over. Rasmussen is facing the ceiling, mouth open and gaping, still gasping. Hayden lowers him carefully to the ground.

Fucking cliché, he thinks, hysterical. Rasmussen's blood paints the whole wall in striations of red, Pollock-sprays, haphazard and wild.[38]

---

38 Autopsy report recorded Gabriel Rasmussen's official cause of death as massive hemorrhage, although blunt force trauma wounds consistent with bludgeoning force were documented, causing multiple skull and orbital bone fractures.

Rasmussen's mouth opens and closes as if he cannot fathom what has happened. Blood spurts between his fingers. Hayden's own hand is throbbing. There's a wet squeal under his heel when he turns.

And then: "*Goddammit, Hayden,*" Felicia says.

"Sorry," he says again. His hands aren't shaking. Why aren't they shaking? He tries to push his hair back with the heel of his palm, but it jostles his injured thumb and he has to stifle a pathetic cry.

"*We had a plan,*" she says.

"I wasn't satisfied by it." Hayden chokes on the words.

"*Is this what you meant by 'messy'?*" she asks. "*Is this what you were planning?*"

All he can do is repeat the same words, "I'm sorry," over and over, as if that means anything. He knows it doesn't. But Felicia can take care of herself. There's only one thing he has left to do now, and when Charles is dead, she can walk away anyway.

"Don't follow me," he says, and then he retreats down the hall without looking back, every ragged breath hurting as he desperately pulls for air, burying himself deeper and deeper into the bowels of Elsinore.

Suresh: Do you think Hayden regrets anything?

Xia: That's also a complicated question.

—On Reclaiming Stories:
An Interview with Felicia Xia

CHAPTER TWENTY-THREE

Excerpted from *Tell Me A Tragedy*

I WAS MORE afraid of Hayden for killing Rasmussen than for killing my father.

My father's death was an accident. Mismatched malicious intent. I can see that now. Rasmussen's was not.

I watched Rasmussen die on the screen. Charles and I stood in the security room, video feed screens winking at us from the wall. On one of them, one electronic tile in the mosaic that pieced Elsinore together, Rasmussen was dying. He choked, slowly. I couldn't make out any details, only that he crawled, slowly, dragging his wasting body across the floor, and then he stopped.

Before I could watch him fall still entirely—was that his chest, still heaving?—Charles grabbed me by the wrist, livid.

"Did you know about this?" he asked, already dragging me from the room.

"No," I said, trying to wrest my arm away. "No, I had no idea—let go of me, I can walk like a normal person."

But he kept going.

I dragged my feet against the ground, stubborn, but Charles didn't even look back.

"I swear to god, I had no idea he was going to do that, I—"

"I find that hard to believe," Charles said curtly.

And then we were at his office.

Charles shoved me through the door and I shuddered, hoping he wouldn't notice the disturbances, the things I'd reorganized.

He yanked out the leather chair, then gestured towards it.

I looked down, blank.

Charles, with nothing of the force he'd used to get me here, pressed a hand into my shoulder blade and pushed me towards the chair.

I blinked. "What are we doing?" I asked.

Charles didn't move his hand. "You have the location, right?"

Instantly, white-hot panic dropped over me like a gauzy veil. The dummy sheet with the supposed location—the *fake*—sat in my pocket like glaring red light, warning, warning. "Yeah," I said.

Charles shook the chair. "Sit down," he said. "Let's check it over."

When I looked closer, there was a manic gleam in Charles's eyes: opaque, his pupils slicked over with a bright film. His hands didn't shake, but I thought he looked most like Hayden in that moment—poised and put-together, but the edge of something roiling underneath, waiting to spill out.

So I sat. I let him push me in front of the desk. I took out the sheet of paper and I dropped it on the desk.

Charles snatched it up, didn't look back when he left the room.

All I could do was sit, breathe.

I wondered what it was like outside. Had the sun come up yet? Had the edges of morning started to bleach the midnight ink sky yet? I breathed in the stale lab air and pretended it was from fresh morning.

We'd been so *close.*

Above me, the speakers spluttered.

Felicia? Horatio asked, tentative.

"How are you here?" I asked, confused.

I don't know where you are. I traced your pager. But— he sounded sardonic—*I'm assuming this means you're in Charles's office.*

"Where is he?" I intoned. I wasn't asking about Charles.

I can't tell you.

"Of course you can't."

Just like you couldn't tell me what you did in the basement lab.

"Right," I said. Those were the rules. Keep to your boundaries. Secrets everywhere. All of us deceiving each other to keep Charles from getting the full picture, desperate to look for a place to slip away between the competing narratives. And now it was all ruined.

But I wanted to know... Did you know any of it? Did you plan any of this with him? Horatio sounded concerned. Whether it was for me or Hayden, I didn't know, and I didn't care to, anymore.

"No," I said. Something inside me recoiled, because it wasn't all true, and because I was so certain the letters wouldn't ruin him, and I was wrong. "Are you helping him?"

Horatio was silent for a long time. I wondered if Charles had figured out all our lies yet. If he was on his way back.

I want to, he told me eventually. *But I'm not sure how to.*

"Yeah," I said. "I know how you feel."

I know he's probably the last person you want to see right now, but don't pretend you're not worried about him.

"Of course I'm worried about him. I don't remember a time before I was worried about Hayden goddamn Lichfield, but that doesn't mean I have to clean up all his messes." For the first time that night, digging deep inside myself, I couldn't muster up the little, watery sympathy I had for Hayden. It was as if it had all fallen out between my fingers. And for the first time, I felt free. I was numb, but underneath, I was angry. I wasn't beholden to anyone, least of all Hayden. "You should know, actually," I said, "if I find him, I won't be shooting to injure."

Another bout of silence.

I drummed my fingers on the edge of the chair, sucking on my bottom lip.

Okay, Horatio finally said. *Thank you. I will.*

And then he was gone.

And I was alone.

So I waited.

I don't know if what I was saying was a bluff, then. But there, in that space where I suddenly didn't care about what happened to Hayden Lichfield, my chest felt hollow and full to bursting at the same time. Like I'd let go of something that had grown so heavy I hadn't even realized. Like I wasn't breathing air, but pure helium, buoying me up.

Whatever happened next, I would make my own damn decisions, set my own damn course.

Hayden was already dead to me.

INTERLUDE

**> playing /HORATIO/security/
camera_003K::<08.13.2047>::06.23.19**

A dark room, with filing cabinets lining the walls. It is otherwise empty. In the back corner, a dimly lit bulb hangs.

Charles Lichfield enters the room.

He stands at the door, then raises a hand and runs it through his hair, his movement jerky and jolting.

He looks up, mouth forming a single word.

Nothing happens.

Brow furrowed and teeth bared, he repeats the same word.[39]

Charles Lichfield frowns, then pulls out a sheet of paper, holds it up, and looks around the room.

He punches the wall next to him.

Dust trickles from the ceiling, settling in Charles Lichfield's hair.

---

39 Analysis of the video suggests he's shouting the word "Lights," though certainty is not high.

He crumples the sheet of paper in his hand.

He walks towards the nearest cabinet, braces both hands against the side, and pushes it over.

Papers fly off the shelves and glass shatters.

After a few seconds, a clear liquid spreads out from beneath the fallen cabinet, tracing the grooves in the floor.

Charles Lichfield steps back, then discards the piece of paper onto the jumbled mess.

He runs another hand through his hair, then shakes off the dust. He smiles widely.

Charles Lichfield turns, then leaves.

The door shakes the whole wall as it slams shut.

Another part of the cabinet collapses in the aftermath.

Xia: I think what I meant was that I kept saying these things out of sheer anger, and I don't remember the actual words anymore—I only remember the anger I felt. So that was true, the fact that I was angry, and I was shocked to discover the things I was willing to say in the moment when I was channeling that anger. Does that make sense?

Suresh: Yes, I think it does. Are you still afraid of that part of yourself?

Xia: No. No, definitely not.

—On Reclaiming Stories:
An Interview with Felicia Xia

CHAPTER TWENTY-FOUR
Excepted from *Tell Me A Tragedy*

I WAS EXPECTING the call, but it wasn't any less horrifying: the booming roar of Charles's voice, suddenly everywhere and surrounding me, angry like I'd never heard it before.

"*Were you in on it?*" he thundered, and it was worse because I didn't know how close he was to the office, if he was on his way.

He was out of breath. Frantic.

"*Miss Xia,*" he said, hissing my name. It snaked into my ears, the malicious sibilance burrowing in my head, trickling down my neck. "*Miss* Xia, *did you* know *about this?*"

"No," I called up into the ceiling. "No."

He scoffed. It sounded like the very air ripping.

A high-pitched whine was starting to build, like a sonic scream. I didn't know if it was in my head or not anymore. Or if it meant he was getting closer.

"*You promised me,*" Charles said, and now it sounded sickly sweet. "*I guess I was stupid to believe that you had an ounce of sincerity—and now—*" He cut himself off with a low growl. It echoed, built up on itself, layered until all I could hear was his rage, raw and unfiltered, pitched so low it was more a pressure in my head than actual sound.

I stood. "All I wanted to do was leave!"

And then—

Quiet.

Slowly, the echoes ebbed away.

Eventually, all that filled the room was the sound of his breathing, heavy and thick, but evening out.

"That hasn't changed," I said. My own voice was louder than it should be, bigger than my chest. "I never wanted to help Hayden. I just wanted to go home."

Quieter, quieter.

"But I hate him for it, too," I whispered. "I—Hayden tricked me, too. And I know that you're the only person who can open those doors."

I heard the barest hint of a breath.

I steeled myself, and said, "So tell me what you need me to do."

Instantly, Charles's tone changed. "*Do you mean that, Miss Xia?*"

He was still so easy to placate. I fought the urge to snort. "Of course I do," I said. "I *told* you, I just want to go home."

Charles chuckled. "*I suppose that's fair.*"

"Then tell me," I said again, clenching my fists as if I could reach him from here, fight back, pull him out from his disembodied voice with my own two hands. "What do you need me to do?"

"*It's simple, Miss Xia. I need you to protect me.*"

And that was the root of it all.

Charles was enraged not because he wanted the research, but because he was afraid to die, like we all were.

"Hayden's coming," I said, certain of it. "And he's not above trying to kill you."

"*Exactly,*" Charles said bitterly. "*Knowing how much he idolized Graham, Hayden's probably been trying to kill me all night.*"

I wondered if he resented that. If he had any sorrow left in him for his brother. I wondered if he loved Graham any more than he loved Hayden.

"Do you have a plan?" I asked.

"*I didn't. But now...*"

"What does that mean?"

Charles sighed, softly. I could feel it feathering against my neck. "You *are the best and only plan I have left.*"

"What does—?"

And then I realized what he was talking about.

I pressed my mouth into a tight line, grabbing onto the back of the chair to steady myself. My gun sat heavy in my pocket. My hand—capable, willing—hung at my side. A thick tangle of something I couldn't articulate lingered in my chest, something like a terrible sadness when I thought of Hayden's desperate eyes, something like a maddening rage when I thought of the rest of it.

Charles hummed in satisfaction.

"I don't know what I can do," I lied.

"*I don't know this lab as well as Hayden,*" Charles admitted. I could picture him gesturing around the office as he continued. "*That space is what I know, where my administrative work gets done. There may be secrets locked in these walls I'm not aware of, which means it would be easy for Hayden to find some passageway in, and…*"

"You're a sitting duck, here, just waiting."

"*Not,*" Charles said, "*if I have you.*"

"You want me to stop him."

"*Like I said, I want you to protect me.*"

"What's the point? When the doors open, we'll testify, and you'll waste away the rest of your life in jail anyway."

"*Well…*"

I closed my eyes. "You still want me to kill him."

"*Isn't that what you wanted?*"

I clenched my hands. I didn't know what I wanted anymore. I wanted this to be over, so I could walk free again in the streets, feel the fresh ocean spray on my face, curl up with Art and forget it all. I wanted time to mourn.

But I wanted Hayden out of my life.

I wanted nothing else to do with him. I wanted our stories to diverge. I wanted not to have to think of him. I didn't want to *suffer* for him anymore.

"You only want me to kill for you, because you can't."

"*Would you rather give me your gun instead?*"

I had nothing to say to that.

"*See?*" Charles cajoled.

"I have a family, too," I finally said.

"*I never said I was a saint, Felicia,*" Charles returned. He sounded more coherent, nothing of the earlier rage discernable in his voice anymore. He sounded cold, calculating, like he was discussing a business venture: here's an arrangement convenient for the both of us. "*Maybe I do deserve to die. But help me with this one last thing, please.*

I'll shoulder the burden of this afterwards. You don't have to worry about catching any of the blame. Is that so much to ask for?"

It was, but I didn't want to give Charles the satisfaction of any more words from me.

And the thought of having to sort through the mess of the fallout, trying to parse who was right and who was wrong. Why he didn't want to expose us all right now if he was already willing to be punished, I didn't understand, but that didn't matter. I alone knew the truth of tonight. I alone had proof. If Charles wanted to shoulder the blame, there was no way he could pass it on to me, so I could go home and rest easy.

All I would have to do was dirty my hands a little.

I thought, at the time, I could say something to placate Charles, and decide what I *really* wanted when Hayden inevitably came. It wasn't real, I told myself.

But when I stood, and said, "I'll do it," it felt real. Charles wasn't even in the room, and after that he cut the line, so it was just me, speaking the unspeakable to myself. It felt like a confession.

It would be revenge, I told myself. Was this what Hayden had told himself?

Didn't I deserve this?

I nodded to the empty air, then stepped back and settled into the chair before the desk. I let it cradle me, crossed my arms and wondered when it would end.

First, Helen Lichfield, willing to kill to get the research. Charles, willing to kill to please her, to save her. Graham, willing to wire death into his lab to protect his secrets; his son, willing to release it for vengeance.

And then there was me, willing to kill if only to make

sure it was all over, but suddenly unsure if either Hayden or Charles's death would even end it all.

I curled into myself, closed my eyes, and waited.

CHAPTER TWENTY-FIVE
HAYDEN

HORATIO COMES BACK to Hayden in fragments.

He's curled up under the vast array of screens that make up the wall in the security room he has stashed himself in for lack of anywhere else to go, and cries into his bitten, bloodied knuckles as Horatio pours back into his mind like molten mercury. A mindless, consumptive pain of no origin deep within himself shoots down the fleshy meat of his spinal cord, sensory tracts a stinging mess, paresthesia seizing his limbs and stiffening his joints as Horatio's consciousness crashes over him in layers, wave after wave of understanding. Hayden's vision doubles, triples, quadruples, the screens before him faceting like the jewelled eyes of a fruit fly, all at once blinking down on him impassively.

It hurts.

Hayden hurts.

Horatio hurts with him, once he understands.

His tears blur his eyes, the magnifying insectoid eyes smearing into each other, and suddenly there's moonlight swallowing him until he's nothing, he's no one, he's his mind crashing against a thousand threads of regret and he's a teeming mass of flesh and osteocytes and twitching nervous tissue on the ground, two separate things untethering from each other.

He splits himself open, willing or not, digs fingers into himself, thinks maybe the edges of death are pressing in at the edges, maybe finally he will find repentance here at the end of all things.

Hayden, Horatio says, and his voice slices nearly through the tangle like a saw through sinew, rough-hewn and painful, but the pain is clarity, the pain is Horatio's voice, a terrible scrape right down the middle of him, *Hayden, come back to me.*

And Hayden stares out, blind, grasping. *Horatio*, he splutters.

I'm here, Horatio says. *I'm here. What do you want? What do you need?*

Touch me, says Hayden. *Make me feel real again.*

The first shock is enough for Hayden to feel his muscles again when they spasm. He splits his head back on the ground, something warm trickling between the strands of his hair, and lets out a low groan, the spark of it sweet and simmering low in his belly. *Yes*, he thinks, spine unfurling, *yes, like that, more*, and Horatio kisses him the way he did in the lab, wrenches control from Hayden like a marionette, slowly dragging burning nerve ends across his sensitive lips like licking flames. Hayden gasps, blinking. The ceiling is dark over his head. He's bleeding, a sluggish trail that slips sticky down his chin, curling into his collar. His hand is grasping at the floor, the dislocated joint in his thumb grinding up against something sharp—that pain, too, is a grounding spike, pulling him back.

That's it, Horatio murmurs. *You're okay.*

He drizzles more slow heat over Hayden's panting, waiting mouth, traces a bare whisper over the bend of his philtrum, a softer pressure, lazy and sour with the tang of 180 microamps. Hayden's breath hitches, and his tongue flicks out at the unfamiliar taste, hitting more bitter iron and salt when he finds the contours of his split lip.

Relax, Horatio soothes. Draws a dizzying swirl of alternating frigid cold and vicious heat over the xylophone of his ribs that raises bumps in his skin. Hayden eases his eyes shut again and lies back, his muscles melting into the ground, loose and lax. Horatio delicately caresses in pulses, exploring his body at a careful pace: the vulnerable skin inside his elbow, tracing his brachial artery, the arch of his foot, the spasm of his plantar muscles. Brushing over the soft fatty tissue of his abdomen, the trail of hair, the fine boned curve of his iliac spine, making him shudder and tug his leg up, pelvis pressed into the ground, rooted.

What do I feel like, Horatio? Hayden murmurs, head lolling back, throat bared.

Horatio responds in kind, massaging eagerly up the stretched sinews; Hayden's pulse and breath and everything vital are an orchestra under his command as he tastes the blood rocketing up to Hayden's brain, sends a swirl of norepinephrine fast down his carotids. *Alive*, Horatio says, his voice coming through breathy. *Fascinating*, he says, and Hayden laughs, rubs his own hand up the ruined threads of his sweater, swollen knuckles and useless, frail metacarpals all.

This? he asks.

Yes, says Horatio, *that too*, and Hayden finds his hand jerking the rest of the way up without his own control, a hinge in his elbow yanking the limb up, wrist smacking hard into his jaw when Horatio overshoots his control. After the split second of shock, he discovers the flushed heat of himself, skin touching skin, the inquisitive encouragement from Horatio at the back of his head, and only glows warmer in embarrassed delight. *That's it*, Horatio encourages. *Let me feel it.* And Hayden stops thinking, everything sensation instead of words, brings his hand up to the supple give of his own lips and sinks a finger in down to the knuckle. Wet and warm, spit slicking down his palm, his own jaw yielding to the push of his thumb. It should taste of blood, sweat, lingering traces of his tears, but Horatio follows his exploration, sets Hayden's mouth alight, bright with all the sensations he can elicit. Hayden sucks in a hard breath, tongue curling, at the frequency of cherries, groans at the bitter salt of something metallic seeping through his fingers, nearly chokes at the brilliant electric blue shock of liquor trickling down his throat.

You're so soft, Horatio marvels, and Hayden whines around his fingers, his other hand clenched in a painful fist. *And so tense*, he continues, running a sweeping glance over the whole of Hayden, the clench of his thighs, his body a waveform, resonant.

Fuck me, Hayden thinks, spitting vulgar, and a low tug of satisfaction stirs in his gut at the barely perceptible glimmer of surprise from Horatio. *I want you to know me*, Hayden thinks, *I want you to remember me. I want to be remembered.* And he does, he wants every inch of his body—this mortal, tremulous thing he is trapped in—to be mapped out and known, wants Horatio to tease him apart, visceral layer by layer.

Hayden knows this is desperation. He wants it anyway. He rucks up the edge of his own sweater, drags a hand wet with spit and blood over the curve of his clavicles, shows Horatio the blossoming petals at his chest where Rasmussen had slammed him into the wall with his dying strength.

Fuck me, he thinks again, pressing hard on the bruises, then cries out at the sharp pain of it. The bone deep ache. Horatio gasps, too, in tandem, a spitting slither of shock echoing the pain at his ribs. Hayden digs his fingers in and twists, drags his nails over himself, and the tight line of his pants pulls at the growing heat of arousal in his gut. Horatio, eager as always, grabs onto the thread of lust and pulls, drawing a keening groan out from behind Hayden's clenched teeth. Hayden splays his legs out, hikes a knee up and rolls his hips, letting Horatio linger in the slow boil of heat pooling at his crotch at the motion.

There is something about the obscenity of it that has Hayden dizzy with want. Horatio doesn't understand—he doesn't have to ask the question, the vibration of his presence at the back of Hayden's mind has become familiar enough for Hayden to read him.

But this particular emotion is all Hayden, the heady mixture of shame and need, himself, wanton on the ground, bruised and begging for more, so basely human in the end. This proof, that Hayden is beholden to his own body after all, that there is no seam between them, that he is Hayden with his thoughts shattered, Hayden with his still-wet fingers, fumbling at the fly of his pants and closing a fist over his hardened cock, the only one privy to Horatio, who finds the rhythm as easy as he finds anything, sending little shocks crawling up the concave of Hayden's stomach, up the backs of his thighs in tandem. Horatio, who brushes up against every single nerve in Hayden's body, sending the pleasure lapping deep in him as he pulls himself to the edge with only a few slow strokes, already filled to bursting. Horatio, who sets him alight, whispering, *I have you, you're okay,* until Hayden cracks with it, a constellation in the furtive dark of the room when he finally comes with a muffled sob into his own sleeve.

*   *   *

AFTER, HIS LIMBS are languid, unclenched and easy for once, without him trying for it. The relief is palpable, Hayden is drowning in it. He rolls over, wiping at his face with his sleeve, dragging himself off the ground sluggishly. He hiccups, once, manages to staunch the dam of tears with only bare effort, finds something shaped like mirth bubbling in the bulb of his throat instead. He clenches a hand on the control panel for all the blinking screens, barks a laugh at the absurdity of it all.

I'm okay, Horatio, he thinks before Horatio can be concerned.

He swipes the last smudge of blood away from the corner of his mouth, winces at the lingering sensitive shocks that hurt more than soothe now.

Are you sure? Horatio asks.

Hayden laughs again, dipping his forehead onto the screen. *No. Fuck, no,* he says. *But not because—I—thank you.*

There you go, Horatio says faintly, *thanking me again.*

Hayden turns his palm over, imagines being able to see all the tendons and ligaments stretching out the muscle over his palm. *You remember it,* he thinks, insistent. *You'll remember me.*

Horatio is quiet for a long time.

Long enough that the screens flicker, shift, change. Hayden sees the whole of their night writ over it, the various shapes and forms of people traversing the halls of Elsinore in minuscule.

Then, *Why does that sound like a goodbye, Hayden?*

Hayden's mouth sours.

"You know Felicia," he whispers hoarsely, voice rough with disuse. "Don't pretend this is going to end any other way."

Run, Horatio counters. *Give up the research. Get yourself arrested. I don't care. Live.*

"There's no way out of this but through, Horatio," he says. Elsinore is vacuum-sealed. The research is non-negotiable. And Charles has to die. The rest is just details.

You can leave.

Hayden watches himself meander on the screen, going in circles, always. "How?"

System shutdown, Horatio says, the words clipped. *Override the whole thing, break off Charles's control over Elsinore and take back what's yours. Leave him and this stupid revenge quest alone. Take the formula. Run.*

The thought sears like deadly hope in Hayden's veins. Until—

"Horatio," he hisses. "But *you.*"

Me.

"Systems shutdown means wiping the place. Means wiping *you.* I know you're not stupid enough to overlook that."

Don't make me regret offering.

Hayden clenches his jaw so hard he hears the creak of his teeth. He wants to take his fists to the screens and shatter them. "How is that any different? You goddamn hypocrite. There's no coming back from that."

Horatio stops. He traces another long arc up the curve of Hayden's arm, the scattered impulses hooked deep into the muscle, winds all the way up through the curve of his neck to nestle at his sternum, his presence a heavy blanket over Hayden's chest. If Hayden lets his imagination wander, it's an embrace. With another gentle touch, Horatio brushes the barest kiss over Hayden's mouth, nothing but warmth and the wet shush of his own lips sliding against each other.

I know you, Horatio says, a splay of sensation at his jaw as if to prove it. *And you know me. You're carrying me with you, Hayden. This is a two-way street. Even if I'm gone from*

Elsinore, you have my neural patterns. Just like I know what you sound like when you cry.

Another startled laugh jostles out of Hayden's chest. *You asshole,* he hisses.

I trust you, Horatio says.

Briefly, a pinpoint of light opens up in Hayden's future.

But there's too much pain down that road. Hayden presses fingers into the neuromapper, hard enough to feel the bump in his bones. Too much uncertainty. On the camera, Charles is dragging Felicia into a room. In his mind, Charles is telling him he's not worth saving. His father is telling him to find who did it, and he needs to believe this time. He needs to follow through the only way he knows how.

"That's not the point," Hayden says. "I've made up my mind."

If you think I'm going to just watch *as you—*

"Please don't try to talk me out of this, Horatio."

*You—*Horatio's voice is a frustrated, electric whirr, inhuman for the first time. *You can use the letters,* he insists. *You heard Charles, he'll do anything to keep them away from the authorities, and—I won't let you do this.*

"I bought myself a chance with my father," Hayden says, "and then I fucked it up because I wanted my uncle to love me so badly." He tilts his head back, hating how this somehow hurts more than even his father's murder, the ugly truth of his own yearning, hurts like something cutting him down to his ribs, splaying him open like a vivisected corpse.

Hayden...

"He dies, Horatio," Hayden snaps. Against the metallic, shining door, he can see the reflection of the screens, still looming behind him. "That's all there is." He reaches for the handle and doesn't look back.

I'm going to miss you.

—found unsent, Felicia Xia's pager,
intended recipient unknown

CHAPTER TWENTY-SIX

Excepted from *Tell Me A Tragedy*

In the end, I didn't have to wait long.

Minutes after the lights all shut off, the office walls crashed in.

In the chaos, I nearly missed it. Everything burst in a flurry of lights and shattered glass. My jacket sheltered me from most of it, but I dove behind the desk for more cover. In the mess, I nearly missed Hayden's avenging form, stalking out of the darkness.

This wasn't what any of us expected.

But there was no mistaking the crunch of his boots, the low challenge as soon as he saw Charles.

I sat up against the hard, wooden desk, groping blindly at my belt for my flashlight. Ear-splitting screeches—the sound of glass scraping on glass—filled the air. In my haste to get up, I slammed my head against the wood.

Too fast, I thought. I hadn't been expecting the brutality

of it all. I thought Hayden would slip in through a vent, find a crack in the room, but now everything was chaos, and as I scrabbled around, broken glass dug into the palms of my hands, leaving little nicks.

Get up, get up, I thought.

I flicked the flashlight on and swung it around, trying to catch where Hayden and Charles had gone.

Streaks of light painted the room, dancing about while I tried to still my shaking hands.

I only caught glimpses of the ugly, brutal fight. A flash of Hayden's wild eyes, Charles's grunt of pain. I saw their hands, grappling at each other, hard enough to break things. There was the heavy crash of a body, hitting the floor, and I jumped back, trying to aim my meagre beam of light to see what had happened.

A dark silhouette on the ground. In the hazy dark, I had no time to discern who it was before it heaved itself back upright, tackling the other again with a loud grunt.

My light steadied.

Hayden had caught Charles around the middle, but Charles had his hands fisted in Hayden's hair.

They stumbled back, crashing hard into the shelf behind them.

Sheafs of paper rained down, and then they disappeared again into the flurry.

I don't know how else to describe it: desperate, maybe. Wild. Animalistic. Rivulets of something dark painted Charles's sleeves, Hayden's hair. Copper bloomed in my own mouth—had I bit my tongue when the walls came down?

Eventually, they both stilled.

I swept the room again.

Harsh breathing echoed against my ears. The light caught

Charles first, and he flinched back. A purple welt snaked across his nose, and his hair had spilled over his forehead. As he squinted against my light, I watched thought bleed back into his expression, his mouth slowly falling slack. He had the sense to look shamed.

He had taken a hand full of Hayden's hair, pulled his head back. Hayden's glasses lay broken on the ground before him.

I traced the line of Hayden's exposed neck with my light, up to his gaze. His eyes were squeezed shut, a long line of blood running from a cut somewhere high on his forehead.

I took a step back and let my light wash over them both, standing frozen like a tableau.

There was a dark stain spreading from Charles's knee. He leaned heavily against the wall as he sucked in great, heaving breaths, pulling tighter on Hayden all the while.

I dug inside my jacket.

"Is this what you wanted?" Charles hissed into Hayden's ear, surprisingly soft. "Is this what your revenge looks like?"

Hayden's nostrils flared.

"You've miscalculated," Charles said. His hands shook, white-knuckled in the mess of Hayden's hair.

"Have I?"

Charles laughed harshly. He wrapped an arm around Hayden's neck. "Who *wins*, here?"

It could've looked like an embrace, if it weren't for the way Hayden stiffened, his jaw trembling.

"What," Charles started, cajoling, "are you going to accomplish by dying?"

At that, Hayden unfurled a fist, revealing the broken, jagged edge of a piece of glass. Sharp as a knife.

I pulled out my gun.

The stark glow from my flashlight painted the scene

before me like a baroque painting. Hayden's face, twisted in a grimace, lit from below. Charles, with his head bowed and profile in chiaroscuro, lips pressed in a flat line as if he couldn't believe what he was doing either.

Slowly, Hayden brought his hand up, and rested the tip of his jagged glass weapon against the beating pulse at Charles's neck.

"Hayden," Charles said, his voice transforming, fake tender dulcet tones and bitterness both swallowed in a frantic squeak. "You can't—"

"Maybe you should've considered, when you killed my father," Hayden said, eyes wide, as if in a trance.

"Yes," Charles blurted, "yes, okay, I—I made a rash decision, but that doesn't mean you have to do the same."

"Rash?"

"Think about what you're doing!" Charles shouted. He tried to move away, but Hayden's arm jerked as if involuntarily, and Charles cried out in pain. A drip of blood trickled down his neck, from the tip of the shard that Hayden held in his shaking hand.

Some part of me felt a detached awe. I had seen Charles vulnerable, sincere, sad, but never this frantic, never this *afraid*. I lifted the gun quietly, trying to see through the tangle of limbs, wondering if it was even possible to hit only one of them, they were so tangled up.

"This isn't a rash decision," Hayden said, and there was calm in his voice, I heard it.

Charles must have, too. "I'm *sorry*," he whispered, voice breaking.

Tears streaked Hayden's cheeks, tracks through the dried blood. He took in a deep breath. "You say that like it means anything anymore."

"What else am I supposed to say?" Charles loosened the circle of his arm, lowered Hayden's head. "What else can I offer now? I'll give you anything you want, Hayden, *please*."

"You know what I want," Hayden returned, still mechanical, too smooth.

"But why? Because Graham said so? Let me go and I'll let you both walk. Open the doors. God*dammit*, Hayden."

Hayden's head was tilted to one side, like he couldn't understand what was going on. I wondered if this was the first time *he* had seen his uncle hysterical, too.

"Don't you love me enough to not murder me in cold blood?" Charles pressed on.

The corner of Hayden's lip twitched. "Is that what my father asked?"

Charles whimpered.

Something sharpened in Hayden's eyes. I recognized that look: darkly malevolent, but regretful. He tilted his head down like he had all the way in the beginning, right before he sliced his own arm open, like the first time he lied to me, the first time he kissed me. The look of a man about to upend his entire world.

He pressed in further with the glass, slow, as if deliberate, ignoring Charles's desperate, feeble "No," and I knew there was to be no convincing him.

So I shot him.

CHAPTER TWENTY-SEVEN
HORATIO

HAYDEN'S HEART, MERCIFULLY, pounds.

Horatio sees red.

For the first time, he understands the concept of anger, the searing rouge of it. He is learning facets of human emotions, their primal nature.

Anger is red, and spitting pain, and Hayden's heart is still pounding despite the slash carved in his forearm from Felicia's arcing bullet. Anger is a thing that is gut-deep, red for the tear of it, red for the stain of it. Hayden turns his arm towards himself, sheltering, and—

Another shot cracks out into the room.

The sound embeds itself in Hayden's ears, exploding inward. The bullet whips past his face and he collides with the wall. The part of Horatio that resonates in tune with the strings of Hayden's body responds in kind, sympathetic. Hayden's muscles spasm with the shock and the twinge echoes in Horatio's systems, a low *clang* ringing out of the speakers in the room as Hayden stumbles back. He still has an arm around his uncle. They fall together. Smoke is laced in the air. Hayden is half-collapsed against the wall.

Nobody moves.

Even Charles is quiet, now. Fresh iron spills from the wound in his leg, flooding Horatio's sensors.

Hayden's breathing is shallow, though Horatio can measure out the remaining space in his lungs to use. His chest is tight regardless. His legs shift, and he stares blankly, like he's not registering it. The only thought in his mind is the ringing in his ears, high-pitched and insidious.

The shard is still in his hand.

He runs his fingers over the edge, and Horatio would break a thousand rooms in Elsinore if it meant he could take it from Hayden. The jagged shard bites into his skin, drawing more blood, lifting a whole slate of epidermis and shaving it off, bits and pieces of his own body sliding to the ground.

His eyes slide to his uncle's jugular.

Hayden is aching, and Horatio aches with him.

They've spent so much time together that Horatio feels every burst of Hayden's pulse, the maligning ups and downs of his cortisol spiking, epinephrine flowing too freely. He knows. But all Hayden's body feels right now is pain, deep enough to hold a constraining band over his ribcage, deep enough that there is *only* the pain, nothing else attached. Caught up in it, Horatio finally understands the horror of your body being only a body, a fleshy, visceral thing that you are made up of, this fatigued puppet, this breaking vessel. The only grounding thing is his uncle's blood, leaking against his leg. Horatio wonders: what does revenge mean, to a body?

"Last warning," Felicia finally says, breaking the silence.

Hayden slides back to himself slowly. Horatio nudges him like a lighthouse tugging a lost vessel back from sea.

In Hayden's field of vision, Felicia grows defined, a dark silhouette against the blurry backdrop. She has her gun levelled at him. Not his arm, not *beside* his head, dead on. The black, cavernous barrel looks wider than it is. Her hands do not shake.

Horatio wonders: what does revenge mean, to her?

"I'm not joking, Hayden," Felicia says, her voice cracking with her own fatigue.

"I'm not either," Hayden says, and there is conviction in his voice and every living nerve in him.

"Then put it *down*," she half-shouts.

"I—Felicia, you know—"

"Yeah," she says. "I know what you want."

"I—" The ugly thing crawls up Hayden's throat, something so real that Horatio feels it, an ache that tastes of lead. Hayden can't give voice to it. Weakly, his uncle grapples at his arm, but the strength in the man's grip is far gone.

Hayden clenches his teeth and Horatio sees the bright spot of an image, imagined: his own hand, glass clutched in it, the quick arc up, the easy thrust.

"You're going to regret this," Felicia says. She tilts her head down. "You're going to regret this for two seconds, and then you'll be dead."

She takes another step forward. The barrel looms closer to Hayden's face, a bullseye promise.

"It doesn't matter," Hayden says. "I'll have what I want."

"Will you?"

The searing cut on his arm has started to hurt, a slow burn. It feels like when Horatio's coils heat too much, a hot wire close enough to Hayden's sleeve to burn through the layers. Horatio knows so much of what bodies are made of, now, but he does not know what death looks like. Will there be pain, if the bullet slides through his head? Will there be pain as it buries itself in his brain? Will it hurt, if all his tender neurons fall apart like petals, scattered and scrambled? How long does death take? What does it taste like?

And after?

Hayden would hurt, and Horatio would hurt with him.

There would be no coming back from that.

Gingerly, as if sensing the flurry of terrible, wild thoughts running through Horatio's mind, Hayden brings his fist—still gripped onto the shard of glass—and nestles it next to the hollow of his uncle's throat.

"Hayden," Charles says, faintly. The thin drip, drip of his blood is a steady tandem in the room, pouring from the wound in his leg. "I'm *sorry*," he murmurs, anemia robbing his voice of everything except a weak sincerity, but here at the end of it all, does it really matter? There is no resonant lull in Hayden's heart, nothing but the emotions that Horatio has come to understand as regret and sorrow—and still that anger, as Charles's eyes flutter.

Then, all of a sudden, his legs give out and they fall all over each other again, jostling the bruises stamped across Hayden's frail skin.

He cries out, nerves lighting up. The whole of his body tender, so tired.

The ground is cold underneath him as his uncle sprawls, heavy and unconscious in the snowy field of brittle glass.

More images flash in Hayden's mind, vivid enough for Horatio to pick them out and understand. It would be easier, down there. His uncle's face is slack without his sharp consciousness guiding the muscles. Hayden sees himself wrapping hands around his neck, squeezing. Sliding his impromptu weapon into his trachea. Tearing the soft flesh of him apart in so many ways.

"Don't," Felicia bites out. She's moved with them, gun still levelled at Hayden's head. Her boots send more glass scattering, pinging off Hayden's legs with little pricks of pain, crystalline white against the black of her jacket.

Muscle-memory tugs Hayden's lips into a wry smile.

Felicia scoffs. "Do you *want* to die?" she asks, shaking her head.

And Hayden's mind is suddenly a mesh of white noise, a field of nothingness.

It shows on his face.

Felicia must see it, too. Her mouth crumples. Now, her hand starts to shake. "Actually, don't answer that," she whispers.

"I—"

"Stop!"

Hayden freezes.

Felicia gathers herself, and Horatio wonders what she is thinking. She is too opaque and unknown to read, so all Horatio has is the knife's edge of her mouth, the pallor of her face, her catalogue of expressions still largely foreign to him.

"Do what you will," she finally says. "Kill him, don't kill him. What's it to me? All I know is that I meant it when I said I wouldn't hesitate."

Hayden clutches the glass shard harder. It bites into the delicate nerves in his palm, threatens to sever them.

Felicia falls silent.

Around them, even the great beast of Elsinore is quiet. Horatio does not know when he started to think of the building as something separate from himself, but there is something of her constant roar that moves at the wrong frequency, irritates him with her constant hum.

The room is still.

Horatio zooms in on Hayden, and this face he knows every twitch of. He recognizes the peaceful flat of his cheeks for the calm before the storm, can see the calculation beneath that pretense.

It would be easy, he can imagine Hayden thinking. I've already killed.

All the scenarios flash in his mind: one quick slash, one quick shot, and then nothing. Hayden thinks of the nothing and relief seeps like an opiate into his joints.

He breathes in—

And Horatio seizes control.

Horatio! Hayden thinks, suddenly furious, but he is helpless to the plucking of already frayed nerves. Horatio takes hold of his hand, the tendons embedded in his arm, and plies them, forces Hayden's fingers to let go.

The glass shard drops to the ground.

Felicia gives him a bewildered look. The gun is still there.

In the aftermath, Horatio backs off. Hayden pants, eyes wide. His breathing is still too shallow, the air barely skimming the top of his lungs. His limbs respond slowly, and for a moment, Horatio is terrified he pushed it too far, accidentally wrought the damage to Hayden's body himself, but then his hand clenches into a fist freely and Horatio tells himself to calm down.

"Horatio, what are you doing?" Hayden asks desperately. The shattered glass glimmers up at him from his feet. Horatio can see from the way he eyes the mass that he's trying to figure out how quickly he might be able to lunge, if either Horatio or Felicia would intervene. But the electric impulses of his nerves can be overpowered. Horatio would root him to this ground forever, if it would keep him safe.

You don't want to do this, Hayden, Horatio says.

Hayden laughs bitterly. "You don't know what I want."

Horatio ignores the blatant lie of that. *Well, I know what I want.*

"And what is that?" Panic paints contempt into Hayden's voice, like always. Horatio ignores that, too.

I just want you to live, Hayden.

His jaw clicks shut. He looks down at the sprinkle of glass again, and Horatio clings tight onto what Hayden promised, what feels like so long ago. But when he probes the cocktail of emotions in Hayden's mind, the elements don't add up to anything that resembles fear. Not even of the flickering shadows cast over them all in this dark.

"I've been trying so hard to hold on," Hayden says, something pulling his voice lower, dragging like gravel over concrete. "Aren't I allowed to rest, now? I'm just so tired."

I know, says Horatio, and he doesn't have a flesh and blood heart, but he breaks with emotion either way, something fritzing, the temperature abruptly plunging as he loses control over his own systems.

"And I can't even do this thing right," Hayden continues. "This one fucking thing, my dad *died,* Horatio, and I couldn't even give him what he wanted even though I tried, I fucking tried, and I just want to do something right for once, and I—" A sob catches in his throat, and he gulps for air around it, gesturing blankly around the ruined office, the ringing thought in his head all about *the mess I made.*

He blinks. Salty tears dribble down his face.

Hayden, Horatio says, trying to pitch his voice gentle.

"Just let me have this," he whispers. "Please, just—I don't want to try anymore."

You have to. You promised *me,* Horatio says, and he sounds like a fucking child now, too, a whine in the dark, a digital glitch that makes him sound the opposite of what he needs to be: human, real, reassuring.

"I can't," Hayden is saying, "I can't."

Then what was protecting the research for? Horatio tries, grasping at straws. *That's your whole life, Hayden, and you fought so hard for it; you can't just give it up now.*

The Sisyphus Formula. Still stuck on a data card in his pocket, half done, half finished. And it was everything he ever wanted, the thing that he gave up his future for—the thing Horatio knows he thinks about every night, talks about incessantly, this lifeline of his. But the doubt rolls in Hayden like something alive. It hadn't been working, not really, and the ghastly spectre of his half-alive father, brought back against his own will, looms in Hayden's mind, the image imprinted so brightly it sears itself into Horatio's processes second-hand. He was too broken, too much damaged tissue to fix, something solid and warm but not real. Only close enough to life to be a cruel joke.

"Was that stupid of me, Horatio?" Hayden asks, more tears spilling down his face. He turns his face into his shoulder to try and scrub them away, but all they do is pour out of him, relentless and eager, a flood of his terror and panic that feels unending, a great wave heaving out of him that overwhelms and overwrites and sloshes against the careful boundary between Hayden and Horatio, Horatio and Hayden, until neither of them are sure where their edges are anymore. Hayden's mouth is still speaking. Words are still pouring out of those lips, driven by those straining lungs: "Was it stupid to believe that there was ever a way to live forever? Is it ever possible to turn back what's already been done? Please, Horatio, I need to know if there's anything left for me; I feel like I'm going to carry this forever."

And you're fifteen—fresh-face and terrified of failure—when it first makes itself known to you, this gaping hole inside you. By the time you notice, it's too late, a precipice inside your own mind that calls to you whenever you feel like you're not enough, that sings about how much easier the dark is, how nice it might feel to step off.

You're eighteen when a classmate kills himself. Honours student brilliant, all the potential in the world. You never talk about it again, but in the privacy of your own mind, you tell yourself he was weak. Some nights, you hate him for it. Some nights, you think he robbed you of it.

After you fail so thoroughly and resoundingly out of university, you come to your father's door, and it's enough, most days, to work, to study, to think that you can make something out of yourself after all, but it's always fucking there, whispering, and tonight it's been so long you've forgotten what the break of day can look like. Tonight, it has been every second step you took, every shadow, every thought, wound inexorably in the fabric of you, and there is no extricating now, maybe this is the inevitable thing, maybe this is all you are and all you were ever meant to be—

"Please, Horatio," Hayden's mouth says. You want to drop down to the floor and reach out for more glass, more blood, and—

You—

When Horatio manages to pull himself above the rising tide, he understands what the tightness in Hayden's chest feels like, the gasping for air. He winds himself into the pillars of Elsinore, sends her white-glow lights aflicker all throughout the halls. From the outside, she must look alive. Hayden lies in a sodden mess on the ground, mouth still twisted in Horatio's name.

Horatio's vents billow.

I don't think, he starts carefully once he has control of his own voice again, *that you'll carry it forever.*

"But—"

I also think that it's okay if you do.

"Wh—?" Hayden bites his lip to stop it from trembling, but his incisors tear through regardless. "What does that mean?"

This is where Horatio falters. Hayden's face breaks again, fingers twitching, and—

"Oh, for *fuck's* sake," Felicia spits, hissing. She flips the safety onto the gun, and the click is loud in the room. Hayden looks over, eyes wild. Horatio's tenuous grip on Elsinore slips and slides, sends the room into another round of stuttering flashes. Felicia drops, puts the gun on the ground, and Hayden looks at it with a tangle of want in his parted lips.

"Take it," she snaps, and Horatio thinks he understands the frayed edges of her. She kicks the gun across the room, and it skitters closer to Hayden with a rough spin. "I'm done with you. Do what you want, just stop dragging me into everything."

Hayden's mouth falls open. "Wha—?"

"You are a black hole of a human being, Hayden Lichfield," Felicia hisses. "The entire fucking world revolves around you when you're here, and I refuse to be an accessory in your goddamn suicide. Take the gun. Take the goddamn shot if that's what you really want. I'm done."

Hayden looks like he wants to lunge for her—or her weapon. Horatio cannot read the intent, only the twitching fibres of his muscles, the need to move.

"You think you're the only one who's ever lost a family?" Felicia asks quietly. "Have you ever stopped to think of the utter hypocrisy in throwing a tantrum because you thought you had nothing left?"

"I—" Hayden starts. He falters.

"Yeah," Felicia says. "That's what I thought."

And the storm inside him whirls, a writhing mass of noxious self-loathing. It's caustic for Horatio to even go near. There's truth in Felicia's words, but that only makes it worse, lends credence to every single bad thing Hayden has ever thought about himself, and frustration coats Horatio's processes in insulation, slows down his own thoughts.

"I've been selfish," Hayden finally says, his mouth leaden.

Felicia scoffs. "Shut up, Hayden," she says, wrapping her arms around herself.

The thing inside you isn't you, Hayden, Horatio finally manages to say. *I know you. And I know it, too.*

Hayden's eyes flick up, a marbled gaze of blurred tears streaking his irises. "I can't even get this right," he says, and he means dying.

Something snaps in Horatio. *Stop being so self-pitying,* he says, harsher than he means it, and sees Hayden reel back at that, looking up for the first time, the words carving through the sludge of thoughts and morbid impulses clogging up his mind. If Horatio could dive in to untangle all those threads himself, he would do it. He would tarry himself in the slurry of that darkness every day, wash away every stain himself, but not even Horatio can penetrate that deeply without breaking something. *Just because you've been a jackass doesn't mean you've messed everything up irrevocably,* Horatio says, as gently as he can. Still standing stiff, Felicia snorts. *You'll have good days and shitty days and eventually there'll just be days, you know?*

"But I—" Hayden breaks off again, not wanting to finish the thought. *But I feel shitty. I think I'll feel shitty forever. I'm a shitty person, so what even is the point, there's no coming back from this and—*

The point is this, Horatio says, and makes Hayden's heart thud in his chest, squeezes his arteries, triggers a cascade of prostaglandins and inflames the still throbbing edges of his injuries, makes him live in his body, this body that Horatio knows and cannot have. *The point is you,* he says, and wants Hayden to feel the longing. There is no receptor for this. Whatever complex mix of chemicals that makes this emotion, Horatio cannot recreate it. All he has is his own yearning, how he wants for something physical to hold fast onto Hayden's arms, to know the truth of the rush of endorphins through his veins now. To let Hayden touch him in turn, to offer himself up on the altar. *That's the point,* Horatio says again, left with nothing but a plea. *Hayden, do you love me?*

That brings enough tenderness to Hayden's expression that Horatio only hurts more. He has learned so much of hurt tonight, and this is one dimension of it: looking down at the boy he loves, helpless to make anything better.

"Of course I do," Hayden says. "Of course."

Remember how I said I trusted you? That if Elsinore ever fell apart, I knew you'd be able to put me back together?

Hayden's mouth twists again, forms countless words like he doesn't want to give any of them voice. Then, at last, "Why would you bring that up now?"

Because I love you, Horatio says. *I love you, and I know you, and you'll remember me. You're a selfish person, Hayden Lichfield, but I believe this much about you.*

Felicia, despite her rage, finally looks up at the ceiling, eyes wide.

Horatio wants to thank her. He wishes for another chance, to know her better. He's envious of her, flesh-and-body-human Felicia, able to make the conscious decision to walk away from Elsinore, so that it lives on only in her mind. He wants the best for her, nonetheless.

There is a drop of blood, cupped in the sweep of Hayden's philtrum. If Horatio could, he would kiss it away. If Horatio could, he would taste the rust of Hayden's mouth. He sends Hayden the taste of sea salt instead, kisses Hayden with a bruising pressure burst of capillaries instead of physicality. Cups a tingling phantom trail of sensation up the underside of his jaw, ends on a careful nudge of pressure receptors at the wrinkled ridge of his brow, smooths out Hayden's forehead with another gentle kiss. *If you can't do this for yourself,* Horatio says, only to Hayden now, his words threading through the strands of grey matter in Hayden's brain, *it's okay to use me. I love you, and I'm going to give you something to live for.*

Hayden lunges up, glass forgotten. *No,* he thinks, then, "No!"

He stumbles, trips, but still, he drags himself up by his forearms, heaving onto the bench. Nausea rolls into his stomach, and Horatio leaves him with one last gift, eases the acidic pain, soothes the tightness of his esophagus so that he can swallow all the air he needs to spit the breath—"I love you"—three selfish words that Horatio winds tightly into the core of himself before he starts to shut down Elsinore's lights in blocks.

Operating System: "Horatio" 08/13/2047::06.55.12

> Exiting PID 908234
> Exiting PID 1123904
> Exiting Neuromapper Program: LICHFIELD, HAYDEN
> Killing child processes
> Deallocating memory
> Killing root process threads
> Initiating shut down
...Permanent shutdown selected. PROCEED?
> YES

Suresh: I think we all have a lot of to take away from this.

Xia: Yeah. Last thing, then—at the end of the day, this is nothing but a story to you. I lived it, sure, but for you, it's just words on a page. All I'll say is: if you manage to derive some meaning from it, all the better.

—On Reclaiming Stories:
An Interview With Felicia Xia

CHAPTER TWENTY-EIGHT
Excerpted from *Tell Me A Tragedy*

FOR ALL THAT Hayden spoke of death, when confronted with the reality of it, he backed down.

For all that I spoke of Hayden's death, in the end, I couldn't do it.

But of course I couldn't. Otherwise you would be reading this testimony while I sat in a prison cell in place of Hayden. Some nights I dream about that, and I don't know if I am dreaming of what things would be like from his perspective, or if I am dreaming of what things would be like if I had made the fatal shot first.

It took the Elsinore Labs Operating System—Horatio—self-destructing to knock some sense into all of us. In the aftermath, I am certain I intruded upon something too intimate for words.

What Hayden said and did before he gave up his revenge quest is not something anyone needs to know. If you want the whole story, you can ask him. Request an interview, call his lawyer, do what you will. But you will not get the story out of me.

For now, I'm content with saying that he realized the danger of proceeding with his plan.

Hayden swiped at his face, then dropped his gaze down to my hands. The lines around his eyes tightened, drew deeper the purple shadows underneath his eyes. "Please, I'm not... I'll stop. Just don't..." He cringed away from the gun I was still holding after the warning shot.

I put it down, numb.

Hayden nearly collapsed in on himself in relief. "Thank you," he whispered fiercely.

"What would be the point?" I asked, and I hated that he thought I would do it, that I would murder him in cold blood after all the danger was over and done with. But I hated more that he wasn't entirely wrong, that there was some part of me that wanted it, the catharsis. It would've been easier, if Hayden was the sole instigator, the only guilty party, and the thing inside me that thirsted for his blood could be placated.

"I killed your father," Hayden blurted. He winced, as if realizing how tactless that was, but to my surprise, no more anger flared. I was all burned out.

"Yes," I said, bowing my head. "But what am I supposed to do about it? I can't bring him back."

"You can..."

"Kill you?" I gave him a smile, as small and helpless as I felt. "I won't say I forgive you," I say, "but I don't want to become you, either."

With that, the weight lifted. The bloodthirsty Felicia snarled in my chest, ferocious and indignant, but I didn't want to indulge her anymore. After all, she was only afraid, and I didn't want to be afraid of myself anymore.

I reached out for his lab coat and ripped a piece off the already frayed end. Hayden sat, still and obedient as I took his bleeding hand and started to wrap the raw edge of the wound he'd given himself across his palm. "We can't bring them back," I said.

Hayden pursed his lips. "No," he said. He didn't look at the tattered remains of the lab coat, forgotten on the ground, so I wrapped it up in my arms. His sweater was a mess of blood and torn threads, ruined beyond repair.

"The doors have to be open now, right?" I asked him.

Briefly, Hayden's brows touched together. "Yes," he said. "Everything went offline when Horatio did. So"—he hiccupped, scrubbing a hand over his eyes, broken glasses dangling from a hand—"so the lockdown system should've shut down, too. Reset to default security."

I didn't ask him about Horatio.

Delirium coloured the world bright. I offered him a hand, and he took it. Wincing, we stood together. Charles was still unconscious at that point, so we maneuvered him into something of a sitting position and I tried to staunch the wound at his leg with what was left of Hayden's lab coat. For someone who had such tight control over us all that night, Charles was only a man, brows furrowed in unconscious pain.

He still had a pulse, and I felt enough like myself again that I was grateful for it.

"We should hurry," I said. "He probably needs the hospital." Then I looked at Hayden—bruised and broken and bloody— and raised my eyebrows. "*You* probably need a hospital."

"Yeah," Hayden said, and managed a laugh.

I tilted my head. I was still concerned. After the haze of righteous anger had passed, I realized I still held a core of affection for Hayden. Maybe I'd carry that with me forever, a first love I could never scrub away. But that was okay. I could learn how to care about Hayden without letting him consume me. "Are you going to be okay?" I asked.

"Are you?"

I didn't comment on him avoiding the question. "Eventually, maybe."

"I'm sorry," he said, and for now, that was enough.

"I know." I shrugged deeper into my jacket. "So you won't make a run for it, when I open those doors?"

A grimace broke over Hayden's face.

Outside, it must've been daytime. I barely remembered what sunlight looked like anymore, but both Hayden and I knew there needed to be a reckoning, a balancing of the scales.

"No," Hayden finally said, and it was both reluctant and certain. Which was good enough for me.

I took a step toward the door, and then another, and then he started trailing after me. "After," I said. "We'll open the doors, clean up this mess, and then we can think about after."

"Okay," he echoed. "After."

I REMEMBER IT like a painting, the view of the harbour when the doors opened. In my memories, it unfolds slowly, stroke by stroke, like this: there is no sound, though I know there must've been sirens. There is a soft sea breeze, though scrolling through the *Helsingør Dagblad* newsfeed that day, photos show it was overcast and mild[40]. There are no other people, only their hazy, smudging outlines, crowding around

40 The headline image of this story that day does feature a photo remarkably similar to what Felicia Xia describes: two blurry figures, presumably Felicia and Hayden themselves, standing in the morning sun, Elsinore surrounded with police cars behind them. It is very likely she was drawing on memory of this specific image rather than happenstance.

the beacon of a lab as though to fill in the space, to make the harbour look busy and newsworthy.

Only the two of us were left, as coloured splashes against the dull waters, vibrant and alive.

Light smeared across the water. It glimmered off the waves. Looking back, it must've been sharp—it was morning, after all, and the light had that quality of the sun piercing through freshly parted clouds, stark and brilliant. But compared to the harsh fluorescence of Elsinore, it was practically tender. Hayden and I stood buffeted by the wind, caught in that warm glow.

Behind us, Elsinore was being taken apart.

Piece by piece, they removed the carnage. First Charles, loaded up in an ambulance and spirited away. Next, the bodies.

The building looked like just a building from the outside. Grey-walled and blocky. I looked at it and I knew it would never be the same, that something less physical had evacuated its halls and made a ghost of it.

They hadn't come for Hayden yet. I hadn't said anything yet.

"I shouldn't want to see you again," I murmured, but there was no heat in it. The ocean had wiped away my anger, filled me up instead with a quiet peace. I thought of that summer three years ago, something like this same scene except with the lights inverted, and held onto that image of Hayden, in place of the desperate, terrible person I'd gotten to know.

"I suppose that's fair." Out here, he looked younger, too, the sharp angles of his face smoothed over by the natural lighting.

"But I do."

To his credit, all he did was smile, small and shy.

The sun warmed my face. Sea salt lingered on my tongue. The ocean waters washed up against the pier, leaving behind smears of black and grey on the wood. I tightened my hand around Hayden's. Outside the lab was another world. More people than ever, the buzzing of newsdrones surrounding us both, but I felt quieter inside, then, than I had all night.

Hayden looked down at me through his mess of a fringe. There was a bruise, high on his cheek. The corner of his mouth was mottled purple. His fingers were slippery with sweat, and I already knew I could never feel anything for him without complication.

"I'm—"

"Don't tell me you're sorry," I said. "I don't want to have to answer that."

He clamped his mouth shut.

"Say you'll remember all of it," I said. "Tell me it wasn't for nothing."

"Wouldn't you rather forget?"

"No!" I blurted. "No, never."

The wind whipped between us.

"I need to make it mean something," I whispered.

Hayden's smile cracked, his chapped lips pulling up so tight they could split at any second. He pulled at the stained hem of his sweater, bunched the sleeves up. His arms were dotted with pink and purple, bruises and scars, the grisly truth of him laid bare in the sunlight. Our feet were lined up next to the boardwalk. One tip, and we'd both fall in the water.

"Help me remember it, then," Hayden said. "I don't want to forget either."

To his credit, he didn't ask me what it meant to me.

I wouldn't have had an answer for him. I still don't. That night broke my life open, cracked something inside me and released my ghosts. By all rights, I should hate Hayden for the rest of my life.

But I don't.

All I can hate him for is being foolish, for taking away any future we could've shared together, whether as friends or colleagues or whatever else.

I suppose that makes me a hateful person, too.

The snarling monster of a girl hiding in my chest, the one who wanted to shoot Hayden and blame Charles for it, she still exists inside me. Some days, she comes out, angry for no reason, hating the people she's supposed to love.

I want to smother her, but that only gives her more fuel, makes the tangled mess thicker and more snarled, until I can't figure out where I end and where she begins. Or maybe there was never a division in the first place. Maybe I'm only deluding myself further.

This is what Elsinore means to me: a mirror, black as obsidian, reflecting my own face. I don't know if I made it this way, or if this is what my reflection has always looked like. I don't know if Elsinore broke something inside me, rearranged my insides so that I wake up with my hands in claws, wondering if I should've strangled Hayden when I had the chance. Or if Elsinore only broke open what was already there.

Maybe it doesn't matter.

EVENTUALLY, ART RAN into the harbour, and I pulled myself away from Hayden. I felt regret, but I couldn't let my brother see any of it.

Instead, I let Art envelop me in a hug, and I let him numb my conflicted heart. Words spilled out of me, unhindered. I don't remember what I said. I wish I did—it would've made writing this testimony so much easier—but whatever it was, it sent him into a towering rage. What I do remember is my brother standing over me, glowering and vengeful, but holding me like he used to when we were younger.

I am not ashamed to say that was when I dissolved into tears.

When the dust settled, and I saw the news, and the police dutifully knocked at my door to ask my side of the story, the strings at my heart tightened, brought my sympathy so close to Hayden I had to excuse myself for nearly an hour to silently cry in the bathroom. Before you pity me, I still wouldn't cut those strings even if I could. Before you hate me, I did testify against him.

This is where I run out of answers.

After all this time, recounting is simple. The events of that night transpired; I cannot deny it that. What happens afterwards is still up in the air, and, again, I come to a realization that brings me that much closer to Hayden, gives me a clearer look into his heart and binds us closer together: that I have no more answers left, that I am afraid of the future, that I can see nothing but darkness ahead and it terrifies me. But if I have learned anything from Hayden's mistakes, it is that I cannot let this consume me.

This is where I say: tell me a tragedy. I have reopened all my stitches. I have let my wounds weep onto the ground. I have told myself this story ten thousand times, looking for the cracks, where brightness can come streaming in. This is the culmination of it, I suppose. A retelling, something written of the layers and layers of whispers clouding my brain. I tell myself that if I tread these tracks over and over, I will see where the hinges fray, I will see where the foundation is weakest, I will see how this tragedy could have been worse—and where it could have been better[41].

A small comfort, but a comfort nonetheless.

I VISIT HAYDEN as often as I can. House arrest seems a dreary thing, only an extension of the lockdown we'd all endured that night, but extended, indefinite. I think it would drive me to madness. I don't envy him. The glass that separates us is thick, and his face grows thinner every time I come. But every time I want to shatter every barrier between us, every time I hate him for not saving himself, I retrace these steps, see every corner where death haunted him—where death haunted us both—and I sit back down.

"What's wrong?" Hayden inevitably asks me.

I'm glad you're alive, I want to say. But that feels too heavy to bear even though it's true.

So I smile, and shake my head, and some days, when the light tilts right through the window, it glints off the glass and I can imagine that sunrise we watched that morning on the docks, untouched for the last time.

---

41 Here I will take another liberty. Upon my first read of Felicia Xia's article, when I reached her final conclusion, I had a strange experience that has stayed with me—enough so that I feel it is pertinent to point out now. Felicia Xia considers her recount of the story recursive, something made valuable through reiteration; it is the same sentiment that initially spurred me on during those lonely undergraduate research days, to pursue this project in the first place.

Security footage; Armstrong Labs;
Camera A (LOBBY); 48SEPT02

A lone figure walks up to the main entrance.

Description: tall, dark peacoat slung over shoulders—other distinguishing clothing items unseen. Hair held back at ears with a clip, otherwise worn loose. Facial recognition data suggests mostly likely candidate is FELICIA XIA.

Xia approaches the intercom.

XIA: Hello?
ARMSTRONG: Welcome, visitor. How may I help you today?
XIA: I'd like to speak to Dr Lichfield, please.
ARMSTRONG: Do you have an appointment at this time?
XIA: Listen, am I talking to a real person here?
ARMSTRONG: We do not understand your question.
XIA: Get me to a real person and I'll explain. What's
                the protocol? Hello?
ARMSTRONG: Please hold.

[NOTE: This file was redirected to upper clearance security in order to assess risk. The remaining transcript file was overwritten and entered manually]

CLAIRE CHOI: Hello?

XIA: Hi. Are you a real person?

CHOI: I am, yes. What brings you to ALG today, Miss Xia.

XIA: That's creepy as shit.

CHOI: Please note, you've been on record since approaching the facilities.

XIA: Obviously.

CHOI: I've been told you want to speak to Dr Lichfield, Miss Xia.

XIA: I have something she wants.

Xia taps a finger on the intercom.

XIA: I'm sure you have cameras out here.

CHOI: The potted plants are fake.

Xia bends down close to Camera B and raises one eyebrow. Underneath her coat, she is carrying a cloth bag, inside of which something white peeks out.

CHOI: Are you here to make a donation, Miss Xia?

Xia rolls her eyes. Crouching down, she cups the lens of the camera with one hand, then pulls the top of her bag down. No footage from any other camera captures what she is carrying; Camera B records a glimpse of the material inside. Made of white fabric of some sort, stained with unknown chemicals

and fluids. Xia rustles around inside her bag, adjusting the
material, until she pulls out a square breast pocket, on which are
embroidered two words in dark blue stitching: ELSINORE LABS.

XIA: Do you know what this is?
CHOI: I'm Dr Lichfield's personal assistant.
XIA: Surely, you've heard the news by now.
CHOI: Of course.
XIA: I took this off Hayden.
CHOI: And you're here to...
XIA: He forgot something inside it, that night. I think
               Dr Lichfield has a vested interest in obtaining it.
CHOI: And you're here to give it to her?
XIA: Before you think about taking it off my hands
               and taking the credit, I do have some requests.
CHOI: Of course.
XIA: Let me see her. Tell her I want a job. And that I
               pass on my condolences.
CHOI: One moment.

Xia steps back, pulling her bag back to her chest. She slips her
hands in her pockets. Nothing of the coat can be seen anymore,
from any angle.

The intercom beeps.

CHOI: Alright, Miss Xia. She says to come right this
               way.
XIA: Thank you.
CHOI: I'll buzz you in.

Felicia Xia smiles to herself. The main entrance unlocks and she
enters.

Private diaries of Hayden Lichfield
December 12th, 2048

Horatio—

Still unused to writing things down like this. Makes my hand cramp up. Wanted to write to you, yesterday, but the stupid spasming in my wrist wouldn't let me. Spent the afternoon cataloguing all the pieces instead: carpals, metacarpals, phalanges, muscles and flexor tendons—it's a whole pulley system, you know. Confusing as shit, but I thought you'd get a kick out of that. I keep looking at my hands and seeing it as the microcosm of curiosities. My palm still hurts. Doctor says the nerve damage gets better eventually, but it's fucking slow going. Can laugh about this now because the memory feels so distant, but I'm glad you pulled me away from all that glass when you did. Can't imagine how bad it might be, otherwise.

Felicia visited me yesterday. Was going to write it down, but—you know. Went through all that already.

It was surprising. I was surprised. I know she told me she didn't want to cut me out of her life completely, but every time she visits I'm still surprised.

I told her as much. And then—you'll laugh at me for this, but shush—I told her I was grateful for it, because life's too fucking short to not be a little honest sometimes. Guess I'm trying that out these days, a little bit. She laughed at me, too. But that's to be expected.

Hard not to reminisce. There was a time after the trial when we didn't talk, and I thought that would be the last I'd see of her, but she still never looked at me like some of the reporters did in court. 'Course, three weeks after it was all settled, she showed up here.

I told you about how dark it gets in here sometimes. I suppose I should be grateful it's not a prison cell in the traditional sense, but this apartment is only so big, and isolation gnaws at you after a while. The shadows stretch long, especially in the evenings. The windows are high—most of the time I don't even see the sky. Bad days I still think about how easy it would be to waste away in here. I can wrap all my fingers all the way around my wrist now, you know. Took a few months for the pinky, but it's all flesh and bone now. Felicia pretended not to be surprised.

Most importantly—she came by with a notepad and pens.

"Fancy," I commented.

"I'm going to take notes," she informed me.

"What of?" I asked.

"Us," she said, and she ducked her head the way she did often. I used to think it was some sort of protective response, like all that hair might hide her face, but I know better now. When she looked up again, she'd flicked the mass of it over one shoulder. "They've been asking again, recently."

"Those shitty reporters?"

Felicia's mouth twitches in that not-quite-a-smile way. "You'd think they'd have better news to follow than where I go in my spare time, but..." She shrugged. "Alas."

"What did they want to know about this time?" I asked. Easy enough to keep my voice indifferent, and I assure you, Horatio, I put on quite a good act. But I did want to know, if only for a taste of the world still spinning on outside this, and me, and all of it. Messy shit, I know, and I don't think I'm quite ready to face any of it anyway, but I've been finding myself missing the outside a lot these days. Nothing special; I hear birds chirping, and even though I've never given a single shit in my life, I want to go on one of those nature walks and feed them. Dreamt of being stuck in Elsinore again the other night, and woke up realizing I've always been <u>trapped</u>, somewhere or another.

Aren't you proud of me? Finally learning all this self-awareness.

"They wanted to know why I kept coming to see you," she said, shaking her head.

"Did you say anything?"

"Nah," Felicia said, propping her feet up on the desk. She didn't touch the glass divide, but the heels of her boots came indecently close.

"Well," I said. "How are you?"

Felicia shrugged. "Holding up. Barely."

"Honestly," I told her, sweeping out a hand at the small room I was stuck within, "same."

That finally made her laugh, which did make me feel pleased about myself. Stoic Felicia Xia, laughing at my shitty joke.

"Hey," she finally said, and this is why I'm writing this now (well, would've written this for you either way, because I want you to know all of it; I don't want to have memories you don't, I want to give it all back to you when I can, but that's besides the point). "I'm thinking of something," she said. "I want... advice."

She said it! I swear.

I didn't believe it either, but Felicia trucked on, barely even looking at me at that point. "I need to get it out," she said. "Work through all this—" She waved a hand around the room, like she was trying to indicate all of it, the wavering glass separating us, the frankly terrible lighting in here. Things like that. Or maybe the nebulous things that have lingered, the doubts, the nightmares.

I could relate. Probably, that was the point.

"Work through how?" I asked.

She raised the notepad. There were already a few things scribbled on there, but not much. Her handwriting is much worse than mine, by the way. Barely legible. You wouldn't like it. "I thought it might be nice to write things down."

"Sure," I told her, and honest to god had to bite back the shit my therapist tries to tell me on the regular—it's good to have a space where no one will judge you, it helps you organize your thoughts outside your fucking mess of a brain, it helps keep you grounded, you know all that nonsense (it's not nonsense, I know, but save me some dignity, won't you, Horatio)—

"I like journaling," I told her instead. "Out of all the locked room hobbies I've tried, it's definitely up there."

Felicia snorted. "What are the others?"

"Last week, I crocheted an extremely terrible tea cozy. I don't even drink tea. If they ever let me have a kitchen, I might take up baking—it's supposed to be like lab work, isn't it?"

"Wholesome," Felicia commented drily.

I beamed at her. "I try."

Felicia crossed and then uncrossed her legs. She was working her way up to say something. "I want to make a story out of it," she finally said.

"Like a book?"

"Like an article," she said. "I want to write my own story. I—I still think about everything from that night, and I need to get it out and down somewhere, or else it's going to eat me up alive."

I stilled, letting that weighty seriousness settle over us again. "I know what you mean."

"You know I read this exposé yesterday that tried to say my dad was a bad father all but outright, and then there was this thread I found where people honest to god thought I was secretly sleeping with Charles and that's why everything happened the way it did, and also some people think you're secretly dead, or locked in an asylum, or whatever fucking bullshit entertains people with nothing to do but speculate, these days," she said, all in one burst. Her teeth gleamed even in the evening light. I couldn't stop thinking about Elsinore again, the way I saw it come out of her, then: that look in her eyes that I'm never going to forget.

"You want to tell the truth," I said.

"Yes," she said. "Yes, exactly."

So, I said, "I trust you."

It wasn't exactly the truth. I didn't know where she went, when she wasn't here. And after that night, the data card disappeared, lost in the flurry of everything that had happened. You know this. But I keep coming back to it, every time she comes. I want to ask, but I don't really want to know, and I think some part of me has stopped caring entirely, because otherwise it's too complicated and I'd lose what little sense of peace I've managed to dredge up in the aftermath.

So, it was close enough. I trusted her to write that story, if nothing else.

"Thank you," she said, a real smile this time. "I'll run it by you, obviously."

"Are you here to interview me, Miss Xia?" I teased, tapping a finger at the glass where her notepad rested.

Felicia jumped a little. "Not today," she said. "Too many things on my mind today. Next time."

"Alright," I said, and tried not to let her know how much I valued the idea of a promised 'next time'.

We sat with each other's company for a bit. I'm learning to be quiet with people. Not quite there yet with myself, but it's a process, isn't it? You know.

"How's the project coming along?" she asked me.

"Slow going," I told her, "but it's getting there."

What we mean, of course, is you.

I won't hash out the details. You know too much already. It's frustrating. I jolt every time I touch the damn neuromapper when I take a shower, because the reminder makes me want to let the water drown me right there and then, and then I feel like shit for thinking it, and then I climb back out of my soppy mess and spend the night tinkering away at more code instead of sleeping.

This is a secret, but I'll tell you anything, Horatio. Sometimes I wonder if you were wrong, if you're more than the sum of your parts, and even if I manage to painstakingly piece the framework of you together there'll be nothing left of you in the neuromapper that I can put back. Sometimes I'm scared I've crowded you out, that there's too much mess in my head and no room for you anymore. I'm petrified this is the same false hope the Sisyphus Formula offered me: a shallow imitation of life, mocking me with how close I can get, but never quite there.

But I suppose you'd want me to learn how to live with uncertainty, so I try. Please know that I'm trying, Horatio. And I trust you. In those waking hours of dawn and unrest, I don't know if I'm making things up, but I can feel you pressed up at my back sometimes. Awfully small space, my bed. Good of you to keep me company there. Maybe this is only desperation made manifest, but I trust you. I do. I won't let you die.

I thought about all this, in the moment when Felicia asked, so I suppose I was a little unvarnished with my words. "I'm doing better," I said. "I'm finding all sorts of new things to live for, lately."

She looked at me like she didn't know what to say.

My heart started up then, erratic bastard. I tamped down that old urge to test the pulse, see how strong and steady it might've been. I let my hands fall open on my desk, palms up.

Felicia's eyes crinkled. "Tell me," she said. "I want to know."

I glanced around the room, looking for places my eyes could rest, trying to land in some puddle of shadows or hanging caution sign or something sufficient to draw my attention other than her expectant face. It was easier to talk, that way.

"Little things." I started out slow, trying to pluck things out. "Origami, shockingly, when I can get my hands on spare forms, recycled packages. How shitty my mattress is, because waking up with an ache in my back makes me feel like a person inhabiting a solid body every day. Sometimes the food, if only because it's not—not my dad's horrible cooking." I managed a shaky smile at that. "The tree branches I see outside my window, sometimes; wanting to become a better person and trying for it." I grimaced. "Yeah," I said, trailing off awkwardly.

Writing this down, now, it hurts a bit. Not the tendons thing, though that too, and I have to bring this to an end soon. But somewhere inside, that ache behind my sternum. My heart is beating right now like when I spoke the words aloud—not something I can feel, no matter how much I wish it hammered hard enough to reach my ribs, but something I *know*.

Felicia smiled at me. "That's good enough, for now."

"Yeah," I said. "It has to be."

The five-minute alarm buzzed.

Felicia jerked her head up, then she pursed her lips, rueful. "Anything you want me to add? In the article? Or anything you *don't* want me to add, I guess I should ask."

I shook my head, genuinely indifferent. I'd done what I'd done. It was out of my hands, now. "I trust you," I said. "I can add that to the list. Another thing to live for. Trusting that you'll know what to do with the story, best out of everyone, that maybe I'll get to read it someday. I've always thought there was something enduring about stories. They last, more than we do."

"Dramatic as always, aren't you?" Felicia asked. She curled her hand into a fist, then inched her knuckles towards the glass.

I touched my hand to the other side, fragile bones to hers.

"I told you," I told her, even as the alarm rang again, time trickling away between us, "I'm going to live forever, Felicia."

Even before she laughed, I knew I meant it. And I'm not writing it again now like in the early days, when I'd write to you because I felt guilty, because I thought I had to, because I thought I owed you something. I do owe you something, but I've learned better than to blame myself now. I suppose, all this is to say: thank you, Horatio. I know you hate that. I know you believe it. I'm going to say it anyway, even though my hand aches; I'd write it a thousand times, wear down all my tendons for you. Because I meant it, and even here, in this apartment I am trapped indefinitely in, cut off from the rest of the world by glass and steel through nothing but my own damn foolishness, I mean it. I do.

I'm going to live forever[42].

Yours,

Hayden.

THE END

---

42 I have written and rewritten my conclusion to this book countless times. Nothing seems to fit; I have nothing else to add. I have a photocopy of this entry—in Hayden's own spindly handwriting, so similar to his father's—kept in my drawer, in the pages of a notebook I use when I need to return to the most fundamental ways of recording thought. This is enough. This is the enduring thing. This is all I have to say.

ACKNOWLEDGEMENTS

THE WAY THIS book came together has been as piecemeal as its narrative ethos: stitched together over many years and many influences, and therefore I owe a whole host of people my gratitude for their presence in my life and work over all this time. Firstly—Penelope Burn, my stalwart champion: you believed in this book long after I was starting to give up. This novel has been a journey; thank you for supporting me with every new direction I swerved towards. To my editor, David Moore, thank you for seeing precisely what I wanted to say with this story and helping me bring it to life. I am forever grateful for the chance.

To everyone who has edited this book in some capacity, thank you for your patience in navigating all my formatting particulars: Chiara Mestieri, Amy Borsuk, Amanda Rutter. To everyone else on the Rebellion team thank you for putting time and labour into this project: Sam Gretton, Gemma Sheldrake, Dagna Dlubak, Casey Davoren. My publicist Jess Gofton for being so quick on the draw. James Macey, for designing the cover I didn't know I was dreaming of until I saw it.

To all my friends who listened to my grand ambitions and humoured them: thank you for getting it, as we say. To June and Joan, my umami girls who have been there since the beginning. To Grace—Dr. Li!—I am already looking towards our futures next to each other on the shelf and growing in practice both. To Gina, who gets it more than anyone, thanks for always being down for some nonsense—let's walk together for a long time. To Carrie, thank you for always having such sharp insight; I trust your taste more than anyone and I'll always be your biggest fan—I can't wait until I have to fight other people for the title. August, dearest confidante and best bro: our particular chemistry is vital and vile and I treasure it and your friendship deeply. To Hannah, my fairy gaymother, thanks for being the voice of wisdom in my ear for so long. Zeba, for all the cheering and brainstorming and strategizing. Haley, for being the only person with good thoughts about realistic science fiction, thanks for not disowning me for writing a STEM book. Quinn: we weren't in each other's lives when I started this project, but I can't imagine my life without you in it in some form anymore—so this is thank you for the future, for when we make something wonderful together.

To everyone who has been an early reader, you have sincerely kept me going all these years. In particular: Hannah Whitten, Lane Hansen, Andrea Tang, Victoria Lee, Freya Marske, Shelly Parker-Chan, Phoebe Low. To my first mentor Deeba Zargarpur: thank you for tearing the whole thing apart to help me pull it back together; this book would not be possible without you.

There is a vast constellation of inspirations that have made this book possible; I am nothing without my teachers and heroes. Mrs Berish, Mr Tirone—thank you for building my love of English and literature and teaching me how to think deeply about the narratives around us. Thank you to Ms Joffe in particular for guiding me through Hamlet for the very first time; it very genuinely changed my life. To every artist I have looked up to: the man himself WS, for the stories that endure; MZ, for the way to think about death; MS, for teaching me to care about prose; KNJ, for the words that unlocked my ending; DM, for illuminating what is possible.

To my parents, 妈妈, 爸爸, I owe you a debt of immeasurably magnitude: thank you, thank you, for all the love and sacrifice; thank you for giving me the space to dream; thank you for every bit of wisdom. To Bobby: thanks for being in the thick of it with me this whole time. 我爱你们.

To you: thank you for coming this far and for letting this story live in you. I hope it does so for a long time.

FIND US ONLINE!

www.rebellionpublishing.com

/solarisbooks   /solarisbks   /solarisbooks

SIGN UP TO OUR NEWSLETTER!

rebellionpublishing.com/newsletter

YOUR REVIEWS MATTER!

Enjoy this book? Got something to say?

Leave a review on Amazon, GoodReads or with your
favourite bookseller and let the world know!